MW00966531

PENGUIN CANADA

BLIND CRESCENT

photo by Louise Mackenzie

MICHELLE BERRY is the author of the novels *Blur* and *What We All Want,* which was short-listed for a Torgi Award and was optioned for film. She has also published two critically acclaimed collections of stories, *Margaret Lives in the Basement* and *How to Get There from Here.*

Also by Michelle Berry

Blur

What We All Want

The Notebooks: Interviews and New Fiction
from Contemporary Writers
(co-edited with Natalee Caple)

Postcard Fictions

Margaret Lives in the Basement

How to Get There from Here

Blind Crescent

a novel

MICHELLE BERRY

PENGUIN
CANADA

PENGUIN CANADA

Published by the Penguin Group

Penguin Group (Canada), 10 Alcorn Avenue, Toronto, Ontario, Canada M4V 3B2
(a division of Pearson Penguin Canada Inc.)

Penguin Group (USA) Inc., 375 Hudson Street, New York, New York 10014, U.S.A.
Penguin Books Ltd, 80 Strand, London WC2R 0RL, England
Penguin Ireland, 25 St Stephen's Green, Dublin 2, Ireland (a division of Penguin Books Ltd)
Penguin Group (Australia), 250 Camberwell Road, Camberwell, Victoria 3124, Australia
(a division of Pearson Australia Group Pty Ltd)
Penguin Books India Pvt Ltd, 11 Community Centre, Panchsheel Park,
New Delhi – 110 017, India
Penguin Group (NZ), cnr Airborne and Rosedale Roads, Albany, Auckland, New Zealand 1310
(a division of Pearson New Zealand Ltd)
Penguin Books (South Africa) (Pty) Ltd, 24 Sturdee Avenue, Rosebank,
Johannesburg 2196, South Africa

Penguin Books Ltd, Registered Offices: 80 Strand, London WC2R 0RL, England

First published 2005

1 2 3 4 5 6 7 8 9 10 (WEB)

Copyright © Michelle Berry, 2005

*Publisher's note: This book is a work of fiction. Names, characters, places and incidents
either are the product of the author's imagination or are used fictitiously, and any
resemblance to actual persons living or dead, events, or locales is entirely coincidental.*

Manufactured in Canada.

ISBN 0-14-301696-2

Library and Archives Canada Cataloguing in Publication data available upon request.

Visit the Penguin Group (Canada) website at **www.penguin.ca**

As always, for Stu.
And for Abby and Zoe,
who make every day shine brightly.

All the meaning of a given life was located in the act of leaning over to untie your shoes and set them in a designated place for the start of the following day.

—Don DeLillo, *Underworld*

Blind Crescent

In the Beginning

WHAT HE DOESN'T WANT is to get caught. Walking through here, through this street, this cul-de-sac. The circle is tight. Once he's in, it seems there's no way out. And he doesn't like to be trapped. Part of all of this, part of the leaving, the walking away, was to disappear, was to move far from the feeling of being squeezed tight by so many people. Too many people. Everyone wants a piece of him and all he wants is for everything that happened to have happened to him instead of the others.

The Others.

It is four in the morning and he's bone tired. His backpack rubs against his hip. It's heavy. Full of cans of food, a change of clothes, a can opener, toilet paper. He walks slowly around the circle, first looking at the hill behind, the trees, the cars in the driveways, and then he looks at the houses. Six houses.

There's a decayed smell in his nose, on his fingers. The stench of life, he thinks, or the smell of death. Sometimes he feels as if he is rotting from the inside out. He rubs his eyes, his chin, his cheeks. Or maybe the smell is coming from the hill behind the houses. Decaying leaves. It's all around him.

He comes upon the first house on the left. There are toys scattered everywhere in the untamed grass. Kids' toys, sandbox toys. But no sandbox. The house is more modern than the others, but overgrown. Everything looks neglected, out of control. The garden is only weeds and scattered bits of garbage. A juice box tipped over. A bubble gum wrapper at his feet. He squints into the darkness and sees something on the front step. A pacifier.

He walks to the second house on the left. The shutters are cracked and chipped. The front porch weathered. A basketball net in the driveway hangs still in the air. Paint cans and hockey sticks rest on the front porch. Two cars. The grass has been recently cut.

Then there is a big house at the end of the circle. He walks up to the front porch and stares at it. It is shifting slightly, the foundation cracked. Its windows are black and gaping. It looks deserted. Empty. He stands for a minute, looking at it. This house, he thinks, looks out at the rest of the cul-de-sac, looks down the street to the road, to the way out, to the city. He thinks a bit about it, about everything. Adjusts his backpack. Stretches his arms out. Continues his tour.

Back down the circle, past a fancy house with landscaped property. Everything freshly painted, swept, tended to. He stops here to look at the furniture on the front porch. Matching. Tidy. The garden smells of pesticides, the grass like a golf green bumps up against the higher grass in front of the deserted house.

Then he comes upon two old bungalows in a row. One lit up like day. The glow makes him blink, gives him a headache. There is a rusty Impala in the driveway of this one. The shades are drawn in the house and so light seeps out from the corners, highlighting the windows.

There is an odd-shaped, large work shed at the front of the other bungalow. Wooden butterflies, three feet high, faded from the sun, are attached to this house like they've flown into it in a high wind. The garage door is open and the garage is empty.

Six houses. An entire street for six houses at the bottom of a hill. The road out is woody and quiet.

All he had to do was walk down Edgerow Boulevard toward town. And then a truck pulled out quietly from this street, this cul-de-sac. The headlights flickered on and startled him. The truck made a right turn and then headed downtown. Before the truck pulled out and drew attention to this street, it was just another throughway jutting off Edgerow. It was just another street. The truck illuminated the street sign on one post—Blind Crescent—and the cul-de-sac sign—a half circle broken by two lines—on the other post.

Blind Crescent. How could he not have walked down here? He feels blind lately, as if someone has turned off all the lights. Nothing in life sparkles for him anymore, there is no glow, no colour.

He walks to the middle of the street and places his feet where he thinks the centre must be. He stands there and watches the sleeping houses. The fullness of the street, with so little on it—six houses— it amazes him. And the empty house at the end. So rundown and overgrown. The front porch sweeps the length of the house. The second-floor porch sweeps half the length.

A good street to disappear on.

And he wants nothing more than to disappear. It's time.

The birds nesting in the hill around the street are quiet. It is achingly quiet. But, he thinks, still, there is an underlying beat, as if the street is just resting, as if it is hummingly alive underneath the quiet. He stands for what seems like hours.

And then the same truck from before pulls softly back into the cul-de-sac and the owner cuts the engine, turns off the lights, and coasts into the open garage. A tall, thin man with an awkward gangly posture walks out from the garage, closes the door quietly, its runners squeaking slightly, and lets himself in through the front door of the house. He doesn't notice the man standing still, frozen, in the centre of the street. Because he's not expecting anyone, he sees nothing.

The man thinks, I am invisible.

Blind Crescent.

Just before the thin man goes inside, he takes his shoes off and holds them in his hand, his soft socks padding the sound of his steps. Then the front door shuts and there is emptiness again punctured by the smell of car exhaust and gasoline lingering in the air, the sound of the truck ticking as it cools.

He takes his backpack off and carries it in his hand. A decision has been made. By not seeing him, the thin man made the idea stick. He takes careful consideration of his own footfalls, mimicking the pad-footed tiptoe of the thin man, and walks toward the empty house, up the large front steps to stand high on the dilapidated porch. With a few choice pushes, listening for any movement or noise, he enters.

Into the empty house.

Dust disturbed by the air from the door skirts past. He wanders around, tentative. Afraid. Is anyone here? He can feel his heart in his chest beating madly. The moulding, the broken sconces, the rugged fireplace, the stained and weathered floor. Marks where it looks as if the movers pulled the furniture out of the house.

Someone wanted to get out of here in a hurry.

The house is most certainly empty.

Outside the kitchen door he finds a rain barrel he thinks he can use for drinking water. Of course there is no electricity. The main staircase has dislodged nails and looks as though someone has tried to steal a wooden step. The basement is choked with spiderwebs, a bird nest. There is a broken window and what looks like the attempt at a bonfire kicked around by kids. He finds a used condom. Pink underwear. An old whisky bottle. There is an Archie comic book in one of the upstairs bedrooms and an unbroken Pepsi bottle in the fireplace.

Under the thickest beam in the basement he finds a small stool. He carries it upstairs and sits on it before a window still draped with a dusty, sheer curtain. He puts his backpack down beside the stool and waits. For what, he does not know.

Here I am, he thinks. I walked onto Blind Crescent, right up to this old house, right into the filth and stench of neglect. I let myself in.

He is looking out now. Not looking in.

When he got the stool in the basement he noticed graffiti spray-painted on the cement. He thinks about it now. About its meaning. On one wall it said, "Back in five minutes. Godot." On the other wall: "Roger Smith." That's all. A name. Large, black letters. A eulogy. A remembrance. Here once, then gone. In child's print. Roger Smith.

Part One

Things to Do

HOLLY WRAY IS SITTING in front of her TV on Saturday, at 8:30 in the morning, in the toy-strewn living room of her house on Blind Crescent. Her kids are clambering all over her, all around her, in front of her face, in front of the TV she's been trying to watch. Holly wants to hear what's being said on TV. Sixth shooting, perhaps? She wonders if there have been any more kids involved. The shooting last month was really bad, two kids asleep in the back of the car. The mother driving. Blood splatter stains on the road. The driver's side window cracked and lacy like a spider's web, or a snowflake, or some other frequently used metaphor.

"Get out of the way," Holly says. "I can't see the TV."

Ever since Ivan left her, the kids have been plain out of hand. But then, they have always been out of hand and horribly misbehaved. Haven't they? Especially Joe. Ivan played no part in changing them because he played no part in anything. Not their lives. Not her life. Not even his own life. Everything, with Ivan, always seemed out of control. And, of course, he'd blame it on her.

Standard Ivan Wray comment: "What'd you do this time?"

He looked so dopey saying it too. His hair was always standing up.

It amazes her, now that she thinks about it, how she ever fell in love with him.

Ivan only knew one of his kids. At least out of the womb. "Things to do," he had said. One moment there. Next moment gone. Just after the Rafferty Christmas party a year and a half ago. Has it been that long? The next week he moved out. Holly was pregnant. So he couldn't have screwed up both of the kids. Holly supposes that one of them is solely her fault. Her two little boys. The big one pushing the other down in front of the TV, the little one crying for help.

One and a half years. That's how old the baby is. The shock of Ivan leaving made her go into labour a week early.

Holly turns the volume up on the TV and says, "Oh, please shut up," for the hundredth time. Maybe if she'd named the younger one they would all be better off. Sweetpea. What kind of a name is Sweetpea for a little boy? Even she knows it's ridiculous. The newborn nickname stuck like glue. Before she knew it, before she thought of a better name, a real name, there was no way out. He became Sweetpea. Fully formed. She even put it on his birth certificate, thinking she would change it later when his real name came to her.

Once, about a month after Ivan left, she got a postcard from him. There was a hyena at the zoo on the front and "Hope the delivery went okay" scrawled on the back. A hyena? Was that supposed to be funny? Holly isn't sure.

Holly scratches under her armpits where the hair is long. No point shaving now. What's the use? Her legs are beginning to look like man's legs. Her armpits look European—Holly hopes even fashionably so. It is getting a bit uncomfortable now, though. It's getting hotter every day out there. Every part of her is sweating. Everything is itching.

Sweetpea has toddled over to the coffee table and fallen. He has knocked his tooth. "Oh, for God's sake," Holly murmurs. She picks him up to stop the tears.

"Oh, for God's sake," Joe echoes.

"Joe, don't swear."

"Joe, don't swear. Oh, for God's sake."

Holly rocks Sweetpea on her lap and gives Joe the eye. Sometimes she wishes she could raise her hand like Ivan did, threaten him, but she knows she'd never do that. Holly jiggles Sweetpea hard until he's bouncing. He forgets about his tooth, stops crying, and looks concerned and violated. Shocked. His tummy moves up and down and his hair whips forward and back in the enforced wind. He stares at his mother.

"Mommy's little Sweetpea," Holly says absently, keeping one eye on the TV. How many shootings is that now? She sees the wife of a previous victim place a plastic rose on the highway.

"Stop shaking him. Shake me." Joe picks up a plastic truck and threatens to smash his brother over the head. "Shake me now. Or else."

One more summer, Holly thinks. At the end of this summer Joe will be starting full-day kindergarten three days a week. Holly and Sweetpea will walk him down through the wooded area, to Edgerow Boulevard, where he will catch the school bus. He will be gone from nine in the morning until three-thirty in the afternoon. Six and one-half hours. A packed lunch and some snacks. And then he will come home for dinner and to fight with his brother. By the end of the summer, Holly reasons, she'll have a name for Sweetpea and she'll be able to get on with her life. Because sometimes Holly thinks that if she could just name the boy, everything would turn out fine, everything would fall into place.

She wishes Ivan had put a return address on the hyena postcard. Just so she could write to him and ask him to suggest a name.

It's just that nothing, not a single name she can think of, sounds right.

Last night there was another murder on the highway. Holly puts Sweetpea back on the floor and Joe scrambles for the toy Sweetpea is eyeing. The TV shows pictures of the truck, the driver's side window smashed in, clusters of broken glass. A bullet lodged in the man's brain. One bullet. "Good aim," the reporter says. The sniper has really good aim. Speeding truck, speeding murderer. One shot. The reporter sounds proud of the shooter, as if he couldn't have asked for a better outcome. Holly thinks of the truck driver's skull and what went through his mind—besides bullet, of course—for the few seconds before and during the shooting.

Holly stands and separates her children who are now on the floor wrestling. Sweetpea is crying again. Holly pulls them apart and sends them each to a corner of the room. "Time out," she pleads. "Joe, stay in your corner." Her finger raised. He is inching back toward the TV. Testing her.

Holly thinks about death a lot. She always has. But more this last little while, since Roger Smith's suicide, since the sniper started shooting. What do people actually think about the moment before they die? Talk of death is not a popular topic, though. She learned that the hard way. The last party she went to, the Blind Crescent neighbourhood Christmas party at the Raffertys', she found herself (her kid screaming, her bra popped open, swollen breasts ready to give milk) discussing this exact matter and all its implications with a colleague of Jill's. Since then she hasn't been to a single party.

Not that she's been invited to one.

A year and a half. No parties.

Now that she has this evening job taking calls at home for the local emergency health centre, finally using her diploma in social work from community college (she knew it would be good for something), Holly can't seem to get away from death. All the disturbed people talking about the sniper. Worried for their safety. As if at any minute any one of them couldn't just die from a heart attack. Holly often has to restrain herself from stating the obvious.

"Okay," Holly says, snapping out of it, looking at her two children. "Your time is up." She touches Sweetpea on the shoulder.

These nights she is getting no sleep. She's been working hard for six months, since the sniper started the attacks. She supposes she should be grateful for his rampage. Everyone is running scared. The call centre wouldn't have needed the extra help if it weren't for the killings. And they certainly wouldn't have let her take calls from home, they wouldn't have wanted to redirect the overload (there was some outcry at the office—"How will we monitor her?" one nosy woman asked). But how, she asked them, can I leave my kids with a sitter all night on the salary you're suggesting?

Holly tells the frightened, angry, often-crazed (although she's not allowed to use that word) people who call all night (often calling for no real reason at all) that if they just think positive thoughts, if they just look at the statistics (one shooting per month in a city of two million) and know that the chance of the sniper shooting them is below minimal, then they'll be fine, then they'll be able to fall asleep, to stop worrying about driving, to stop drinking, taking pills, or pulling their hair out. Organize your thoughts, she tells them. Control your mind. It's that simple.

Of course, she can't take her own advice.

She looks around at her living room. It looks like someone threw a grenade through the front door.

Holly begins to fold the wrinkled laundry she took out of the
dryer last night, and Sweetpea comes over to help. Joe knocks him
down. They begin to roll on the floor and then Sweetpea starts to
scream. Holly raises a sock in her hand and smashes it down on
the coffee table. Her hand smacks. Her old, dirty mugs jump. The
newspaper on the table jumps. The fashion magazines with hairless
women jump. Sweetpea and Joe jump.

"Just be quiet for a minute, will you? You'll get another time out
if you don't just be quiet. Please."

When everyone is shocked into a second of silence Holly hears
the reporter say again that the number of highway murders this year
is six. Six people shot point-blank in the head while driving on six
different highways during six different months. This does not
include the two children in the back of the one car, or the number
of people who were in the line of the cars when they spun out of
control, or who were pedestrians run over by the careening vehicles,
or in other cars that got knocked off the road. The reporter sounds
amazed at this. The number six is emblazoned on the TV screen.
Holly feels she can see it hovering just out of his mouth. *Six, six, six.*
The reporter says the police are trying to put together a profile.
Create a man out of his actions.

That's how many years Holly has been married to Ivan. Six damn
years. One year and then Joe was born. Three and a half years
married, and then Sweetpea. And a year and a half without Ivan. It's
hard to believe. The minute she got huge and awkward again,
Sweetpea kneeing her in the gut, the groin, the bladder, the ribs, the
minute she couldn't bend to pick up Joe anymore, that's when he
walked out. "Things to do," he said. And he left.

If Holly closes her eyes, she can remember a time when she was
happy with Ivan, when he was happy with her, when they loved one

another. But the last few years of their marriage was all about hurting one another, seeing which of them could make the other more miserable.

Strange how these things happen, Holly thinks. Strange, because she doesn't know how they happen. There is no logical explanation. No connect-the-dots answer.

Holly thinks about the questions she would ask if she were the police officer on the Highway Murderer Case. She can see herself, sitting in an office somewhere, dressed in uniform....

What does he wear when he swims, who are his parents, are they still alive, what kind of cereal does he eat in the morning, does he wear pyjamas to bed or sleep naked, is he sexually frustrated, does he brush his teeth up and down or back and forth, does he kill for fun or because he is angry, is he right wing, left wing, or politically inactive, vegetarian, a beer drinker, left-handed, flat-footed, is his back covered in moles, hair, spots, how old is he, is he prematurely balding, does he take Prozac or Viagra, does he listen to country-western music, does he Q-tip his ears, trim his nose hair, wear overalls, does he have a girlfriend, a boyfriend, a pet poodle, a goldfish in a bowl, did he ever serve in any war, is he black, red, white, yellow, has he travelled to a foreign country in the last year, does he have an accent, is he an immigrant, is he patriotic, is he schizophrenic, did he do well in high school, did he go to college, has he ever shot an abortionist, taken part in a political rally, does he go to church, and if not, why not, if so, why, does he have any friends at all, has he ever had a friend ever ever ever in his life...?

Holly looks at the sock still in her hand, blinks, and then rummages through the pile of laundry, trying to find its mate. No luck.

Holly thought Ivan meant errands. She thought that "things to do" meant he was running errands for himself (always for himself, never for her or the kids). Buying beer, checking out new cars, buying himself clothes. It didn't occur to her at the time that he wouldn't take his suitcase while running errands. She wasn't thinking. She forgives herself for this because she was almost nine months pregnant.

She matches a brown with a dark blue sock. Good enough.

"It's hard to believe," Holly whispers, and this is the signal that it's time to start yelling again. She looks around the room. The laundry is half folded at her feet. There are snack packs and juice boxes and toys everywhere. Newspapers. Magazines. Books. Holly stands to stretch. Her back cracks. She catches a whiff of her underarms and marvels at the smell. Human and animal mixed. The things she had to avoid when she was with Ivan. Smells and farts and burps. Loud conversations with yourself. Picking your crotch, masturbating. Joe catches Holly sniffing her armpits and gives her a sourpuss look.

"What?" she says.

Ivan drove down through the cul-de-sac, through the newly fallen snow, as if out for a Sunday drive, and turned right on Edgerow Boulevard and was gone. Just like that. "Things to do," he said.

Raccoons

COMING HOME SO EARLY in the morning, driving his truck onto Blind Crescent, Jackson Kern had been tired. He had turned the lights off the truck at Edgerow Boulevard and Blind Crescent and then driven through the pre-dawn, down the street, and pulled into the empty garage. Mr. Walcott's lights glowed from his house next door. They had blinded Jackson when he had gotten out of his truck and quietly shut the door to the garage. He had taken off his shoes and entered the house. Jackson's right hand had hurt slightly, he must have pulled a muscle, and this made it hard to open the door, hard to concentrate on getting inside, on not waking his aged parents.

Once inside, Jackson had turned to shut the door of the house and saw movement on the street. His heart stopped in his chest. He had peered out into the odd light, the half haze between night and day, Mr. Walcott's lit-up house confusing his vision even more. He must have imagined something moving in the night. Maybe it was a cat or a raccoon from the hill out back. He had made a mental note to put the bungee cord back on the garbage cans in the morning. The smell of the cans attracts raccoons. They topple the cans and

wake people in the night. People on the street who come to the
window to see about the noise.

And then, maybe, see him.

Jackson had put his shoes down on the mat by the front door and
tiptoed quietly into his bedroom. He'd heard his father snoring
down the hall. He'd stripped out of his clothes, put them away in
drawers, and climbed into bed wearing only his underwear. He lay
there for what seemed like hours, shivering, staring at the ceiling.
His head had begun its slow ache, the dull creep of it starting at the
base of his spine and moving up and up. It would land, the full pain,
at the top of his forehead.

Now, in the morning, Jackson lies in his bed, still staring at the
ceiling. Recalling the night drive. Thinking about the things he sees
when he drives at night: the people out on the streets, the other cars
cruising carefully along, the drunks coming out of the bars, the prosti-
tutes on the corners, the police drinking coffee, sitting in their cruisers,
waiting for some action. He thinks about the open highway, how the
wind whistles through his hair, how glad he is that summer is approach-
ing and the air is warmish and sweet smelling. It's fertile. Alive.

For six months Jackson has been feeding his father pills, coping
with the cancer he has, the cancer Jackson's mother doesn't believe
he has. And his father, Shannon, is getting weaker and angrier.
Esther wanted to be sick first. His mother wanted someone to take
care of her. So for six months everything has been complicated and
strange for Jackson. Too many responsibilities. So much pressure
and stress. His mother. His father. But summer is coming and
Jackson knows things will get better. Shannon has had the last of the
pills and his symptoms have steadied somewhat, have remained
consistent and treatable for now. It's been a long, hard winter.

Smell the Fire

Jill McCallan is at home, in the kitchen, on the computer. Oliver Rafferty is downtown, at work.

"Now you are mine," Jill types into the computer. She deletes it. "No, no, no," she says. Jill reaches over and grabs a small silver bottle of perfume, elegantly shaped, and sprays it into the air. She sniffs. She almost retches. "Jesus," she groans.

"Now you make me throw up," she types. Her mother had a perfume like this. Jill remembers watching her spray it in front of her and then walk through the curtain of rain. Jill remembers the smell was strong, too sweet, a little citrusy. A rotten lemon.

Jill deletes what she has written. She wipes her hands on her silk bathrobe.

"Now, now, now … now what?" she whispers. "Why do I have to start with *now*?"

"You used to be mine," she types.

Delete.

"It's called 'Now.' That's why. Really. Concentrate."

"Here and Now. Now's the time."

19

Delete.

"Now this perfume is horrid."

Jill hears footsteps in the hallway. She shudders. A lipstick tube rolls off the desk onto her lap. She looks at it. The name of the lipstick is Red Fire, and Jill wonders if she could use that in her ad for the horrible perfume. She bends over the computer, trying to look serious and busy. Maybe if she looks busy, Pearl will leave her alone.

"Now. Smell the fire." Jill pictures people buying the perfume. She pictures them smelling it and it smells like fire. Like a dirty campfire. She almost laughs. Delete.

Pearl walks across the Italian tiles. She pushes the button on the coffee maker, which she filled with coffee and filtered water the night before.

"You could've pushed the button," Pearl grumbles. "That wouldn't have been hard."

Jill looks up. "Button? Oh, the coffee maker."

"Well"—Pearl shuffles around the kitchen—"every morning, same thing. Pushing a button. Not hard. Although I suppose you could break a nail."

Jill looks down at her nails.

"Every morning," Pearl says. She helps herself to the first bit of coffee coming out of the machine. She scowls at Jill.

Jill scowls at Pearl.

This battle has been going on from the moment Pearl stepped into her house. Jill can't remember a time when there wasn't someone arguing with her first thing in the morning. Jill has a block about the coffee maker. It's not her fault.

If it's not Oliver making her mad, it's Pearl. Kate never makes her mad. Not really mad, not hopping, smacking, screaming mad.

But the minute Oliver walks into the house, well, Jill just has to have a drink in hand—not that she's a drinker, she thinks, just a small, small drink—or she'll start up with him. When she's not with him, like now, Jill can't remember why she's mad at him all the time. But she can always remember why she's mad at Pearl.

Pearl sits down at the kitchen island and opens the newspaper. Jill sighs and stands and helps herself to coffee. What, for the millionth time, does she pay Pearl to do? She stretches. Her head aches and her stomach is raw. Too many glasses of Merlot last night. Or was it shiraz? That's Oliver's job—to know the type of wine. And, unfortunately, to give her a lesson with each bottle. It's the straight red wine all night. If she were to mix, say, white, red, maybe a cock-tail first, an after-dinner drink, then she wouldn't feel sick in the morning. But staying with red—those tannins—well....

"Wait a minute," she says.

"There was a fire in Jamaica," Pearl says. "A bushfire." She rustles the paper.

"I've got it." Jill sits at her computer and begins to type. "Shush. Quiet for a minute."

"The mongeese ran for the hills," Pearl says. "Lord, that'd be a sight to see." She guffaws.

"*Mongeese?*"

"Mongoose," Pearl says. "For the snakes."

"Isn't it mongooses?" Jill says.

Pearl grunts. "What do you know about Jamaica?"

"*Drunk on Now*," Jill types. She imagines the campaign. Happy couple (no one arguing, or sitting far apart on the sofa, no one watching TV by themselves at night), giddy, drunk on love. The here and now. The moment—*now*—to be grabbed and savoured. Maybe a beach somewhere.

Jill pauses. Hard to write romance, she thinks, when you've got none of it in your own life.

"Jamaica never has much luck," Pearl mutters. "Barbados, now they have all the luck."

The Caribbean. The woman in a simple white bathing suit. The man wearing rolled-up pants and a white shirt unbuttoned. All white. Maybe they are drinking martinis. Wait, that's too Calvin Kleinish—the all-white. Maybe they are wearing colourful clothes, blues to match the water. Pinks. Yellows. Sitting in violent-pink beach chairs with purple cushions.

"Them jellyfish," Pearl says loudly. "Stinging all the time."

"Jellyfish?" Jill looks up. "What are you talking about?"

"In the water."

"But what does that have to do with fire?"

"Nothing."

Maybe the picture fades out from the beatific expression on the woman's face as she leans in to kiss the man, and fades in to the woman in her office at work as she smells the bottle of Now that has just arrived on her desk. No, she smells her wrist after she sprays it on. Even better. Associate the actual smell with the image.

"But they sting," Pearl says. She gets up and helps herself to more coffee. Jill looks at her empty mug. "They sting bad."

"I don't understand, Pearl." Jill stands and gets her own coffee again. Again—what is she paying Pearl to do? Kate is all grown up. Pearl won't even get her a cup of coffee. And talk, talk, talk, the woman can certainly talk.

Of course, Oliver says they are made for each other. Jill and Pearl.

"What's to understand? A sting is a sting. And look—the price of oil has gone up again. That's why I don't drive."

"You don't have a car, Pearl."

"Another reason I don't drive."

Jill goes back to her computer.

"Always clack, clack, clacking on that thing. Never time to just take it easy."

Jill looks up. She can think of nothing to say so she continues to type. Her last two ad campaigns—a nice one for Kleenex and a highly unprofessional one for a used-car lot on Edgerow Boulevard (where they got the money to hire her, she can't imagine)—were not successful. She must do a good job on this perfume ad. Even if the liquid stinks like her mother.

Jill's mother. She never had an unsuccessful moment in her life. The only thing unfortunate that ever happened to her was that she died with only one breast. A perfect breast, of course. Newly implanted. Dr. Swain did do an amazing job.

And then Kate clomps into the kitchen in oversized, second-hand sandals.

Oh, Jill thinks, her mother did have one other bad thing happen—her only daughter marrying Oliver Rafferty. That drove her to the grave almost as fast as the cancer.

"Hey," Kate says. She pours herself some coffee, barely able to see from the curtain of blonde that is her hair. Kate sits beside Pearl at the island and picks up the paper.

"*Hey?*" Jill says. "What happened to hello? How are you, Mom? Pearl, you look lovely today."

Pearl snorts.

"Hey," Kate says again.

"Well," Jill sighs. "*Hey* to you too. Did you sleep well? You're up early."

Kate shrugs.

"What happened to the new sandals I bought you, honey?"

"Too tight."

"What about the new summer outfit, the one I bought last week?"

"Too big."

"That girl," Pearl says, almost to herself, "spoiled rotten."

"No she's not," Jill says. "She's just growing."

"Growing big and small at the same time?" Pearl hoots.

Kate glares at both of them. "Don't bother me," she says. "I'm reading the paper."

"When did you get so surly?" Jill says.

"Teenagers," Pearl says. "They'll be the death of you."

"I just got up. I haven't had my coffee. Leave me alone."

"Coffee? You're sixteen."

"Look, Mom, just leave me alone."

"Coffee," Pearl says. "I drank it when I was seven. Up with the goats, I was. Drinking coffee, tea. I had gruel for breakfast and gruel for lunch."

Jill and Kate stare at Pearl. Then they look at each other and shrug. They've heard this story so many times. Sometimes Pearl calls it gruel, other times it's porridge. Sometimes it's goats, other times it's cows. Any way they hear it is far too many times.

Jill turns back to the computer. Kate turns back to the paper.

Kate thinks it's typical that her mother puts her computer desk in the kitchen so she can be in the centre of everything, so she can show everyone how hard she works, so she can make everyone move quietly around her.

"Done," Jill says. She closes her computer with a quick flick of her wrists. She swivels on her chair and turns, beaming, to Kate. "I've done it, I think. I've finished the ad campaign for that perfume."

"That's what I smelled," says Kate. "I thought something had died."

"Smells like rotten chicken in the garbage can to me," Pearl says.

"Yes, well, that's the perfume."

"If you can sell that stink," Pearl says, "you're a genius."

"Is there anything to eat in this house?" Kate says. "I'm starving."

"You could get yourself a bagel," Pearl says.

"Or you could get me one." Kate smiles slyly from her curtain of hair.

Pearl glares at the girl, but instead of rebuking her, she gets up and starts to toast a bagel.

"Can I have one?" Jill asks, but Pearl ignores her. How, Jill thinks, does Kate do it?

"Did you read this, Pearl? There's been another highway murder." Kate holds up the paper.

"No."

"Yes, that's six shootings."

"Not another. My Lord."

"It's totally cool," Kate says.

"What highway murder?" Jill asks. "What's that?"

"I've told you before, Mom. Don't you ever listen?"

"I'm very busy, Kate. You know that. I can't remember everything you say."

"Don't you ever listen to the news on the radio or read the paper or watch the news on TV? Six months and—"

"I have more important things to do than watch TV. Do you mean that highway sniper? Is he still at it?"

"She watches the commercials, doesn't she?" Pearl says, and Kate laughs.

"That's not true." Jill stands and walks over to the island. She sits next to Kate. "I often watch other things. Just last month I watched a show all about movie stars and their houses. It was magnificent."

Jill gets a dreamy look in her eyes. She wishes it were cocktail hour. She could use something to drink right now.

"I saw that show," Pearl says. "The one with the pink fountain in her front hallway? Now, she was something, wasn't she? Pink champagne in the fountain, Katie. Can you believe it? I watched it from my dungeon."

Pearl calls her above-grade apartment in the basement a dungeon just to make Jill angry. The money Jill and Oliver spent in renovations (sunroom, floor-to-ceiling windows, light paint colours) was substantial. That was back when Jill was making lots of money from her great campaigns. Not that they're suffering now, but really, she must concentrate on this perfume one.

"Always flowing," Jill says. "A continuous flow. Running twenty-four hours a day."

Kate rolls her eyes and bites into her bagel. She doesn't care about movie stars. "How would it stay carbonated?"

"Most of them had pictures of themselves all over their houses," Pearl says. "Imagine that."

"Anyway," Kate says. "The highway murderer. Again. Last night."

"No," Pearl says again.

"Tell me," Jill says. She is ignoring Pearl's comment about the pictures. She has pictures of herself all over their house. Pearl knows this. It was an intentional jibe. What's wrong with having pictures of yourself up? They were taken by professionals. Highly respected photographers. The frames themselves are worth thousands. They are black and white. They are art. Fine art. And there are pictures of Oliver too, and of Kate as a baby. And Jill thinks there might even be one of Pearl holding Kate when she was a baby. Yes, in the back hallway, off the guest room.

"That's six. Six people dead." Pearl wipes off the toaster oven with a rag.

"No, six shootings. There was that family—the kids—last time. Remember? That would make it eight. Six drivers. Then the two kids."

"I hope your father is okay," Jill says. "Should I be worried about your father? He sometimes drives on the highway, doesn't he?"

"This guy only shoots people at night," Kate says. "Dad doesn't take the highway to work. He takes Edgerow downtown. Besides, he shot someone last night. He won't do it again for another month at least."

"His timing," Pearl says, "is fine."

"I'd be more worried Dad would crash drunk anyway," Kate mumbles.

Jill looks sharply at her daughter. "Why would you say that? Drunk? What are you talking about?"

Kate shrugs. "I'm just joking."

"No, really," Jill says. "Why would you say that?"

"I don't think," Pearl says loudly, "that that movie star ever drank the champagne from the fountain. She wouldn't need to keep it bubbly. It was just a fountain. To look at. Filled with champagne."

Curiouser and Curiouser

IN THE KITCHEN Holly stares at the grease-splattered stove. She tries not to look down at the dirty floor. She hears Joe turn the TV channel from the news. There is quiet while the boys settle into watching *Sesame Street* or something. Something with stuffed animals masquerading as perfect people. People you'd really want to know. People who were kind and considerate and really, really cared how you were. Holly wishes she lived in a world where her best friends were purple stuffed creatures, fuzzy and warm, small wires attached to their arms and legs so that if you hugged them, you got all tangled. Because Holly would like to be tangled in the arms of something kind and cuddly. Anything. Even a big purple dinosaur or a damn sheep. There is a sudden appreciation in Holly's mind for people who have sex with animals. She wouldn't do it, but she can kind of understand. Holly never realized how much she would miss sex. It certainly wasn't the first thing she thought about when Ivan left. But now she craves it, needs it, wants it. Holly takes a tray of chicken meat out of the freezer and looks at it. She puts it on the counter. It is freezer-burned and grey. Sex with animals? Maybe not, she thinks, looking at the meat. She shivers. What is she thinking?

Maybe that's what Ivan is doing right now. Screwing a sheep. He grew up in the country. Where they shot guns and herded sheep and cattle. Holly pulls a plate out of the cupboard and picks off the dried-on food. In the summer, Ivan said, as a boy, he would tend to the sheep. Holly assumed that had meant shearing them, feeding them, walking them, cleaning up their poop, whatever the hell you do with sheep. But now she wonders what he really got up to.

Holly looks at the chicken on the counter. Then she throws it back in the freezer where it has stayed for about six months. There's that number again. Six. She rifles through the fridge for lunch. Why can't she just feed them? Holly often gets stuck in the most menial of chores, as if her brain were discarded with the afterbirth in the hospital. She's taken to feeding the kids anything that is packaged in snack-size containers. Yogurt tubes, Jell-O and pudding in lunch-size plastic bowls, noodles that go in the microwave for three minutes. Anything she can find at the grocery store that means she won't have to wash pots or pans. Holly serves them this food in these little containers and then, once a week, goes through the house with a garbage bag collecting all the crap. Every so often she runs the dishwasher. She is fed up with the whole process of thinking about what to eat and then cleaning it up. There's no point to it. Any time she tries to make something, like last month when she forced a lasagna onto the table, the kids just spit it up and screamed. She ends up eating it all herself and then feeling bloated for days afterward. When you are used to pre-packaged food coated in preservatives, Holly thinks, it's hard to get your stomach back into accepting anything fresh or green.

She opens two yogurt tubes, a snack pack of crackers with spready cheese that she can already see coating the living-room carpet, and two grape juices in boxes. And then she slips on the floor. There is a wet patch near the fridge. Holly picks herself up. She looks down at the water. She wonders where it's coming from. There are footprints leading from the water around the kitchen.

"Joe," Holly calls out. "Were you getting water from the fridge again?"

Joe ignores her.

Holly carries the tray into the living room. "Well, here's your lunch," she says. "Don't squeeze the juice box. Oh, never mind, Sweetpea, honey. It's all right, Joe. He didn't mean to squeeze it. Don't yell."

Holly goes back to the kitchen for a cloth and slips again. She rights herself. She goes back into the living room. Good thing her carpet is dark. She imagines it beige or white like Jill's carpet, and what it would really look like if it were covered in red ketchup and other sticky substances. It might look a bit like modern art, Holly thinks.

"Oh, for God's sake," Joe says, looking at his lunch. "Oh, for God's sake."

Holly thinks Joe is much too old for his five years. She bends to clean the carpet. The extra weight she is carrying squeezes out around her waist, making her feel twice as fat as she really is. Organize your mind, she tells the callers each night. Ha.

Sweetpea is making a mess of his yogurt tube. It is all over his face. Holly puts the dirty cloth on the toppled clean laundry pile and sits back on the couch and watches him. She begins again to fold the laundry. One chore, she thinks to herself, if she could just finish one chore. She wonders if they'll have yogurt tubes in the future. But there will be something more convenient. There always is. The designers will have come to the miraculous conclusion that a yogurt tube is impossible for young children. Like a light bulb over their stupid heads. Mouths full of the goo, kids tend to cough it up, splurt it everywhere, they'll say. They are hard to open, and when they do open, half the tube gets all over your hand. There will be meetings about this every day for a year. Some young female designer with a full-time, live-in nanny and housecleaner will say, "My kids make a mess with these. I think."

Holly finds another brown sock and a blue sock, and instead of reaching to separate the ones she'd mismatched earlier, she puts these two together and now has two mismatched pairs. And, Holly thinks, who invents those new feminine products? Men, that's who. Who else would invent pads that are impossible to put on, little wings that stick together, or stick to your leg instead of the underwear, slippery glue, black thong pads—and what's with those nighttime pads? The ones that are ten feet long? The first time Holly bought those she thought she was wearing diapers to bed. She wanted to shout, "You don't bleed from your belly button!" but she was all alone. There was no one to complain to.

She does miss Ivan sometimes, if only to have someone nearby she can complain to.

"Clean your face," Holly says to Sweetpea. She takes up the dirty cloth and wipes at him. He throws his yogurt tube down and smears his face on the couch.

Ivan was out of control with his life, he was verbally abusive, and never around really, but when he *was* around he was a clean freak. He couldn't abide yogurt tubes. He would have known what was going to happen when you put them in a kid's hands. It was as if he had a little TV in his head, always revealing the future—"You're going to spill that," he'd say to Holly just before she spilled some-thing. "I'm going to leave you," he should have said to her on that last day. Not, "Things to do."

Holly often wonders if she would have stopped him.

When they first moved into this house, Ivan used to take the double mattress off their bed once a month and strap it to the top of their car. He would drive around and around the cul-de-sac, airing out the bed. "You can't shake it, it's too hard. You can't hang it out to air." His reasoning was frightening. Holly can remember the horror she felt, the creeping fear up her back, behind her neck, as she watched her mattress—sex stains, period stains, sweat stains—going in circles around the neighbourhood. Mr. Walcott watching from his front window. The Quimby kids, young then, sitting on their front porch, laughing. And Jackson Kern peeking out from his shed. Sometimes Ivan beeped the horn and waved out the window of the car. Like it was a goddamn parade. He loved drawing attention to himself.

And then he'd forget about it and leave the mattress on the roof of the car and go off and do something, and Holly would find herself struggling with it, pulling it down, dragging it up the stairs into their house, all by herself.

Holly takes Sweetpea's empty lunch containers away and puts them on a high shelf so he won't play with them anymore. He begins to holler.

"Shut up," Joe shouts. "Can't you see I'm watching TV?"

It's only eleven-thirty and they've already had lunch.

Holly hates Saturdays. Although all the days bleed into one another now. There is no relief, no break. Except maybe the drop-in. She occasionally takes the kids to the drop-in down at the library. But then the other mothers are so happy and bustling with their little children—all of whom are named—that Holly feels outnumbered and alone.

Leaving the laundry, Holly stands in front of the picture window in the living room and looks out at the street. Gavin Quimby is going around and around the cul-de-sac with a basketball. Like one of those hamsters in a plastic ball. It's a nice day. Sunny, bright. The grass at the Raffertys' is lush. It's almost summer. She supposes they could walk to the park or something. They could walk to the grocery store—they need bananas. Holly peers at the Raffertys' perfect heritage home, the sweeping front porch. She narrows her eyes. Her own porch needs a coat of paint. There are plastic cars and buckets and broken toys in her front yard. An empty juice box and a pacifier on the stair. The Raffertys' nanny, Pearl, probably sands and paints those front porch railings once a month. It's amazing what they get her to do. Watch the kid, make the dinner, shop, clean. The Rafferty family is so beautiful. Picture perfect. Nothing wrong over there. Ever. They should put a sign up on the front door that says, "Welcome to the Land of Perfection. Don't bother to feel good about yourself."

That party. She is still sure she had something going with Nelson Quimby that night. She's sure she did. She felt something strong between them. Then Nelson went off and quickly got himself a girl-friend or two. And then Ivan left Holly. Everything happened back-wards. Ivan should have left first and then Holly would have snagged Nelson. Now Holly thinks about Nelson several times a day. She finds herself spying on him through the window on her staircase. Lately, whenever she does, his live-in girlfriend, Lindsay, is standing there looking back. Only six months together and Lindsay has taken over. And Holly waves back. What else can she do? About a week ago, late at night, Holly had placed a folding chair by the side window. She was sitting in the dark, sipping wine and waiting to catch a glimpse of Nelson, hoping he'd pass by her line of vision, maybe run his hand through his streaked grey hair, maybe look at her with those green eyes, his shoulders proud and wide. She was thinking things like this, when suddenly Lindsay appeared directly opposite and waved. Holly thought she was invisible. There, in the dark. Her heart stopped. Then she realized Lindsay was waving at Nelson's daughter, Grace, who was walking toward the house, coming around from the side where, Holly is sure, Grace must have been up to something. She's always out at the side of the house, or up the slight hill behind the houses. Sometimes with her brother. Sometimes with Kate Rafferty. Sometimes alone.

Looking out the front window at Gavin, Holly suddenly sees a slight movement coming from behind a window in Roger Smith's empty house at the end of the street. She sees a shape, a shadow. This house has been empty since Roger Smith hanged himself. It surprises her that there is someone inside, especially since she's seen no For Sale sign, no indication that the house was available. Celia Smith had a moving company pack up the house just after the funeral and then she moved off. Holly heard she went to England to live with relatives. Holly never saw her again and the house has remained deserted. It has become weathered, in need of repair. Occasionally the local high school kids hang out in it until the police come and chase them out. But this shadow, in the daytime, is very unusual.

Holly feels movement by her leg. Joe is standing beside her, looking out.

"Someone's in the haunted house," he says.

"It's not haunted, Joe."

Joe looks up at his mother. He arches his eyebrows and then sighs.

"Do you know," Joe says, "what Alice says when she goes down the rabbit hole?"

"What? What did you say?"

"Alice in Wonderland. What she says."

Holly looks out at the house again. Then she looks down at Joe's vulnerable head. She puts her hand on it and thinks of the highway sniper and those poor parents. Because there's almost always a parent out there, mourning, grieving. She sees no more movement in the house. Holly thinks, This is how lonely I am. I'm seeing things.

"What, Joe? What does Alice say?"

Sweetpea begins to cry. He has spilled his juice box again, squirted it out the straw, and is covered in purple drink. It's a mournful cry. A cry Holly feels welling up inside her body.

"'Curiouser and curiouser,'" Joe whispers, looking through the window at the haunted house. "That's what she says. 'Curiouser and curiouser.'"

"I don't think that's a word, Joe," Holly says as she scoops up Sweetpea and carries him upstairs to his bedroom for a change of clothes.

Joe remains at the window, looking out. "Of course it's not a word," he says to himself. "It's three words if you count the 'and.'"

And then, after a pause, he says, "For God's sake."

Shape Junkie

FOR MR. WALCOTT, getting out of bed is harder than sitting up. It requires his complete and total concentration.

Last night he heard the engine on the truck outside. Then he heard Jackson coast the truck into the garage just beside his own house.

Mr. Walcott tries to turn over to his other side but his arms have fallen asleep and he needs his arms to push his body up. He blinks rapidly to clear his eyes and looks at the clock. Bagel with cream cheese. It's late. Still Saturday, he assumes. He can never be sure of what day it is until he has forced his bulk into the kitchen to cross off another day on the calendar.

Swivelling his legs around until the weight of the legs props the rest of him into a sitting position, Mr. Walcott thinks about Jackson Kern. He supposes he should be kinder in thought to the boy. After all, he does deliver his groceries and occasionally checks in on him. Mr. Walcott rubs his arms to get the circulation going. Jackson has helped during power outages, he cuts his grass in the summer, he hangs his Christmas lights above the door each year. One year he even got Mr. Walcott a tree and helped him decorate it. Yes, Mr. Walcott should be nicer. Even in thought. If the Kern boy just wouldn't wake him in the middle of each night. Over twenty years he's been waking Mr. Walcott. How does the boy survive with so little sleep? Waking up twice a night has certainly taken a toll on Mr. Walcott. He finds his groin aches if one night passes without being woken. A little cramp in his bladder area from not peeing in the night. Mr. Walcott wonders if his continuous and increasing overeating has anything to do with not getting a full night's sleep in twenty years. And he sleeps later now. Some mornings he doesn't wake up before noon. He could conceivably blame everything that's gone wrong in his life on Jackson Kern's early-morning rambling adventures if he wanted to.

Every night he tells himself to speak to the boy about it. But every morning he forgets, or if he doesn't forget, it just doesn't seem the right time to complain.

Mr. Walcott assumes Jackson has a girlfriend. He assumes he drives away each night to sleep in the same bed with her. This made sense when Jackson was a teenager but the boy is going into middle age now.

Mr. Walcott reaches out to steady himself on the side table and he uses all his strength to pull and balance and manoeuvre himself into a standing position. Knees bent. Back crooked. He feels as if he's going to topple. One foot in front of the other. Steady. Mr. Walcott holds on to the wall with both hands, palms flat. Spider-Man. He wishes he had suction grip. When he makes it out into the hall he glances out the side window at the car, sitting like a metal giant, in the car park. The gold Impala. Judy's baby.

Lemon meringue pie.

It makes him sad to look at this car but every morning he looks at it. He studies the licence plate, the side-view mirrors, the gold paint, scratched and faded. Mr. Walcott thinks of how Judy would get in the car every day and drive places. Just for the sake of it. She would drive downtown to the stores. Lose herself in the mall. He knows she would drive in order to get away, away from the house, away from the cul-de-sac, the neighbours with their noisy kids, the smell of the dirt from the hill behind them. "Fetid smell," she'd say. Like something dying back there. And now she's dead and the car sits still, under the covered car park beside the house. Fifteen years now. Nothing but bones. Rust.

His Judy.

"Ahhhh," Mr. Walcott sighs. Testing his vocal cords. He rarely talks to another person but he thinks it's important to test his voice at least twice a day. In case of emergency. Most of the time he whispers to himself. But occasional full-throated, open-mouthed testing is necessary. "Me, me, me, me, me."

Making his way slowly down the hall toward the kitchen, Mr. Walcott uncrooks his back and walks straighter. It just takes a few minutes. There is a stoop to his huge shoulders, an obese sway to his moves. His belly follows a pattern of movement that is surreal, the sudden tumbling of a half-empty jam jar turned upside down. *Slide, slide, plop.*

He can hear the basketball coming around the cul-de-sac. That damn boy across the road, single-minded basketball humper, noisemaker. Words scatter in Mr. Walcott's head. In the kitchen there is the stench of stale garbage. He turns on the radio.

Euphobia is the fear of hearing good news.

"Highway murderer …"

Mr. Walcott fixes himself a very late breakfast. He'll call it brunch. Four eggs, fried, half-pound bacon, three glasses of orange juice, a stack of buttered toast. He putters around, almost light on his feet. Creating his meal. Eating toast while waiting for the bacon to fry. Eating raw bacon while waiting for the eggs to cook. Mr. Walcott dips his finger in the fry-oil, the bacon fat, burning himself, and sucks on it. In the oil, out of the oil, suck. It's too good to wait.

Several years before Judy died she took Mr. Walcott to a specialist. On advice from their doctor. He was always hungry, she said. The way he couldn't stop eating. Everything reminded him of food, she complained—the oblong shape of her eyes, the square TV, the rectangular rear-view mirror in the Impala.

"This will fix you," she said as they waited for the specialist.

"Synesthesia, perhaps," the specialist said. "An alternate perception. A unique wiring of the brain. Some people see the written word or maybe numbers in a burst of colour. Some hear the spoken word as a mental rainbow. Others, like you, Mr. Walcott, see shapes as flavour. Sensations are heightened. Your senses work differently."

Mr. Walcott was relieved a name had been given to it, but didn't think that would change anything. There was a diamond-shaped picture on the wall of the specialist's office. Olive oil, he thought.

"But he's eating us out of house and home," Judy said. "We're retired. We can't afford this. He'd eat the kitchen door if he could. He says it reminds him of chocolate or grapes or sometimes asparagus. It's getting worse. I get thinner and thinner and he gets fatter and fatter."

"Jack Spratt and his wife," Mr. Walcott said. "But the opposite."

"He's left-handed," the specialist said, ignoring them. "They are all left-handed."

"You're Jack," Mr. Walcott giggled, pointing to Judy. "I'm the wife."

"This isn't funny, Murray," she said.

Mr. Walcott began to read about it then. He read of a university professor of medicine whose synesthesia helped him learn the complex words of math and science during his studies. The professor sees *two* as blue, but he sees *2* as orange.

And then Judy got sick and so worries about the synesthesia took to the back burner. Easier to forget about it, concentrate on other things, like chemotherapy and radiation.

Mr. Walcott wishes that his synesthesia took a different form. He wishes that he could hear a human voice and see a rainbow. He's a flavour addict. A shape junkie. The fix is a necessary part of his life.

If human voices were multicolour, Mr. Walcott might want to go outside again.

Sitting down at the kitchen table with his plate of food, Mr. Walcott tries to reach behind and scratch his back. But his arms are too short to go around his waist and so he rubs himself up and down the chair to ease the itch.

Agoraphobia. He has that too. What doesn't he have? He makes his way around his plate. One bite of each item. Agoraphobia, synesthesia, obesity. Liver problems, probably. Kidney and heart problems, he's sure. He holds up the bacon and looks at it. Studies it. Maybe he's just a hypochondriac. He wonders if anyone is ever diagnosed as a hypochondriac. Because if you have been diagnosed as one, then you can't really be one, can you? Then you'd have something, some ailment, and therefore wouldn't have an imaginary illness. The bacon shape reminds him of peppermint for some reason. It all comes down to words and their meanings.

This line of thought is ruining his brunch. He swirls the orange juice in his mouth.

"Six drivers shot, point-blank."

"What does 'point-blank' mean?" Mr. Walcott whispers to the radio, a boxy square that makes him think of chicken livers.

Thunk, thunk, thunk—the damn basketball freak outside his window.

Six drivers shot by a highway man in a flatbed truck with a window that opens out of the back. He shoots out both sides of the truck. Mr. Walcott is disgusted. He shakes his large head over his toast. Now he's making a sandwich with the final bacon and egg. Bacon-and-egg sandwich with his buttered toast. Loads of salt and pepper. Might as well eat lunch. It's almost noon.

High blood pressure. That too.

Mr. Walcott chews. Chewing the fat, he thinks.

He must remember to call Jackson and get him to buy some groceries. Tomorrow is Sunday and some of Mr. Walcott's favourite stores are closed on Sunday. Mainly the specialty shops—the best sun-dried tomatoes, the Brie and blue cheese, the stinky Stilton, the racks of lamb from the new Greek restaurant, the tempura from the Japanese supermarket on Edgerow toward downtown. Good thing he has a little money left from retirement, from inheritance, from Judy's life insurance, from her parents and his parents—dead and gone. Good thing he doesn't have grown children to take care of. If you're going to die of fatness, Mr. Walcott thinks, then you might as well depart this world eating only the best. Grilled shrimp on skewers, roasted red pepper, beef tenderloin, rib-eye steak.

Athazagoraphobia is the fear of being forgotten.

"Point-"—Mr. Walcott points to the end of his sandwich—"blank." He wipes his hands on his pants and then stands up and walks to the kitchen counter and stares at the radio in front of him.

Back when his wife was alive, when Mr. Walcott worked at the supermarket deli slicing meat and Judy taught kindergarten, when they first bought the house and then started trying to have kids, when, at the end of a long day, they would come home from their jobs—Judy smelling like chalk and sticky things like lollipops, Mr. Walcott smelling like slow-roasted ham and back bacon—and they would lie together in bed, holding hands but thinking separate thoughts, Mr. Walcott assumed the world would be fine, that he would be fine in this world. He figured that if the actual planet just kept revolving at the same speed it revolved all the time, then everything would turn out okay. There was nothing much more that needed to be done, if the planet just turned on its axis.

Now? He's not too sure about that anymore. Although he likes to try to stay optimistic.

Mr. Walcott is all done. He cleans up, wondering what he'll eat for dinner. Jackson has to take the garbage out because it stinks. Rotting bones and shrimp shells and the pizza box from last night's snack, which he ordered in.

That reminds him, Jackson will have to do some banking. Mr. Walcott is running out of bills.

Square pizza boxes from Italian Delight have the flavour of ricotta cheese.

He reaches around again to try to scratch his itch. Damn annoying itch right in the middle of his back, directly where he can't reach it. Grabbing a spatula, he tries again.

Giving up on the itch, he sways his bulk into the living room. There he catches a glimpse of something different outside the front window. He looks again. He walks toward the window and peers out through the sheer curtain. Opens it slightly. Quimby kid with his basketball. But also, there is movement in the Smith house. Movement on the second floor. A shape moving.

"Oh," Mr. Walcott says. He grunts it.

He watches until his legs ache from standing but there is nothing more from the house. This is intriguing.

The boy goes around the circle.

Lygophobia is the fear of being in a gloomy place.

Mr. Walcott turns to his chair and eases himself in. He rubs his back on the chair, but it's slippery material and so doesn't do the job he needs it to do. He picks up the remote and turns on the TV. Saturday cartoons. Almost over for the day.

It bothers him that someone is inside Roger's house. It couldn't be Celia, could it?

Mr. Walcott misses his wife. Fifteen years now, and he misses her as if it were yesterday. He misses Roger too. And Roger's wife.

Mr. Walcott can never remember what the shape of a coffin is called but he knows it tastes like those sour candies he used to eat as a child. He thinks they were called Sours. Standing before Judy's grave, fifteen years ago, Mr. Walcott remembers drooling. That's all he remembers. The humiliation of drooling. Sour drool coming out of his mouth and dribbling down his chin. No tears. The Kerns were there, Shannon and Esther. Esther talking loudly, saying, "Well, poor, poor Judy. Poor Judy. But if she'd just stopped smoking. Well." Jackson stayed back with the crowd of Judy's friends. Old hens. Ladies from the bridge club, the book club, the teachers she worked with at the school. They all watched him drool.

"Ah, well." Mr. Walcott looks at the TV. A cartoon mouse is chasing a cartoon dog around and around a tree. The dog's leash is getting more and more tangled. The mouse is laughing. Soon the dog is so tangled its neck is squeezed and its head bulges.

Roger Smith. This reminds Mr. Walcott of Roger Smith. So he stands again and looks out the window.

Feeding Time at the Zoo

JACKSON KERN has spent a good part of the morning watching the movements in the old house at the end of the cul-de-sac. His heart has sped up, his headache pounds. He noticed motion first when he was carrying the breakfast tray to his mother. Two eggs, runny but not broken, the yolks jiggling obscenely on the plate like female breasts, a piece of slightly toasted bread, not burnt, and a cup of white tea, two tablespoons of sugar.

His mother, Esther Kern, greeted Jackson with a shout.

"Six murders. And then those poor kids last month. Just asleep in the back seat. Poor, poor children."

She was watching the black-and-white TV in her bedroom and Jackson could see a truck with its driver's side window shattered on the screen. He could see the number six in the top right corner. He could hear the reporter sounding excited. Six shootings. Speculation. Who was the shooter? Jackson's mother sounded like a screech monkey. In the paper this morning Jackson saw an article about screech monkeys, about how you can hear those monkeys from miles away.

Jackson's ears hurt. Sudden loud noise troubles him greatly. As if someone is hammering nails in his brain. He's always had severe headaches, migraines, ever since he was young, but they seem to be getting worse all the time now. His mother's voice is particularly bad. Jackson has been taking plenty of painkillers. Acetaminophen. Ibuprofen. He goes through a large bottle of something or other every week. He drives every night to take the pain away.

"You'll get your blood pressure up. You'll wake him," Jackson said.

"I don't care if I wake the whole street," Esther shouted. "Six drivers shot. What has the world come to? You can't take a pleasant drive anymore without getting shot."

Jackson watched his mother get all worked up.

"I can't stand this place anymore," Esther said.

"What place?"

"The world. I can't stand the world."

NOW JACKSON IS STANDING in the front window in the living room, hidden behind the drapes, watching the movements from down the street, watching Gavin Quimby with his basketball. He is sure there is someone in the house. Every so often he sees a shape move across the windows. Early this morning, when Jackson came home, coasting the pickup truck quietly into the garage, engine off, he didn't notice anything out of the ordinary at Roger Smith's empty house. The street looked the same as it does every night. Everyone's lights were off, except Mr. Walcott's, but he sleeps with his lights on and so Jackson knew the cul-de-sac was normal. The Raffertys, the Quimbys, Holly Wray, everyone was asleep. As it should be. The only sound was the early call of birds.

And the raccoon. He thought that movement, that shape, was a raccoon out messing about in the garbage. It drifted across his vision. And now it worries him that perhaps someone was on the street or in that old house looking out at him, watching him come home. Someone watching from behind the black windows. Someone moving slightly. The movement catching his eye. Perhaps it wasn't a raccoon at all.

It can't be Celia Smith. She and her children moved to England after Roger died. They haven't been back since. And the house has been deserted for a year and a half. Jackson always expects nothing from it. It's just an empty shell at the head of the cul-de-sac.

"Get away from the window." Jackson's father comes into the living room. Jackson moves away from the window quickly.

Shannon Kern says, "It's rude to stare. You know that. Didn't I teach you anything? Leave people alone. Give them their privacy."

Jackson moves toward his father, tries to help him lower himself into the chair.

"There's someone in the Smith house," Shannon says breathlessly. "I saw from my bedroom window."

Jackson nods. "I know. That's what I was looking at."

"No one's lived there for a while now."

"Do you want breakfast?"

"Roger Smith and his family used to live there. Have I told you about him?"

"I was there," Jackson says. "When he—"

"He killed himself, the stupid bastard. I remember."

"Do you want a late breakfast or do you want to wait for lunch?"

"Don't go bug the new neighbours, Jackson. Don't go over there. Leave them be. We don't need anymore Christmas parties around here."

Shannon's stories swirl around Jackson's head like lice, nipping his scalp, digging into his brain. For some reason, his father's stories all have sad endings. And Shannon likes to laugh at the sad ending. It depresses Jackson.

Jackson begins to move toward the kitchen.

"His kids found him."

"Yes."

"Saved himself the trouble of getting old, I guess." A phlegmy cough takes hold of Shannon. "That's what happens when you get old, Jackson. You turn into a useless piece of crap. You know that. Everything you do right now will amount to nothing when you're old. Look at me. I was something. Boy, I was something." Shannon coughs some more. "Big man in construction. I was"—Shannon stares down at his hands as if they will tell him something—"a big man. Powerful."

Jackson nods. He leaves the living room and goes into the kitchen where he leans on the counter and stays as still as he can. He tries not to breathe. His head pounds. His stomach roils.

"Where are you going?" Shannon shouts when he's regained his breath. "I was talking to you. You're always just walking out of conversations. That's not polite, Jackson."

Jackson stares at the fluorescent lights in the ceiling.

"Not nice, that's what it is. Always ducking out of the room just because I can't move quickly and follow you. We were having a conversation, you and I, and you up and left. That's rude. Just plain rude."

There is someone in that old house.

"I'm old, Jackson," Shannon moans. "Old."

Someone watching.

Jackson imagines the feel of a rope around his own neck. Tightening. He holds his breath.

"Jackson!" Esther screeches from the bath. "Come here. I need help getting out of the tub."

Squatting

PEARL AND KATE AND JILL are in the living room. Pearl is sitting beside Kate. She puts her hand on the girl's head like she used to when Kate was small.

"It'll be warm today, Katie. You can feel it in the air."

"It's already warm."

"It'll be even warmer. Nice to have your hair off your neck. I could braid it up for you."

Kate shrugs off Pearl's touch. "No, thanks."

Jill is standing by the window, admiring her garden, wishing she had one more cup of coffee, staring at her beautiful front porch, the twig furniture placed in a cozy diorama, meant to look both comfortable and friendly. Too bad the furniture hurts when you sit in it. It's wobbly and pokes you in the back. Jill keeps meaning to replace it with some wicker, but she just never has the time. Besides, it looks so cozy there. And really, she sighs, that's what counts, doesn't it? The impression.

"If I were dressed," she says, "if I were presentable to the world, we could sit on the porch."

"Bah," Pearl says.

"When have we ever sat on the front porch?" Kate laughs.

Kate, from her position on the couch, can't see him, but she knows Gavin has his basketball and is going round and round the cul-de-sac. She can hear it. *Thump, thump, thump.* It's like a mating call, only it's not quite working on Kate. She wonders if Grace is home. On Saturdays Grace hangs out in front of the bus depot downtown with her friends. Smoking. Bumming cigarettes from the travellers. If Grace sees Kate at the depot, she ignores her, but if she's back on the cul-de-sac, she's as sweet as sugar. Especially when Kate steals booze for her. Puts it in a jam jar. Siphons a bit out of every bottle in the house. Kate calls it "shit mix," and Grace swallows it, feels the burn, gasps.

Sometimes Kate loves Grace so much it hurts. Other times she hates her with just as much passion.

She feels nothing really for Gavin. He's like a mosquito. Always around. Annoying. Grace makes life fun. And life really isn't that much fun when you are sixteen years old and have a curfew.

Jill looks over at Holly Wray's house. It certainly needs some upkeep but at least it's not as much an eyesore as every other house on the block. She really should hire a gardener. Jill doesn't know how many times she's taken her gardener's number over to Holly and suggested it. She doesn't know why the stupid woman doesn't just phone him. Money, she guesses. He is kind of expensive. Holly's kids are always running around half-dressed, their mouths open. It makes Jill sick. They look so dumb. If her child had been a mouth breather, Jill would have had her sinuses looked at. She's heard they can stick a little camera up the nose and check everything out now. Make sure all the parts are working.

It's like braces. You don't let a kid with uneven teeth grow up without having braces. No matter what the cost. That's what loans are for. Jill had braces when she was little and it did wonders for her teeth, even though the memory of the tightening still gives her headaches. It amounts to some kind of child abuse to have runny nose and bucktooth kids.

Jill's mother had no sympathy for the tightening of braces. None whatsoever. In fact, Jill remembers she used to have the cook serve the toughest roast beef the nights of Jill's visits to the orthodontist. Just to watch her suffer.

The woman really wasn't very nice, Jill thinks.

Kate walks over to her mother at the window. She sees Gavin. She sees him looking at her house. He waves. What does he want with her? Always at her, asking her to do things, blushing, stuttering sometimes. She's sick of him. She knows he has a huge crush on her but she doesn't understand why. She's done nothing to encourage him. Just hung out with him last summer, that's all. But that was after he pissed himself and the whole school was talking. Kate just felt sorry for him. Or felt guilty. After all, she did tell people. She was the reason they all knew. He means nothing to her. It's Grace who always lets him hang out with them.

Pearl joins them, looking out front. "Ah," she says, "I see your boyfriend out there. Playing with his ball."

Jill raises her eyebrows at Pearl.

"I said 'ball,' not *balls*."

"Pearl."

"He's not my boyfriend," Kate says.

Pearl laughs.

"He does seem to like you, sweetheart. Remember the Christmas party? My God, he followed you around like a lost puppy dog."

All three women glance nervously over at Roger Smith's old house.

"More like a snake than a dog," Kate says. "Oh, my God—look. Someone is in that house."

"What?" Jill says.

Pearl says, "How could someone live in there? It's disgusting. Rundown. There are rats in there. I saw a rat one night when I took the garbage out."

"Since when," Jill says, "have you ever taken the garbage out?"

"Wow," Kate says. "Someone moved in with rats?"

"I wonder why we didn't know it was for sale?" Jill says. "Oliver and I have always thought of buying it and tearing it down, making some money off the property. I would have liked to have known it was for sale. I should speak to someone about that. Surely someone should have told me. Celia Smith should have called. I asked her to call if she wanted to sell."

"It's a cursed house," Pearl breathes close to their necks. "Cursed and damned."

"Oh, don't be silly."

"Maybe someone is just squatting there," Kate says. "I can see movement. Did you see that?"

"I can't see anything," Jill says. "Move your head, Kate."

"Lord," Pearl says. "This spells trouble."

"I've heard that in London they just squat everywhere," Kate says dreamily.

"Who is 'they'?" Pearl says.

"Look. Someone is moving about. On the second floor."

They all duck a bit at the window. They move back. They don't want to be seen snooping. It's okay to snoop, Pearl thinks, as long as no one sees you do it.

"Ghosts," Pearl whispers. "Roger Smith."

Jill laughs nervously. "Don't be ridiculous. I really should call Oliver. This is the kind of thing he'd really like to know all about."

"Maybe," Pearl says. "Maybe you should call the police. Maybe it's the highway murderer hiding out in there."

Kate stares at Pearl, wide-eyed. She takes her mother's hand. "Do you think?"

Burned

GAVIN QUIMBY'S MIND. It scares him sometimes. Like today. He notices some movement in the house at the end of the street and immediately, in his mind, he sees Roger Smith.

Around the cul-de-sac again. He's counting. Sixty-seven times already. He's been out since 9:00.

It's been a year and a half, it's almost summer again, and still Gavin can't get the image of Roger Smith's distorted face out of his head. That face and his mother's face. They are unconnected but still he can't forget her face either and he'd sure as hell like to.

Her face pops up in his mind all the time.

The basketball pushes against the pavement and then his hand. Back and forth. The motion is soothing. His hands are callused. He switches often. Back and forth. Up and down. The ball thumps, makes a nice rhythm. Clears his mind.

But then he looks up again and sees the shape of a person in the house. Someone must have moved in last night because there was no one there yesterday when he got home from school. Someone is now living in a house where a man killed himself in the basement. Gavin wonders if the new owner knows this. He wonders if the new owner can feel it in the walls, feel the sorrow, the horror.

Maybe it's Roger Smith's ghost. Haunting the place.

Maybe it's the sniper and this is his hideout.

Gavin stops bouncing the ball for a minute and stares at the house. Then he goes back to bouncing. Good thing he doesn't drive yet, he thinks. He's sure, with his luck, that he'd be the sniper's next shot.

Mr. Smith wasn't a sad guy. Really. And only sad guys would haunt, if there were such a thing as ghosts. Mr. Smith was pretty happy most of the time. Gavin still remembers when Mr. Smith helped him start the Raffertys' lawn mower, he remembers when Mr. Smith pretended to race him shovelling snow one year. He remembers Mr. Smith with his kids, laughing and playing with them, even rolling in their front grass together, tossing footballs. Gavin remembers this the most because he always wished his dad would play with him.

But now Gavin's too old to play with his dad and he wouldn't play with his dad if he were paid all the money in the world.

When he remembers Mr. Smith in these scenarios, Gavin remembers the face that was hanging.

That old Jackson Kern is peering out of his shed. And Mrs. Wray and her stupid kids are looking out the window. The whole neighbourhood is remembering, Gavin thinks. Of course they are. They see the movement in the house and they remember, too. They were all there. Mrs. Smith howling like an animal caught in a trap. The ambulance drivers forgot to turn the sirens off and they blasted for what seemed like hours into the rain.

Jackson Kern. He's so strange. Gavin thinks he could be the sniper. In fact, so could Mr. Walcott. This neighbourhood sucks.

Gavin lives on a wacked-out street. Everyone's insane here.

Sixty-eight times around the cul-de-sac.

His dad has a new girlfriend. His mom left a little over two years ago and hasn't been back once. She hasn't even called or sent a letter or anything. She sent divorce papers, though, so Gavin knows where she's living. Gavin hates his mom. But he loves her, too. And misses her. But he would never tell anyone that, even if he had someone to tell. Someday he will go and find her. He will take the address he copied down out from under his mattress and he'll go to that small city a bus ride away and he will find her and ask her how she could do what she did. How she could just pick up and leave her own children.

This is when his wrists really start hurting. Burning. He likes the sensation. It clears his mind. Supposedly his mom was a long-distance runner when she was a kid and Gavin remembers her telling him about the burning. He remembers her saying that once you reach that burning and run through it, you don't want to stop.

Maybe that's what she did. She ran through the burning and took off.

Zoom.

But Gavin sometimes stops because he doesn't want to go through the burn. He wants to feel the burn and take it with him into the night.

He knows that if he were in the car with his dad driving, and he saw the sniper point his gun out the window and take aim at him, Gavin would piss his pants then too. Like he did when he saw Mr. Smith. Anything scary, in fact, makes him want to piss.

Grace just left for downtown to hang out with those kids from school and smoke. Gavin threatened to tell on her, but he knows, and she knows, their father doesn't really care. He's still in bed with his girlfriend and doesn't give a damn what his kids do all day as long as they don't rock the boat.

Grace is changing so much it worries him. She used to be fun. Now one moment she's sour and unhappy and sly. The next moment she's laughing her head off. She dresses like a slut, Gavin thinks. But she sleeps with a teddy bear. And she smells all the time of cigarettes and perfume and booze. It's like she's a little kid and a grown woman all at once. At the same exact moment.

Don't rock the boat, Gavin thinks.

"Don't rock the boat, Gavin," Gavin's father says all the time. He whispers it. Sometimes he shouts it. Gavin's dad shouted it when Gavin accidentally called Lindsay Michelle. At the beginning he couldn't keep his dad's girlfriends straight. It wasn't his fault. They both looked the same and his dad was dating both of them at the same time. But apparently Gavin's father didn't want either of them to know that. "Don't rock the boat," he says.

Gavin passes the Raffertys' house. He wonders what Kate is doing. He saw her earlier, looking out. Summer is coming and the three of them, Gavin, Grace, and Kate, will be off school for two months. And, like last summer, they'll have nothing to do. Just hang out. Gavin will stare at Kate. Grace will act cool. Smoke a lot, flirt with anything that is wearing shorts at the beach. Kate will be rich and aloof and above it all. As usual. Although lately she's been wearing a lot of second-hand clothing and looking a little bit scuzzy. Gavin doesn't know what that's all about. He also doesn't know how he can still be in love with her when she told everyone about him crying and pissing his pants.

He knows love is strange. Kate laughs at him most of the time.

Passing Jackson Kern's house, Gavin sees him go up his front steps and into his house. That guy is a freak. The sniper? Maybe.

That's what happens, Gavin supposes, when you live at home with your parents all your life. Gavin knows his dad will want him gone the minute he turns eighteen.

And he'll oblige, Gavin thinks. The minute he turns eighteen.

White Sand

IN THE SMALL ROOM attached to his shed, Jackson sifts the dry, white sand through his fingers and a sense of weightlessness moves over him, as if the boulder that sits on his shoulders in the house has rolled off. The dehumidifiers are humming around him, blocking out all sound.

Jackson's work shed is at the front of the house. His father built it there long ago to house the lawn mower, the rake, the snow shovel. Jackson thinks that originally his father wanted to feel part of the neighbourhood, he wanted to be able to look out from the shed and wave to the people living on the street. That's why he built the shed out front. That was back when Shannon thought he might like his new neighbours. Back before he realized that not everyone thought the same way he did, not everyone was like his son, not everyone's opinions were so easily swayed and manipulated. No matter how much he yelled. Too many of the neighbours created too many problems for him—whose lawn was growing out of control, whose dandelions were creeping up, whose sidewalk was covered in leaves that turned to mush in the rain.

Later, Jackson added a small second room to the shed, the drying room, and put on a good door, sealed it tight to keep the moist air out. He hung dim lights and put up shelves.

Jackson vaguely remembers a time when everyone was happy in the house, or if not happy, at least peaceful. A time when his mother baked, his father smoked a cigar in front of the football game on TV, when Jackson had projects he did in his bedroom in the quiet that surrounded him. When his headaches were manageable. Lately, Jackson doesn't try to understand it, though. Too many years have piled up. Jackson himself is getting older. There are some things, Jackson thinks, that aren't worth thinking about all the time. Some things that make no sense no matter how much of your brain you use. All Jackson can do, really, is his best. Even if his best isn't ever, according to his father, good enough.

In the drying room Jackson feels the heat of the closed space under his arms and on his back. It warms him. After a while he can hear past the dehumidifiers, he can hear the sounds of the street. He can hear the Quimby kids, Gavin and Grace, arguing somewhere outside. Standing in the street. Between the whirring noise around him, Jackson can hear a faint "Fuck you" coming from Grace. He can hear Gavin mumbling.

"I'll tell."

"Fuck you."

Jackson continues to sift. Releasing all his tension.

A bouncing ball on the street again and then the sound of Grace stomping off, Jackson can hear her high-heeled sandals clatter. Gavin's basketball, *thump, thump, thump*. A heavy shuffling noise. He is close to the shed, making his way around and around the cul-de-sac, his weekend solitary game as predictable as the moon.

The sand rains down upon the flowers in the box in Jackson's shed. They are lying in two inches of sand and he sprinkles more down upon them like snow. Jackson thinks about the whiteness of the sand. His headache comes back briefly, glowing red, and then recedes into blackness, pinpricks of light dance on the inside of his eyelids.

Six houses on the cul-de-sac. Five families. White like snow. Grace Quimby and Kate Rafferty with their blonde hair. Grace's raccoon eyes, lined with makeup to look frightened or beaten. Holly Wray and her little kids. Sticky kids, covered in juice and dust and dirt.

Six highway shootings.

Jackson stops sifting for a minute and looks around him, blinking, as if coming out of a tunnel. He has to concentrate. He can still see the tops of the tulips, red and yellow, inserted flat into the sand, stems removed. He knows there are fairy roses in the corner shelf in a box, almost dry, their long stems left on for balance and symmetry when they are arranged. There are boxes of yellow daffodils in the shelves above him, cut before the pollen dust appears in their centres. They have a week left to go. It will take two weeks for the tulips to dry once they are covered with the sand.

Once, when he was young, Jackson saw a book in the library on flower drying—just pictures of the before and after of live flowers, white-haired ladies holding up stunning bouquets—and it seemed as if that book reached out with hooked hands and grabbed him. There was something so delicate and unusual about the flowers once they had been dried. It was as if they were reflecting life back on the world even though they were dead. When he used to work at the flower store, just out of high school, Jackson spent years experimenting with different ways of drying different species of plants.

Now, in his modified shed, it's a refined science and Jackson has grown it into a very small business.

Jackson finishes this box and moves on to another box of tulips. Sprinkles more sand. Delicately. His hand still hurts. It aches like the muscles inside have been pulled out and snapped back. Stretched a little. He doesn't remember what he did to hurt it. The sand he is sprinkling will hold the flowers in shape while the moisture is wicked out. Labelled boxes are stacked all around him. On his table are several perfectly dried flowers stuck in Styrofoam, each flower waiting to be wired into the hollow stem of a dried daisy. The daisy straws are stacked in orderly rows at the back of the workbench, looking like green children's straws. Jackson picks one up and sucks on it, trying to make a soft whistling noise. But the stem is too narrow and no sound escapes. He can hear Gavin's ball come around the cul-de-sac again. *Thump, thump, thump.*

The ceiling of the drying room is empty. But the shed ceiling is like a bat cave, those hanging flowers that can take some moisture sway upside down on hooks or nails, attached to rings cut from Jackson's mother's old pantyhose. When Jackson is in the shed he likes to look up at his flowers. He sometimes feels as if the flowers are watching him, making sure he is fine. There is a beautifully odd stillness to their appearance. The flowers sway only when the door to the shed opens and a breeze passes through. They are spiritual flowers, heavenly somehow. It's uplifting, Jackson thinks, the way that, with a bit of care, fine-tuning, they retain their beauty in death.

Jackson is always awed by what happens to his flowers when they dry. The colours change but stay vibrant. He knows now, after years of doing this, what he will end up with, he knows how to control the end result. Jackson uses some blues to get purple. Delphiniums stay blue, only go darker. Larkspur too. Orange roses dry to red but other orange flowers stay orange. Yellow fades quickly. So does green. Green is the hardest colour to dry, it doesn't hold its colour and fades more quickly. But there is a leafy plant grown on the West Coast that works well.

Jackson sells the dried flowers and the daisy stems to the arrangers who put them together. They use them in banquet halls and for political receptions and dinners, sometimes as wreaths for funerals. Oftentimes, when Jackson is watching the news, he'll catch sight of flowers placed near the podium where a politician stands, and he'll know those are his. They've been sprayed with a fixative, of course, he can tell, but he is sure they are his dried flowers. An arranger once told him that Kern Dried Flowers are the only dried flowers so brightly coloured and vibrant that they still look alive. She told him that his flowers make her stop and stare, get close to the arrangement and feel, smell, just to be sure.

The other day he watched the funeral of one of the highway murderer's victims replayed on television and there, on the oak casket, was a wreath of dried flowers.

Jackson's head pounds.

The basketball goes around the cul-de-sac. Jackson goes back into the drying room, into the sound of the dehumidifiers.

When he was a teenager, when his headaches began, Jackson would slip out of the house at night. He would disappear down the street toward Edgerow Boulevard, just keep himself moving in order to clear his head of the pain. He would try to fade into the darkness. For hours he would walk, taking note of the still world, coming back to the silent house only to slip into his pyjamas in time to appear in the kitchen for breakfast. He would pretend to wipe the sleep from his eyes. Stretch. His head finally clear. He would catnap in the day, sleep several hours after dinner. Fall asleep at school.

Gavin moves around the cul-de-sac again and Jackson stops thinking and sifting sand through his fingers and walks out again, into the shed, toward the door, toward the *thump, thump, thump* of the ball. He opens it a crack and looks out. He looks at the house at the end of the street, the once-empty house. The noise of the ball stops. Gavin is looking at the house too. A gangly boy of about fifteen, a boy waiting to be as handsome as his father, Gavin slouches over his ball, a scowl on his face. He is squinting through the sun. Jackson turns his head minutely and there is Holly Wray in the front window of her house looking out at the house up the street. Jackson shuts his door again, walks back in to his boxes of flowers. All this opening and closing of the door. He should stay in one place.

When he was young, time was slow. But Jackson supposes it's that way for all children. He remembers lazy summers, stretching into the distance. Because he rarely had friends, his summers were solitary games of the imagination. Scaling the hill out back of his house, pretending he was immersed in war, ducking down, shooting. Thumb up, pointer finger straight out. *Bang.* The squirrels would jump.

He used to wish he was like his father. Big, muscly, confident, loud. Shannon had friends who would come around on Sunday afternoons for beer and they would sit on the front porch laughing about things that happened at work the week before, talking about women they knew and places they wanted to go.

Look at him now, Jackson thinks. Shrivelled up like one of those apple-head dolls.

Jackson's watch beeps suddenly, 12:00 noon. He sighs and the noise of the air expelled from his lungs works back up to his head and his head pounds. Feeding time at the zoo. It doesn't matter when they have breakfast, lunch always has to be eaten at 12:00. It's amazing how quickly time passes when he's working.

Leaving the drying room, and then the shed, he is blinded by sunlight. He stops for a minute, his eyes adjusting, the hot burn of midday on his face, and he feels the happiness of his work leave his body. His headache has fully reappeared. It is the small things, like the silence or the dry heat in his shed, or the sunshine, or the wind in his hair as he drives through the night, small things like that that make a difference.

Thump, thump, thump, Gavin moves around and around. He won't look up at Jackson and Jackson won't look at him. Jackson goes up the front stairs and into his house. He shuts the door on the ceaseless ball sound and turns to face his father in the reclining chair. Shannon looks up from the TV.

"Soup and crackers," he says. "That's what I always have. You don't have to ask."

"Jackson?" Esther calls from somewhere in the house. "Is that you?"

Jackson's head throbs. The ache moves up his spine and soon encompasses his whole head. A giant hand squeezing hard.

"Jackson!" Esther shouts. "Where are you? Where are you when I need you?"

The Thirty-fifth Floor

OLIVER RAFFERTY IS SITTING at his mahogany desk in a black leather chair on the thirty-fifth floor of the black-glass office building downtown that boasts his law firm. He's really only a partner, it isn't solely his law firm, but Oliver calls it his law firm whenever he is given the chance. "My firm is having a party"; "my firm has organized a retreat"—that kind of thing.

Oliver has been sitting with his head in his hands and his elbows resting on his desk for half an hour. He is trying not to look out the windows at the lake below. It always makes him feel nauseous. The cost of success is that you have to work high above the world, Oliver thinks. His father-in-law told him that. Jill's father always had the corner office in the firm. The one with all the windows. Oliver would much rather be in a bottom-floor office. Street level. Where he didn't have to feel the sway of the building during high winds. Where his ears didn't pop when he took the elevator up.

God, he feels ill. He shouldn't have had so much to drink last night. Or he should keep drinking right now, postpone the hangover another day. But that's what he always does, and he's starting to think that he should get a hold of his life, he should stop drinking

65

so much. The area where he assumes his liver is hurts. It's tender. If he presses hard on it. And his pee seems so thick these days. Funny smelling. And it's very yellow. He pees all the time and drinks lots of water, so he assumes his pee should be watered down, but it isn't. It's yellow. The same yellow that is on Kate's walls in her bedroom. A lemon yellow.

Lately, all Oliver does is think about his pee, his liver, his drinking, and his marriage. And then he returns home at night and has a drink. He argues with Jill. He can't seem to hold on to his convictions, keep them with him, stand by them.

Oliver raises his head and looks at his computer. His screen saver is the New York skyline at night. With the World Trade Center towers lit up beautifully. It makes him so depressed and scared to look at it, but he doesn't know how to get it off his computer. Oliver is useless when it comes to any kind of machine. He can turn his computer off and on, he can surf the internet, even check out porn sites surreptitiously, or buy Christmas presents, but he has no idea how to change his screen saver, or how to download a virus program, or if he got the virus, how to avoid spreading it. He has an assistant at work who calls the IT man and things get done. Oliver has no idea what "IT" stands for and, really, he doesn't need to know. At home Oliver has a simple computer he's been using for years. He's never felt comfortable with machines. He has trouble with the barbecue and with the lawn mower. Jill's father spent most of his time around Oliver mocking his inability to grasp the concept of machines that make men macho. Thankfully, Jill thought of hiring a gardener a couple of years ago. Oliver's own father couldn't do much with lawn mowers either and no one laughed at him. Oliver always imagined mowing his toes while cutting the grass, and the mental picture of this would leave him paralyzed on the front lawn, until the Quimby boy would eventually come to rescue him, take the lawn mower from his frozen hands, and cut around him. Oliver always paid the boy and it seemed to stay their little secret, as no one in his household, or the Quimbys', every mentioned it to him. And then Jill did an ad for cereal that featured a lovely garden and so she hired the gardener for their place.

Oliver is suddenly very hungry. Cereal. He'd like french fries right now. Something greasy.

He stands, and holding on to the wall, he looks down at the street below. Hot-dog vendors are out. A french-fry truck on the corner. He sits again. He holds his stomach.

Oliver can never remember how it starts. The drinking. Sometimes it's because work has been great, he's won a big case, someone in the office has clapped him on the back. Sometimes it's because, driving around the cul-de-sac toward his house, he sees the beauty in the design of it, the money he put into it, and he's happy to be home. But then sometimes it's because he gets home and sees Jill and Kate and needs a drink to keep the mood high. Or because Pearl just instinctively brings him the first of his martinis or a glass of Australian shiraz. And then because she keeps coming back with fresh ones. Maybe it's because Jill is complaining about something at work, or about Pearl, her red lips flashing. Jill nagging him. There's often Jill's cleavage involved—with Jill it's all lipstick and cleavage. Because maybe Kate is getting older and wiser every day, moving away from him emotionally, and because he wonders where his little baby girl has gone. Or maybe, especially lately, because he sometimes sees Nelson's daughter, Grace, hanging out on the sidewalk, her tight tummy flashing, her blonde hair glowing—too much skin showing—her tight ass, her tight jeans. Her lipstick. Why is her lipstick so much more alluring than Jill's?

Because Grace's lipstick isn't always forming the words, "Why did I marry you?"

"Fuck," Oliver says to himself.

The phone rings, startling him, and Oliver jumps and knocks his knees on his desk.

"Fuck, fuck, fuck." He rubs his knees.

It's Jill. She has an uncanny way of knowing he's been thinking about her. Or around her. Or including her in thoughts he shouldn't be having.

Someone is in Roger Smith's old house. Jill thinks Oliver should get angry. She thinks he should call the real estate agent and find out why they weren't told the house was for sale. She thinks Oliver should contact Celia Smith and find out what she got for it. Harangue her for not phoning them first.

"Harangue a woman whose husband hanged himself in the house for not calling us before she sold it? Come on, Jill. Don't be ridiculous. Besides, I don't even know where Celia went."

"London," Jill says. "She moved to London."

"You can call her if you want," Oliver says. "I'm staying out of it."

"I assumed," Jill says, "that the house wasn't on the market. Didn't you assume that?"

"I wasn't really thinking about it. I didn't assume anything. And, if you think about it, why would a wooden sign indicate whether or not a house is for sale? People sell privately. If you wanted to purchase it, Jill, you could have bought it any time. You could have contacted Celia. You just want it now because someone else has it."

"Don't use your lawyer voice on me. You sound like my father."

"I'm not, I'm just—" Oliver thinks Jill sounds like her own mother, but he's not about to say that.

"Kate says someone might just be squatting in it."

"Call the police then."

"You call the police."

Ah, Oliver thinks. He knows so well how good they both are at avoiding things, at arguing around and around something and never doing anything about it.

"I'm not calling the police on our new neighbours until we know the situation," Oliver says.

"As if you'll do anything then. You're always putting things off. My mother always said you were lazy."

Oliver says nothing.

"Fine then," Jill says. "When are you coming home? You can introduce yourself to them. You can ask them things."

"*Things?*"

"Like how they knew it was for sale. How they bought it. How much they bought it for. I went on the internet and it's not listed anywhere."

"Why don't you just go over now? You're right there."

"I'm not going over there. It's disgusting. Besides, I'm working. I'm writing a campaign for a perfume. I do have a job, you know. Just because I'm not at the office doesn't mean I'm not working. Our office just happens to be closed on Saturdays, unlike yours. Our office staff get weekends. Holidays. There's no one to photocopy, or if I had a computer problem, no one to help me. Labour laws, I—"

Oliver rubs his temples. "All right. All right. Why don't you take something over?"

"Rat poison?" Jill says.

Oliver smiles. He looks out the window and again feels nauseous and faint.

"We're the only normal people on Blind Crescent," Jill sighs. "That's a fact."

"I wouldn't be so sure of that."

"What's that supposed to mean? We're normal."

"Listen, I have work to do. Either call the police or go over and say hi."

"Or," Jill says, "just forget about it."

"I have to go."

Oliver gets off the phone. He leans back and reaches into his jacket pocket and takes out his flask. He unscrews the top, counts to thirty-four, one count for each floor his office is above, and then swallows a large gulp. It burns going down. His eyes water. The New York skyline on his computer monitor flickers slightly. He thinks of Grace Quimby for a minute, imagines her in front of him, hovering like a holograph image, all long legs and blonde hair and perky breasts. Oliver clears his throat, tightens the lid back on his flask, and gets down to work.

He knows why his father-in-law drank himself to death. He knows why his own parents moved to Florida. Everyone was running from the wives.

Five Minutes

GAVIN SEES MRS. WRAY and her bratty kids come out of their house.

"Time to quit," Gavin whispers to himself. He knows that the minute that stupid little kid, Joe, catches sight of his basketball he'll start following him around the street. And then there'll be yelling and crying. There'll be no chance to feel the burn, or even to get through it, if that's what he wants to do today.

Gavin stops. He sees Kate and her mom and her nanny standing in the front window of their house. He waves. Kate ignores him. Gavin shrugs. He moves once more around the cul-de-sac, *thump, thump, thump,* and then up the front stairs of his house and thumps his basketball into his house. He thumps it hard in the front hall. He hopes he wakes Lindsay and his dad. He hopes he rocks the boat. Things are slow right now, Gavin thinks.

As he shuts the door Gavin looks once more at the empty house and the shadow at the window. It doesn't matter to him who lives there now. The only thing that matters is that the new owner doesn't go and hang himself in the basement.

Upstairs, Nelson has his hands all over Lindsay. He can't help it. Saturday and she's naked there beside him. She is fifteen years younger than he is. He marvels at his luck. Anna did him a big favour by leaving him. Nelson couldn't ask for anything better. Lindsay is tight and lean. Almost wiry. She works out all the time.

"Cut it out, Nelson," Lindsay purrs—or Nelson likes to think of it as a purr. His mind is always adding things to their relationship. Purrs and velvet touches and alabaster skin—when, in fact, Lindsay is a little bit angry and she has a few pimples on her back. "Let me wake up slowly," she says. "Cut it out."

Anna used to read Harlequin romances and Nelson laughed at her. For their whole marriage, he teased her, using the words that he now can't live without. "Oh, baby," he'd say, "your eyes are like diamonds, your stomach is as soft as silk, your hair flows like water." Now Nelson watches Lindsay and this kind of crap, these words, keep popping into his head. It's all he can do to keep his mouth shut.

Purrs, she purrs.

"Fuck," Lindsay says and puts the pillow over her head. "Tell your stupid kid that basketballs aren't for inside the house. Doesn't he know anything? What—was he raised by wolves?"

Nelson hears only half of this because Lindsay's voice is muffled by the pillow. He moves his hand over her breasts and then reaches down with his mouth and pulls at her nipples. Like candy, he thinks.

Lindsay rolls over on her stomach and buries her body under the quilt. "Leave. Me. Alone."

"Come on," Nelson says.

"No. If you want to do something, get me a coffee."

Nelson stretches. He stands. Coffee, he thinks. Not a bad idea. He walks over to the side window and looks out. "Nice day out," he says.

"Do I look like I care?" Lindsay murmurs.

Nelson sees Holly Wray in her front yard with her kids. The boys are running around, knocking things over. Holly is weeding, or at least sitting in the dirt at the front of her house, picking at the grass. That woman, he thinks, is a mess. Used to be a time when she was attractive. Now she's gone to pot.

In the kitchen, Gavin is making peanut-butter sandwiches. He was going to make peanut butter and honey, he tells his father, but he settled for jam because the honey was too hard. Nelson sits at the table and watches. Gavin's face is covered with pimples. Too much peanut butter, Nelson thinks. He yawns.

"Oh," Gavin says. "Someone moved into Mr. Smith's house last night."

Nelson stands. "What?" He goes over to the living-room window and looks out. "How do you know?"

"I saw a shape in the window."

"You sure it's not kids again? Fooling around? I should call the police."

Gavin shrugs. "I don't know. If it's kids, they are quiet. Besides, it's the daytime. No one is ever there in the daytime."

"Who'd want to live there?" Nelson asks.

"The weird thing is," Gavin says, "how could we not have known someone was moving in? Everyone on the street has been sneaking looks out their windows all morning. I could see them. No one else knew."

"It wasn't for sale, was it? I don't remember a sign."

"It's just weird."

Nelson peels a banana and eats it in three bites. He looks at his son. Studies his face. Gavin stuffs the sandwich into his mouth as he stands up by the kitchen counter. He talks with his mouth full.

"It's like whoever is in there is looking out at all of us. Studying us."

"Aliens?" Nelson says and laughs. "You should wash your face more, you know."

"Yeah, right. Aliens."

"Four years ago you would have believed that."

"I wash all the time. And four years ago I was stupid."

"Yeah, well. Wash more."

Gavin and his father look at each other and then quickly look away.

"Maybe it was a private sale," Nelson says. "Surely Celia needs the money from the house by now. Where'd she move to again? China?"

"London, Dad. England."

"Oh, right. She had a sister there, didn't she? No money or something. What a guy, that Roger Smith. Leaves her with nothing but debt."

Gavin shrugs. He washes his sandwich down with milk. He pours it into a glass because his father is there. Normally he would drink from the container. Gavin picks at a pimple on his face nervously.

"What are you doing today? Don't pick."

"Same old thing," Gavin says.

"Ah, the basketball."

"Yeah. I might go downtown."

"Where's your sister? She up yet?"

"She went downtown."

"To do what?"

Gavin shrugs. He puts the peanut-butter knife in the dishwasher.

Nelson stands up and begins to make coffee. Who would live in that house? It's a mess. Needs tons of work. He uses the espresso coffee in a filter coffee pot. This is the way Lindsay likes it, although, to him, it's so thick this way it tastes like sludgy cigarettes. Gavin nods to his father and heads out the front door into the sunshine.

Nelson pauses and watches his son go. Ever since Anna left him, whenever he looks at Gavin, Nelson feels a pain in his chest like he's been stabbed. A buckling sensation. It knocks the wind out of him and he often has to steady himself and breathe carefully. He wishes Gavin's face would clear up. He wishes the boy would stop shrugging so much.

"Hey, Nelson?" Lindsay calls downstairs. "What's taking so long? Is the coffee ready yet?"

"Five more minutes," Nelson whispers and continues filling the coffee filter. He remembers that his face was like that when he was a kid. It'll clear up. "Five minutes. That's all I need."

Call Me Esther

MR. WALCOTT FORCES HIMSELF out of the chair again to look at the Smith house. Nothing new. He can't see the shape and now wonders if he was imagining it. Since he is up, he might as well phone Jackson. Ambling out of the living room toward the phone in the kitchen, Mr. Walcott clears his throat. "Me, me, me, me, me." He trills a bit and hums to get the frog out, to get the stiffness in his vocal cords out. He'd better tell Jackson to get more light bulbs from the grocery store. In case any burn out.

"What?"

"Esther, it's Murray."

"Jackson's not here. He's out. I don't know where he's gone. I need help and the boy is never around."

Mr. Walcott sighs. "Maybe he's in the shed?"

"What he does in that shed, I'll never know."

Mr. Walcott holds the phone away from his ear. Esther's voice is pitched high and loud. She knows what her boy does in that shed. She knows that's how he makes the little money he does. For them to live. Mr. Walcott doesn't want to argue so he says nothing.

"Could you tell him I need some shopping done?"

"Drying those flowers. As if there's nothing else to do. The house is a mess. A pigsty. He should be vacuuming."

Ah, Mr. Walcott thinks, she's on the right track.

"I need my groceries before Sunday. Before the stores close."

"I'll tell him. If he'd just buy us groceries every so often, then maybe we wouldn't have to eat soup all the time."

Mr. Walcott can hear something from Shannon in the background. He hears Shannon's voice from the phone and, just faintly, he thinks he might hear it from outside the house. But that's not possible, is it?

"Shannon says he likes soup," Esther shouts. "He says it's good for his digestion. But what about me? No one seems to care what I like."

"Tell him to call me, Esther."

"Okay, Esther," Esther laughs. She cackles. "Get it? Call you Esther?"

Mr. Walcott pretends he didn't hear that and hangs up the phone.

"Me, me, me, me." Always keep your spirits up, he thinks. Easy to feel down about things.

Eremiphobia is the fear of being oneself.

He can't believe Esther and Judy used to be friends. He can't believe the four of them used to play bridge once a month. He hasn't seen much of the Kerns (except Jackson) for a while. Since that Christmas party, he guesses. Shannon is sick. Jackson told him. Esther is ornery and old.

Strange family, the Kerns. But then Mr. Walcott spends so much of his time assuming he is the strangest person around that he often forgets to open his eyes and look at the rest of the world.

Bending slightly at the knees, creaking, groaning, Mr. Walcott uses the side of the counter to scratch his back. He can't get far enough down.

Has Roger Smith come back? Is that it? Mr. Walcott moans. His heart breaks.

He has no luck with the itch and just bears the pain alone.

Said the Spider to the Fly

JOE SAYS TO HOLLY and Sweetpea, as they sit in the front grass, pretending to weed but really watching the house at the end of the street, "Did you know that the average person eats eight spiders in a lifetime?"

Holly says, "That's disgusting. Where did you learn that?"

"On TV."

"Ah."

"While they sleep," Joe says. "Imagine."

"I imagine all eight of those spiders are eaten in the first three years of life," Holly says as she reaches over to Sweetpea and pulls grass out of his mouth.

Please

ALL MORNING the street has been alive. Everyone watching everything. Watching him. And he is watching them.

A hand opens the curtain slightly from the bungalow across the way. Just the hand. He watches as the curtain opens quickly and then closes. The hand opens the curtain again. Closes it again. Several times. And then the hand doesn't come back for a while.

He thinks, The things you think you would miss, in the long run, you don't really care about. The things you take for granted, most of the time, you miss the most.

His mind is clearer. He slept some. On the floor. He ate half a can of beans. Washed it down with stale water from the rain barrel.

There is a sound coming from the third floor. A scurrying noise. He heard it in the early morning and can hear it through the ceiling from his perch on the stool. Rats. Mice. Then a heavy thump. He jumps. Then nothing. A raccoon nesting in an upstairs bedroom? A creak on the stairs. His mind moves quickly through all the possible scenarios.

A boy with a basketball dribbling around and around the street.

Then he sees a small shape in the hall. The shape sees him and freezes, stays perfectly still. They stare each other down.

Small eyes, beady, head twitching, moving, everything shaking, whiskers fluttering, nose circling, sensing air, smell, sweat, human.

A rat is a rat is a rat is a rat is a—

The rat moves fast toward him. Suddenly. It's so sudden that he doesn't think. He just lurches off the stool in fear of being bitten and strikes his foot out ineptly. He makes contact and the rat scurries in circles, squealing, and then is gone. Out the door. Down the stairs. Away.

At least it's rats, he thinks. He can deal with rats.

Back on his stool.

There is a woman sitting in the grass outside her house. Her two children run around her. Occasionally she reaches out and hugs one of them.

He thinks, No matter where I look, I can't find them. Any of them. The Others.

He's taken to thinking of them as "The Others." It's easier this way. He'll name everything, he thinks, but them. He can't bear to think of them. The Others.

"Please," he whispers to this cul-de-sac, and the sound seems to come from way down deep in his hollow insides. The sound scares him. The people out there, moving about their business. "Please." Teenagers and adults. Small children. A Saturday morning. And here he sits on his stool, waiting for one of them, or for all of them, to come and get him, ask him to leave, order him out. But so far no one has put one foot on the steps of the empty house.

He makes lists in his mind to occupy his time, to keep his brain busy. His lists began before he entered Blind Crescent and have become habit now. Catalogues of pain.

A teddy bear, blue dolphin pyjamas, a night light shaped like a bear (his paw in a glowing, yellow honey jar), a toy train, dirty sneakers, a baseball cap faded from the sun, an unopened bag of diapers, earache medicine, children's Tylenol, a red T-shirt with a stain on the front, a winter coat like Christopher Robin's, an old baby doll, a bear with a half-chewed ear and stretched-out-of-shape neck, a ring from a plastic bubble out of a vending machine, glow-in-the-dark stars for the ceiling, books, videos of Disney movies, a cup with a sippy straw and bear face, a spoon for yogurt, reams of pictures scribbled, smeared, painted, sloppy attempts at first works of art, handprints and footprints on a ceramic tile, a photograph album, baby shoes in a little cloth bag....

His hands, the veins purple on white skin, a scar on the knuckle, his wedding band white gold, his wrist thick and covered in black hair, his forearm weak from little exercise and hardly any food, the skin draping off like cloth, his bicep the same, a shoulder rounded, his neck, Adam's apple protrudes, unshaven chin and neck and cheeks, thick stubble, wide nose, heavy eyes, prominent eyebrows, hair shorn close to the scalp, and behind that scalp a brain, a twisted mass of material with ganglia, veins, bone structures, and matter incomprehensible....

And moving through all of this—blood and water.

Blood is thicker than water, beat around the bush, cut through the red tape, done to a turn, minding your p's and q's, chew the fat, getting the short end of the stick, turn the tables, rule of thumb, stone cold, keep your eyes peeled, face the music, fine-tooth comb, read him like a book, rock the boat, roll with the punches....

Part Two

Bottoms Up

"WHAT ARE WE GOING TO DO this afternoon?" Joe asks his mother.

"I don't know. You had lunch so early today."

"I want more lunch."

Sweetpea starts to cry.

"Oh, for God's sake. We had lunch. Why did I say 'lunch'? If I hadn't said it, you wouldn't even be hungry."

How many years has she been a mother and Holly still can't remember to keep her big mouth shut. She blurts things out all the time, starting arguments, she cajoles when she should really discipline. It's ridiculous. She wishes that her brief stint in community college could have taught her things like how to be a mother. "Motherhood 101." "After Divorce." What good was her education when it taught her nothing practical?

Holly's college education was almost left unfinished. She met Ivan and he insisted she drop out and join him in what he called "the real world." What a dope. What an idiot she would have been. The real world would have been begging money off her mother when the two of them couldn't scrape together enough for food. Not that her low-paying social work position in the government gave them much. Eventually they did beg off her mother—but they called it a loan—and they managed to save enough to buy the bungalow, which they slowly grew into a two-storey, fairly modern house (with another loan from her mother, who intended to move in when it was completed). Then her mother died, two kids came, maternity leave all used up and no money for a babysitter, Ivan left, the postcard came—and now she's right here, sitting in the grass on a Saturday.

"Things to do," he said.

"Here she comes," Joe says.

"Who?"

"Her." Joe points up the cul-de-sac and Holly groans when she sees Jill come out of her house, walk down her front porch, and head straight through the circle toward Holly's house. Down Jill's fancy, fixed-up, moneyed front porch and over to Holly's dump.

"Why does she get dressed up on Saturday?" Holly mumbles. "It's Saturday, for God's sake."

Joe laughs.

"Don't you go repeating that, young man."

Joe laughs again.

Sweetpea toddles off toward what were once nice flower beds and begins picking all the weeds.

"Don't pick the plants," Holly says. "Come here, honey."

"Holly," Jill calls out. "Hello, Holly." She saunters up to the threesome in the grass. She tiptoes toward them, her sandals, Holly notices, impractical. Suede perhaps, Holly can't tell. But it's obvious that Jill doesn't want them to get dirty.

Pearl stands on the front porch of Jill's house and calls out, "Ms. McCallan, you left the coffee pot on. Can't you turn anything off?"

"First she wants on, then she wants off," Jill says to herself. She waves back at Pearl, waves her off, and then looks at Holly. "I don't know where I'd be without her," she says.

Pearl slams the door when she goes back in.

"Hello," Holly says.

"Hello, little boy," Jill says. "Joseph, right?" She bends a bit at the waist to touch Joe on the head. Joe backs up. Sweetpea comes up close to Jill and Jill backs away. It's like a choreographed dance. No one wants to touch anyone else. Except Sweetpea, who is determined to wipe his dirt-covered hands on Jill's silk skirt.

"Joe," Joe says. "Not Joseph. Joseph is a baby name."

"Really," Jill says. "I would have thought it was the other way around."

"He likes Joe," Holly says.

"I was wondering if you knew who moved in over there?" Jill points to the big house at the end of the cul-de-sac, all the time pushing Sweetpea away from her, her hand squeezing his little head, his arms swinging toward her. "I didn't see a sign. Did you see a sign?"

Sweetpea has enough of this game and moves off toward his mother. He climbs all over her, wiping his hands on her face, snuggling his dripping nose into her shirt.

"No. I didn't see a sign."

"Because if there was a sign," Jill says, watching Joe, who is staring at her hard and making her uncomfortable, "I would have seen it. Wouldn't you have seen it?"

"What's that smell?" Joe says. "You stink."

"Joe! I'm sorry, he's just—"

"No, don't worry. It's perfume, dear. Your mommy probably doesn't wear perfume."

"I wear perfume."

"Oh, I didn't mean—it's a new perfume. I have too much on. I've been spraying it all morning. I'm doing a new ad campaign—"

"I have lots of perfume," Holly says. "And lipstick, believe it or not."

"What do you mean by that?" Jill looks at Holly.

"Nothing, I just—"

"Clowns wear lipstick," Joe says. "Did you know that?"

The women look at each other. Holly has a streak of dirt and snot on her shirt. Her hair is falling out of its clip. She pushes Sweetpea off her lap and stands up.

"Anyway," Jill says after a moment of awkward silence. "About the house. I just wonder who our new neighbour is and I wonder if you've seen him."

"Him?"

"Well, him, her, whoever."

"It's probably a family," Holly says.

"Why do you say that?"

"I don't know. The house is big, I guess."

"I don't know when they moved in," Jill says. "You would think we would know."

Holly nods. The two women face the house at the end of the street, their hands crossed in front of their chests.

"Are you a clown?" Joe asks.

"What?"

"Joe, that's rude."

"No, it's not," Joe says. "It's being honest. You told me to always be honest."

"Yes, but—"

"That's okay. Don't worry about it." Jill sighs. She truly can't stand these bratty children, this woman who is an insult to femininity, to womanhood. Why can't she balance her job, her kids, her money, her looks, and her house? Jill knows plenty of women whose husbands have taken off and they always manage to pull their lives together. Sure, it's not easy, and most of them already had high-paying jobs. But they also don't dwell on their problems, don't lose themselves in self-pity. Instead, they take the bastards for everything they've got, don't let them off with any money, and they don't let their houses fall apart, or let their gardens disintegrate. It can be done, Jill thinks. It can always be done. You just have to want to pull yourself together. You have to struggle a bit at the beginning. Jill should know. It's as if she runs her own household without a husband most of the time. Oliver is always at work, but does Jill let that bother her? No. In fact, like this morning, she balances by working at home. Like a good mother. It's good for Kate to see her working. It will empower her in the future. Kate will never fall apart like this woman here before her has done. Kate has a wonderful role model.

Holly is watching Jill, who is noticeably puffing up her chest and starting to smile. It's a strange thing to watch someone as they think. Their bodies change so slightly. But if you are perceptive, if you really watch, you can sometimes guess exactly what they are thinking. Holly wonders if that is why people avoid her. Maybe her body language tells them that she's mad all the time. Maybe the men stay away because she's always thinking about Ivan and where he's gone off. She wishes her kids were more perceptive. If Sweetpea and Joe would notice when she's mad, she wouldn't have to yell at them all of the time.

"Why would we know?" Holly asks.

"What?"

"You said that you would think we would have known if someone moved in."

"Well," Jill says. She says it slowly, as if she's talking to someone with a brain impairment. She was trained at work to talk this way to people who don't have a good grasp of English, the Japanese clients, the German ones. "Most of the time, Holly, a sign is put up in the front yard of someone's house. Then people are aware that the owners are selling. Clients come in to see the house. Eventually it sells and there are moving trucks. Usually in the day. Not at night, which must have happened in this case." Jill signals toward the house. "That's why I think we should have known. It makes sense, don't you think?"

"But there isn't any furniture in there, is there? No drapes. I can't see anything from here."

Sweetpea starts to cry.

"You are a clown," Joe suddenly cries. "I think I've seen you on TV."

"Joe!"

"Silly boy," Jill says. She sniffs. "I am not a clown. Grown women wear lipstick. Mature, grown women with careers, with husbands, with … well…. We wear it on our lips, not around our lips like clowns."

Joe looks down at the ground.

Holly thinks to herself, Don't say it, don't say it, don't say it. But he says it. Of course he says it:

"My mom doesn't wear lipstick."

"Well," Jill says. "You should teach this boy some manners, Holly." She tries to laugh, as if this is all one big joke, but it comes out more like a cough.

"He has manners," Holly says. "More than some."

Sweetpea is still crying. Holly picks him up and cuddles him.

"Listen," Holly sighs. "I don't know who moved in there or even if someone moved in there at all. If I find out, I'll tell you—"

"That's fine. That's great. I didn't mean—"

"I have to go inside now."

Holly carries Sweetpea and pushes Joe ahead of her up her stairs and into her house. She shuts the door quietly behind her, and leaning against it, crying child in hand, she slides down to the floor.

"I can see your underpants," Joe says. "Big, fat underpants."

"Bloody hell," Holly murmurs. "Manners. Bloody hell."

"Oh, hell," Joe says as he walks over and turns on the TV.

OUTSIDE ON THE GRASS, Jill stands with her hands on her hips and surveys the street. She can't believe that woman. A clown. No control of the children. Jill can still hear the dirty little one sobbing.

It's as if, Jill thinks, she lives in the slums. Everywhere she looks on this street there are people who make her sick. She tried to persuade Oliver to move to Wedgwood Hills, or even to the Uptown region, but he said that this house has character, that the neighbourhood has character, that the cul-de-sac and the hill behind it has character. Character-schmaracter. It's just trash, Jill thinks. That's all it is. White trash. And now the new people have moved in and they are probably just more added garbage. Surely, if they were sophisticated, cultured, et cetera, they would have had all the renovations done on the house before they moved in. Now what are they going to do? The house needs a complete overhaul.

Sometimes, Jill thinks, she should just up and move. With or without Oliver.

Jill looks at her watch: 2:30. Ah, she thinks, that's perfect. Oliver should be home soon. If she could just get Pearl to fix them some drinks without complaining about something Jill overlooked— groceries she forgot to buy, appliances she forgot to turn on or off— then all will be fine. Although it wouldn't hurt to have a drink herself right now. It is 2:30, almost 2:34, actually. It is Saturday. And she did come up with a brilliant ad campaign this morning. If she can just sneak past Pearl. Jill can't stand one more confrontation today.

Jill tiptoes off the grass and walks up the street to her house. She walks up the stairs onto her large porch. She opens the front screen door and peers inside. She enters and heads straight for the liquor cabinet.

"Ms. McCallan?" Pearl calls out.

"Shit," Jill says.

"Ms. McCallan? Is that you?"

"Yes, Pearl."

"Come here for a minute. I'm in the kitchen. I want to teach you something about peanut butter."

"Peanut butter?"

"Margarine, really."

"Margarine?"

"Come here."

Jill sighs. She walks into the kitchen, her shoulders slumped. Kate passes her as she goes upstairs to her room. "Watch out, Mom," Kate whispers. "Pearl's in a foul mood."

Sometimes, Jill thinks, it's as if she is paying for punishment. Sometimes it's as if she's paying for her own mother to nag her again.

"Why did you put the knife into the peanut butter and then use the same knife for the margarine? What were you thinking? Look at this mess. I've had to scrape all the margarine from the surface here and…."

Jill sits down at the kitchen counter and watches Pearl as she cleans the margarine, as she complains about hygienics, about contagion. As if peanut butter were a disease instead of a spreadable oil product. Jill looks at her watch several times but the minutes seem to have stopped.

IN THE EARLY EVENING, Jackson Kern emerges from Mr. Walcott's house. He goes into his garage, starts up the flower delivery truck, and drives down the road toward Edgerow Boulevard. Mr. Walcott watches him go from behind his curtains. His fingers are crossed. He is hoping that the specialty shops won't be closed up this late in the day. He is cursing Esther and Shannon for being almost bedridden, which kept the boy from attending to his shopping. Mr. Walcott wants pesto for dinner, pesto with roasted pine nuts and aged Gorgonzola cheese. He wants artichokes and baby snow peas and grilled salmon slathered in dill.

NELSON AND LINDSAY leave the house and drive down the cul-de-sac toward dinner engagements in town. Co-workers, friends of Lindsay's. The kids can fend for themselves. Gavin sits in front of the TV for a while. And then, fifteen minutes later, his sister, Grace, creeps down the cul-de-sac on her way home, a lit cigarette burning proudly between her lips. Oliver Rafferty drives past her, coming home from work, astonished at Grace's legs, those long legs, coming out of her miniskirt. He doesn't notice the cigarette. He forgets she is the same age as his daughter. Her legs are white and shaped and curved. They are strong. She looks at his car, the roof off, and thinks that she should get some of that, some car that drives fast, a man. Something like that. Grace wants anything that Kate has. Even if she has to get it her own damn way.

HOLLY WRAY IS TRYING to put Sweetpea to bed. She's kept him up, not let him nap all afternoon, even after his crying jag with

Jill McCallan, hoping he'll start going to bed earlier. She is sitting in the rocker in his messy room, smelling the old rot smell of his diapers in the pail, listening to the sounds of TV from Joe below in the living room, and holding Sweetpea tight. He is making sad-sounding sighs, his little lips pressed against her neck, his body heavy with exhaustion, tight with trying to fight sleep. Every time she puts him in his crib he begins again to cry and Holly is frustrated beyond hope. She turns the rocker slightly toward the window and sees the backyard, the steep hill climbing up to the rest of the world. She sees the trees bending ominously in the weight of the creeping night. And Sweetpea's weight becomes hugely solid and her arms ache. A car door slams outside, footsteps echoing across the street at the Raffertys'. Nelson's laugh.

Another Saturday over and she didn't finish one chore. One of so many Saturdays she has done by herself. She will answer calls tonight after Joe goes to sleep. She will have a glass of wine and sit before the phone, ready to soothe the crazy, scared people, and she will work to the glow of the television. Maybe she will try to finish folding the laundry. Holly wishes she were going out somewhere nice with Nelson Quimby, or even staying home with her hand on his tight stomach, her head on his shoulder. She wouldn't mind anything like that, anything at all. But for now she stands slowly, slowly, slowly, the rocker tilting her forward, the rocker rocking back quietly, and she tiptoes Sweetpea toward the crib. And then bending, bending, bending until half her body is with him in the crib, she puts him in there and covers him up, his lips pursing and sucking, sucking and pursing, as if he's on her breast.

Why, Holly thinks, why me?

"What's for dinner?" Grace walks into the living room. She kicks Gavin's feet off the coffee table and sits down next to him. She reeks of cigarettes.

Gavin shrugs. He's watching an old episode of *Star Trek*. Captain Kirk and Spock are down on some planet, looking confused and angry. He thinks they are always confused and angry and wonders why that is. If he were on the *Enterprise,* he certainly wouldn't be mad—except at the uniform he'd be made to wear. Totally gross.

"Where's Dad? Where's Lindsay?"

"They went out for dinner."

"And they didn't leave us anything? Fuck. Sometimes I wish Mom were still here."

Gavin looks at Grace. She is scowling. When she is mad he can see his mother in her face.

"Let's order a pizza." Grace gets up and walks into the kitchen. "What do you want on it?"

Gavin shrugs again.

"We'll use Dad's credit card."

"Where'd you get that?"

"From his wallet. This morning."

Gavin laughs. "How's he going to pay for dinner tonight with Lindsay?"

"Who cares." Grace peeks around the corner into the living room. She is holding the phone and waiting for the pizza place to pick up. She smiles.

There is jackson kern settling his parents down for the night. Eventually he'll take the food over to Mr. Walcott, but for now he has to give his father his medication, feed them both an evening snack— They're like children, he thinks—put them to bed. Jackson works around their noise, he shuts his ears to it. When he was downtown he almost bought earplugs. He saw them in the pharmacy, foam ones, but they were orange and would draw attention. If his mother saw him with earplugs in, Jackson doesn't know what she would do. Talk louder probably.

Jackson knows that Mr. Walcott is most likely drooling over there. He probably watched Jackson come into the house empty-handed and thought the stores were closed. But Jackson left the groceries in the back of the truck for now. He must remember to get the few things he bought for himself with Mr. Walcott's money out of the bags. He bought a box of chocolates for some reason. He bought a new flower-drying magazine, *Air Time*. And he bought himself a pack of Juicy Fruit gum because the flavour reminds him of his long-dead grandfather.

The fact that his grandfather has been dead so long makes Jackson utterly sad. Everything, lately, has been making him feel down.

Jackson is always tired, he never sleeps, but there are still chores to do. He feels anxious tonight. He must remember to shut the shed, lock it up for the night. He must remember to keep the garage door open so he can go out driving without waking anyone. He longs for the fresh air on his face and arms, the release of the ache in his head. If he just drives freely, his headache will disappear. Lately, though, he's had to drive farther and for longer. And now, in the daytime, he's more tired than ever. Twice he's been stopped by the police, who searched his truck looking for any evidence that he might be the sniper.

The telephone rings and rings. Jackson is afraid it will disturb his parents. He creeps into the living room and waits until it stops ringing, then he picks up the receiver and places it on the table.

The *beep, beep, beep* is barely audible when he puts a pillow over it. Mr. Walcott is calling about his groceries. Jackson is sure of it. He'll get to the fat man. In time.

A stabbing pain through his eyes. Jackson sits for a moment. Then stands again.

He listens for movement in the house. There is none. His parents are asleep. He takes up his keys and leaves. Pausing on the front lawn, he looks around the cul-de-sac. Lights are on everywhere. Mr. Walcott's house is glowing, lit up brightly. There are no lights in Roger Smith's house, but Jackson is sure someone is in there, sitting just behind the window. He thinks he can see a dark shape. Jackson shivers.

Jackson takes his belongings out of Mr. Walcott's grocery bags and then heads over to his house. He doesn't even have to touch the bottom step before Mr. Walcott, his huge bulk shadowing the doorway, blocking light, hurries him inside.

"Where have you been, Jackson? Where have you been? I'm starving. Famished. About ready to faint. Die, my boy. Die." Mr. Walcott talks as he shuffles away from Jackson and into the kitchen, lugging several of the bags with him. Jackson follows with the rest. "When a man my size is as hungry as I am, Jackson, you must watch out for your own safety. I could eat you." Mr. Walcott laughs. His humour returning with the wealth of delicious things he begins pulling from the bags.

Everyone, Jackson thinks, needs me.

Jackson once read about a woman in Japan who has barely seen her son in six years even though they live in the same apartment. He leaves his room only when he is sure she is out or asleep. The article said that as many as a million Japanese are shut-ins, refusing to work, or to see people for up to ten years. And most of these people,

Jackson remembers, showed no signs of any mental illness. They just didn't want to see anyone.

Jackson begins to leave.

"Wait," says Mr. Walcott. "Wait, Jackson. Why don't you stay for something? A bite, maybe? It'll only take a minute. I've got pasta and—well, you know what I have."

"No, thanks, Mr. Walcott. I'm busy tonight."

"Busy boy, busy boy," Mr. Walcott mutters. He turns back to the stove. "Suit yourself."

Jackson stands for a minute at the front door, watching Mr. Walcott move about the kitchen. The fat man grunts and groans and sighs and moans. Jackson remembers Mr. Walcott's wife, Judy. She was tiny. Thin. She was so sick at the end that, when Mr. Walcott would wheel her out to the garden for air, she looked like wax paper.

Jackson leaves the house quietly and heads for his flower shed, for his dried beauties, for his slowly dying brood. Everyone he's in contact with these days is slowly dying. His mother, his father, Mr. Walcott. Even the store owner at the delicatessen who, when cutting into the salmon, coughed up phlegm that speckled his apron with blood. Slowly dying. Quickly dying. Roger Smith's tight noose. The sniper's victims.

Jackson's headache blacks out his vision for a minute and he thinks quickly (and then shoves the thought down deep) that maybe he, not his mother, not his father, but he, Jackson Kern, will be the first to die.

MR. WALCOTT EATS FETTUCINI with homemade pesto, pine nuts and Gorgonzola sprinkled copiously on top. He eats an entire baguette. He drinks two bottles of red wine and then begins to sing. He wishes Jackson had stayed. The company would have been nice.

He grills two pounds of salmon lightly and then tops it with fresh dill. A salad of radicchio and arugula. Roasted red peppers. An entire pecan pie for dessert with freshly whipped cream on top. He licks the pie plate clean. While he's washing up the dishes and whistling quietly, Mr. Walcott looks out the kitchen window of his house toward the hill behind. He thinks how peaceful it is in this cul-de-sac. How quiet and lovely. The trees sway in a slight breeze, it's like looking out on a forest. Mr. Walcott washes everything up and then retires to his bedroom to read before he sleeps. On the way there, he circles the inside of his house, turning on every light in every room that wasn't already on. In the bathroom he even turns on the fan. He finds the white noise helps him settle, takes his mind off things.

OUT ON THE HILL behind the houses, behind the Raffertys' house in particular, Gavin Quimby sits high in his favourite tree and watches the houses he can see. He watches his father and Lindsay come home from dinner out. They are arguing. Then he watches Lindsay pull the blinds closed in his father's bedroom. He watches the glow of the TV Grace is watching in the living room. A blue room flickers out into the street. He watches Jackson Kern leave Mr. Walcott's house and go back to his own. Gavin stares at the house next door to the Raffertys', tries hard to imagine the man behind the dark windows. The man is at the front of the house, Gavin is at the back. He wishes he could see through walls. X-ray vision.

The tree is fairly comfortable. The branch he is on is thick and flat. Gavin swings his legs. Back and forth. He looks at the Rafferty house and hopes for any sign of Kate. Once he caught sight of her hair as she moved through the kitchen, the back of her. Once he saw her on the second floor, but only as she turned a corner to go into a room that was hidden. Gavin can see Mr. and Mrs. Rafferty. They have been drinking heavily. He can see them in their living room. Gavin sees Mr. Rafferty stumble to the liquor cabinet. Then suddenly he sees Kate turn on her bedroom light and look out through the window. Then she rapidly closes the curtains. Thick, dark curtains. She erases herself.

Gavin is cold and clammy. He is momentarily aware of the temperature. A cool, pre-summer evening. He can hear crickets in the underbrush. His senses are heightened. His palms are sweaty. He is afraid that he might fall and so tries to adjust himself, steady himself. He tips a bit and then climbs out of the tree. Kate's light goes off. The Raffertys shut the light off in the living room. Gavin straightens himself up and stretches high. He starts to creep off, past the Raffertys', toward the empty house that's not all that empty anymore, when a face in the Raffertys' darkened kitchen window startles him.

"You shouldn't be spying, mister," Pearl says. She has the window open and she's peering out at him. Hissing. Whispering.

Gavin jumped high when he saw her face. He stands still now, like a fox caught in the headlights, his hand on his chest, his heart beating rapidly. His eyes white with fear.

"I saw you watching." Pearl shuts the window and closes the blinds.

Gavin stands there, afraid to move. His heart aches, it's thumping so fast. He begins to run, then hightails it fast, sprints, out of the backyards and into the street, onto Blind Crescent, and then up his front porch, through the unlocked front door, up the stairs, and into his bedroom where he slams his door loudly and dives onto his bed and buries his head under the pillow.

In the next room Lindsay jumps to the sound of the door slamming.

"Why can't he just shut a door like a normal person? Why all the slamming?"

"He's a kid," Nelson says.

"Your kids need rules. Rules you enforce, Nelson."

"The credit card was an honest mistake. Grace said so. She thought she had my library card."

"And you believe that? She used it to buy pizza."

"I'll pay you back, Lindsay."

"That's not the point. Library card—honestly."

Lindsay and Nelson stare at each other.

"Well, forget it," Lindsay says. "Forget it."

Nelson looks at her. She is standing naked by the bed. She pulls on an old sweatshirt and track pants.

"I'm going to sleep. Just forget it."

Even in frumpy clothes she is mesmerizing, Nelson thinks. The glow from the window sliding off her hair, lighting parts of her face.

Nelson reluctantly climbs out of bed and puts on his boxer shorts and a T-shirt. He climbs back into bed. He turns toward Lindsay, facing her back, and wonders what he's doing wrong. His wife, his new girlfriend. Even his daughter. It seems he has a hard time making women happy. Maybe it's not him, though. Maybe it's his kids. Kids in general, they do make a mess of things.

Part Three

Blink

THE STREET IS BEGINNING to astonish him.

He has been watching the movements back and forth between houses, movements out and into the cul-de-sac. The thin man he saw the night he walked into the crescent seems to take care of someone in the bungalow. He works in the dark of his shed with flowers. His truck says, "Kern Dried Flowers." Every night, late, he drives off and doesn't come back until early morning.

The woman with the young children sits up late into the night in her living room, the TV flickering around her, turning her walls blue. The children get on her nerves but she loves them. The tilt of her head when she's listening to them, the way she moves her hips to settle the small one in her arms, the touch of her hand on the other one's head when he's crying.

He has watched the two men in the cul-de-sac who have steady jobs come and go every day like clockwork. The blonde woman next door drives her fair-haired daughter to school and then disappears for the day herself. They have a woman who cleans and cooks for them. She is often sitting on their porch in the day, drinking from a mug and talking on the phone. The teenage children on the other

side walk down Blind Crescent together toward school. A woman
with black hair often comes out mid-morning and drives off in
her car. She is young and has a carefree look to her. To the man
watching out, she looks nothing like the teens.

Blink.

Wink, flash, twinkle, gleam, spark, flicker, glimmer....

In the evening the street is lit up.

What is most spectacular, he thinks, is the fact that no one has
approached this house yet. To welcome him. Or to tell him to leave.
No one has even come close. They have forgotten he exists. They
took note of him the first few days, stood in their front windows to
watch, but they did not approach.

The rats have welcomed him. A new one was sitting on the
floor beside where he was sleeping this morning. He woke to see
it looking at him, curious. It had chewed a hole into his canvas
knapsack, straight toward the cans of food as if it could smell
through tin.

He isn't afraid of the rats anymore. It's the nightmares he is
afraid of. Nothing else scares him. The rats are just a nuisance. His
food will run out someday, but he will deal with that when the time
comes. He has water from the rain barrel. The bathtub serves a
purpose it wasn't designed for. It ashames him how dirty he has
become. How disgusting with his habits. Everything about him
smells. Unwashed, unshaven. His fingernails are long and snagged,
his toenails cut at his legs in his sleep.

Black nights don't bother him. But when he finally closes his eyes
and his life floods through, that's when he wakes screaming.... It
feels as if leeches are covering him, his mind, sucking all sense out.
He is terrified to dream.

Blink.

His lists save him for now. His lists ground him to some reality. The lists make the memories easier, make the pain lessen slightly. He goes through the rooms in his mind and picks out the things he remembers.

A small blanket wrapped about a finger in the casket, a bunny with floppy ears, a yellow summer dress, pink diapers with smiling bears and stars on them, a crib with a mobile of bears in dresses, silky angel wings on their backs, baby dolls, a dollhouse, a cup that, when tipped, fills with sparkle stars, a Beatrix Potter plate and straw and spoon, on them bunnies in blue coats, old jars of baby food, bottles of milk, pictures scribbled, zigzag lines of colour across the page, soft books for squeezing, a plastic book for a bath, bath toys, baby shoes in a cloth bag, a pillow shaped like a heart, hair clips that shine, baby oils and powders and diaper creams and eczema creams and sweet-smelling shampoo, baby-nail clippers and toothbrush, a night light of a princess with a pink glowing skirt, a plastic frog, an orange beaded necklace....

The anger overwhelms him. One day he caught a rat, one of the smaller ones, and he slowly beheaded it with the lid from his baked-bean can. The rat struggled throughout the process and finally went limp in his hands.

Hands covered with blood. The iron smell permeates the room. The sorrow, the anger, is too huge to register. He cries.

Postcard from Ivan

HOLLY STARES AT THE POSTCARD. On the front there are four women lying on a beach. They are on their stomachs on beach towels, their gold hair fanned out to the sides. They are each wearing a different colour bikini bottom and no top. They are tanned and silky. Their skin shines. Holly stares at the four colourful bums, blue, red, orange, and yellow, poking up at her. The caption on the front reads, "Don't you wish you were here?"

She turns the postcard over. There is no stamp, no postmark, nothing. Holly takes down the last postcard she got from Ivan, the one sent just after Sweetpea was born, the one with the hyena on the front, and looks at it again. She notices for the first time that this postcard also has no stamp, no postmark.

Ivan is dropping them off. Putting them in her mailbox.

Why didn't she notice this before?

Holly looks around. She goes to the front window and looks down the street.

Then she turns the new postcard over again and looks at what he's written.

"Sometimes," it says, "life is full of surprises. Hope you are well. Say hi to the kids. Ivan."

Holly reads it over and over again. She studies his handwriting, looking for clues. Angry scrawls? Happy swirly letters? Does the *Y* look like a monkey tail or is it straight and direct? She shivers. Then she puts it with the other postcard, high on a shelf in the living room, and sits down on the couch and stares at the TV.

School Is Out

SUMMER. SCHOOL IS OUT. Grace, Kate, and Gavin begin to hang around together. There is nothing better to do. Occasionally they ride their bikes to the local beach and Grace smokes a lot, wears a string bikini, and stares at the boys. Gavin digs his hands in the sand, sifting, and sometimes he swims. Kate watches Grace and wishes she could be her. She copies the other girl's loose style, her flair, her laughter. Everything Grace does is better, Kate thinks. At the end of the day they ride back onto Blind Crescent and survey the street. They prop their bikes against their thighs and stand in the centre of the cul-de-sac and look around. Grace looks at Kate's bike a lot. She wishes she had it. She wishes she had Kate's hair and her house and her mother and father. When Gavin is annoying, Grace wishes she were an only child.

"He never leaves the house," Gavin says. He is looking at Roger Smith's old house. "How do you think he gets food? How do you think he gets water?"

Mr. Walcott is watching the teenagers from his front window. He is snacking on iced coffee, topped with whipped cream. He has a cookie in his hand. It is hot in his house and he is sweating profusely. Every so often he uses his cookie hand to wipe the sweat off his forehead.

The teenagers are talking. Mr. Walcott watches their mouths flap open and closed. The radio is on behind him. Jackson Kern is due over any time now with more groceries. Mr. Walcott sees the glint of something metal in the window where the man sits at the end of the street. Creepy, Mr. Walcott thinks. Strange and bizarre and odd and peculiar. Staring out.

"I think he sneaks out at night," Kate says. "I think he probably has a night job and no one sees him go." She looks at Grace.

"No," Gavin says. "I would see him."

"Yeah," Grace laughs. "From your tree."

"How'd you know?"

"What tree?" Kate asks.

Grace laughs. Gavin turns red.

"I think he's the highway murderer," Grace says. "I think he rents a different truck once a month and shoots people down. This is his hideout." Grace looks over at her house, her father's car isn't there. She lights a cigarette. "In fact," she says, "we should sneak in one night and check it out."

"No way," Kate says. "There's no way I'm going in there."

Gavin likes the idea. He imagines skulking through the house, confronting the man inside. The idea intrigues him.

Mr. Walcott moves. Gavin sees him in the window.

"Fatty's watching us. Checking you out, Grace."

Grace turns toward Mr. Walcott's window and gives a little wave. She sticks her hip out. She shows her legs.

"Grace," Kate says. "Don't." Grace's sexuality makes Kate nervous. She wants to be Grace, but then again, she doesn't. Kate flicks her blonde hair over her shoulders. She's seen the way people look at

Grace. Men. They look at Grace like she's candy. Like they need her. Kate wishes men would look at her like that, and then again, she wishes she were invisible. As it is, Gavin's the only one who stares at her and she's had quite enough of that.

"Is that a new top?" Grace says, sucking on her cigarette. "You seem to have new clothing every day."

Kate shrugs.

Mr. Walcott bustles away, back into the recesses of his house.

"Let's do it," Gavin says. "Let's go in there."

Oliver Rafferty drives down the cul-de-sac in his convertible. He stops before them. Grace puts her cigarette out quickly.

"Hi, there. What are you three doing?"

"Just getting back from the beach, Dad," Kate says. Men, Kate thinks. Even her father looks at Grace like he's drowning and she's the life preserver. It makes Kate sick. Her dad.

"Well, then." Oliver clears his throat, smiles at them, and then drives on and into his driveway. He sits in his car for a minute, staring down at his lap. Grace Quimby, he has noted, is wearing a bikini top and cut-off jean shorts.

"Your dad is cute," Grace says.

"Fuck off," Kate says. "That's gross. He's my dad."

Grace smiles.

The teens split up, walking their bikes onto their separate properties, shrugging each other off. Tomorrow they will go to the beach again.

"Who cares about the man in that house?" Grace says to Gavin. "I don't, do you?"

"Well, if he's the highway murderer, we should probably do something about it, don't you think?"

"What?"

"Call the police—I don't know."

Gavin follows Grace up the stairs and into their house.

"And tell them what? That a weird guy has moved into a house on our street?"

"I think we should try and go in there. Check him out."

Grace groans. "We aren't the Hardy Boys, Gav. I was joking when I said we should go in there."

Grace turns and looks out the front-door window. She sees Mr. Rafferty getting out of his car. He walks over to Kate and they climb the steps of their perfect house together. Mr. Rafferty puts his arm around Kate. Grace wonders where her own father is. With Lindsay, of course. Where else would he be?

Gavin laughs. "Cool, the Hardy Boys."

"HE SEEMS TO HAVE STOPPED at six, Jackson. That's what they say on the news."

"It hasn't been long enough, Mother," Jackson says. He's dishing up the peas. His father sits sullenly at the table. About a month ago Esther insisted Shannon come to the table. "No more eating like an animal in the zoo," she had said. "Get away from that TV."

"What's that supposed to mean, Jackson?" Esther says, her mouth stuck together as she gums the peas.

Jackson cuts her meat into tiny forkfuls. Then he turns to his father's plate and begins to do the same thing.

"It's only been a week," Jackson says quietly. "The highway shooter usually waits a month before doing it again."

"How do you know that?" Shannon says. "And don't cut my damn food. It's my food. I can cut it. I'm not a baby."

"But—"

"Let him cut your food, Shannon. You drop the knife every time. Let your son take care of you."

"I'm not a baby. It's demeaning."

"Oh, for God's sake," Esther says. "Get over it. You're an old man, Shannon. The sooner you admit that, the better. Jackson, cut your father's meat."

Jackson reaches for Shannon's plate again and Shannon pulls it back from his son. The knife, balanced precariously on the side, falls to the floor.

"*See*," Esther shrieks. "Dummy. You're such a dummy."

"I am not," Shannon shouts. "How dare you say I'm stupid."

Jackson stands up and begins to empty his plate into the garbage under the sink. He scrapes it off, all his food, right into the garbage. Esther looks at him. Shannon looks at him.

"Wasting good food," Esther says. "You're the dummy."

"You think we're made of money?" Shannon shouts.

Silence.

Jackson is slumped over. His shoulders and neck ache. He looks at his parents. "I'm going out to the shed."

"Don't leave us here," his mother whines. "You need to help me take a bath tonight. I haven't had one in days. I'm stinking, Jackson. I'm starting to smell."

"She's right," Shannon says. "Old-lady smell. Phew." He waves a hand in front of his nose and then pushes a spoonful of peas into his mouth and mulls it around. Jackson thinks the old man looks like a cow chewing its cud. In six months his father has changed so drastically.

"I'm working for a bit, Mother," Jackson says. "Then I'm getting some groceries for Mr. Walcott and then I'll come in and help you with your bath. Watch TV with Dad for a while. Please."

"You're always doing things for Murray," Esther says. "We ask for nothing and he—he asks for everything." She scoops peas into her mouth and glares at him.

Jackson walks toward the front door. His body feels achy and old. He feels stiff, as if he's been running. His legs hurt. He's lost ten pounds in the past month. He must try to eat, keep his strength up. He needs his strength now. It's crucial. But every time he swallows anything it threatens immediately to come back up.

"I think the highway shooter will do it again soon," Shannon says from the kitchen table. He isn't talking to Esther. He's talking to no one in particular. "I think he's getting daring. I think he'll take risks and then we'll catch him. That's what will happen. He's not smart. Mark my words. He's like Dahmer or that Bernardo guy. What about Bundy? You think I'm stupid, Esther? They are stupid. Murderers are stupid. All of them. They get caught eventually. I can feel it in my bones. You wait and see."

"Charles Manson," Esther says. "Remember him? Cutting that poor baby right out of—"

Jackson shuts the front door quickly and walks down the stairs, out into the warm night, and into his shed. He pauses as he shuts the shed door and he looks out across the quiet street toward the house at the end. He must watch himself. Someone in there, he is sure of it, is watching him. He has to be careful in the early mornings these days. Jackson wouldn't want anyone to befriend his mother and father and tell them what he's been up to. He wouldn't want to have to stay in all night. He wouldn't want to sleep in his own bed. Jackson's bed hasn't been slept in straight through the night for years. He catnaps there, but he has no intention of starting to sleep there, now or ever. Whenever he lies flat for more than two hours his head feels as if it's going to explode.

Mr. Walcott is signalling to him from his window. Jackson raises his hands. Ten minutes, he mouths, and goes into his shed, ducks under the hanging flowers, and enters the drying room.

He begins to sift the sand through his fingers over a new batch of tulips and he checks his daffodils on the shelves. He whispers to them as he sifts. He whispers sweet nothings, soothing words, lovely compliments.

"My pretties," he whispers. "Pretty, pretty, pretty." But then he thinks that he sounds like the wicked witch in *The Wizard of Oz*. Didn't she call Dorothy "my pretty"?

Pretty, Jackson thinks. There is nothing in the way he runs his life that leaves room for anything—anyone—pretty. Even if there ever was anyone out there who could look beyond his stick legs, his sallow complexion, his thinning hair. Once, driving late at night, Jackson saw a woman in a car beside his. He watched her. Stared at her profile, her small nose, upturned slightly, her long eyelashes. He was that close, driving that parallel, able to see her that clearly. And then she felt his stare, he could see her feel it, and he watched— almost running into the other lane—as she turned toward him, ready to smile.

But then she got a look at him. His ball cap slung low over his brow, his unwashed hands—later he noticed a smudge of dirt on his cheek—and she turned quickly away. He saw her face. Saw what she did with her face. As she tried to compose herself.

The story of his life. Jackson's never met anyone who really looks at him, sees him for who he is.

But then, who is he?

The boy with his basketball isn't out tonight. Jackson's head is clear for a minute. Clear enough to think of old movies, *The Wizard of Oz*. Come to think of it, the boy hasn't thumped into his head lately. It's been still on the street. That's fine with him. Fine with Jackson Kern. His mind needs time to rest, his headaches need to go away. Maybe, just maybe, if they go away for good, then everything else in his life will iron out into one long, flat road. All the bumps gone. Driving down a straight highway, the wind in his hair, all the ground even beneath him.

"My nice flowers," he whispers, "such beauties." He feels like a fool. No matter what *Air Time*, the flower-drying magazine he bought, tells him, Jackson knows for a fact that he won't ever get used to talking to the flowers. He might as well give it up right now. The writer in that magazine is crazy. When his flowers are slowly dying, Jackson is one hundred percent sure it doesn't help to talk to them. Help what? Help the colours? That's ridiculous. He wasted Mr. Walcott's money on that magazine and the advice is worth nothing to him. Serves him right to listen to anyone. Jackson has spent most of his adult life trying not to listen to anyone about anything. He just got momentarily sucked in, taken in by the pictures of the author's dried flowers—so lifelike, so real. But talking to them didn't get them that way. Hard work and diligence got them that way. And a little bit of photo touch-up. Airbrushing. Magic.

It is getting dark. From his front window, Mr. Walcott tastes a rainbow of colours as he watches Jackson drive the truck into the street and get out. He tastes the curve of the steering wheel, the half circle of side mirror, the straight-arrow, ramrod posture of Jackson, the dip at the bottom of the hubcap, the rectangle of the broken back window, Jackson's L-shape bent leg, the circle of tires as they stop rolling. He tastes the white door of the truck and he tastes it vanilla and wonders if colour is affecting his synesthesia—but then he can taste slight rosemary in the pale orange shirt Jackson is wearing and thinks he is wrong about any colour connection.

Mr. Walcott's synesthesia is out of hand these days. It is because of the beginning of summer. It is to do with the closed-in carpeted feeling he has in the summertime. In the winter he is fine. In the winter he is supposed to stay inside, someone retired like him would stay inside. But the summer feels like the time he should be out in the fresh air, smelling the cut grass, the bloom of flowers, the hot, sticky breeze, the soft scent of dirt.

He misses Judy so much. Oh, so much.

And his back is itching. Insanely. Rubbing himself endlessly on furniture and counters, desperately scratching with an umbrella and the fireplace poker, Mr. Walcott does everything he can to control the itch. But then it occurs to him that maybe this back itch is something else, something deeper. Something more than an itch. Everything, big and small, has potential meaning.

A couple of days ago Mr. Walcott put his foot out the back door. Just the toe of his right foot. Touched the mat, touched the decking. His heart sped up. His itch stayed steady. Then he took his foot back in, kept it for himself, shut the door, and disappeared within.

"JACKSON, BOY. How are you?" Mr. Walcott lets Jackson in.

"It's hot in here." Jackson carries the grocery bags to Mr. Walcott's kitchen counter. Is it his imagination or is Mr. Walcott getting bigger? Is that possible in the one week since he was here last? "Don't you have an air conditioner? What about opening some windows?"

"Oh, no, no, I can't open windows. Would you like something to eat?"

"Why not? Why can't you open the windows?"

"People will get in."

Jackson scratches his head. This reminds Mr. Walcott of his itch and he picks up the old barbecue tongs he's been trying to use on his back.

"I can't stay."

"Just a bite. I would adore the company." Mr. Walcott puts down the tongs and begins to bustle around the kitchen, unpacking his bags, turning on the stove.

Jackson pauses for a minute and then surprises himself and sits down at the kitchen table. Mr. Walcott turns toward him. "Oh, goody," he says. He claps his fat paws together. "This is good."

Jackson doesn't know why he's sitting down. He has to bathe his mother. That's why he's sitting down. Perhaps Mr. Walcott's food will go down his throat. It always smells so good. Perhaps this food will make Jackson hungry.

"If you open up your windows," Mr. Walcott says, "it's an invitation to criminals. You might as well stick a sign on your front lawn that says, 'Come on in and rob me.'" He laughs.

Jackson shrugs. He looks around. He can't imagine anyone finding anything worthwhile to steal in Mr. Walcott's house.

"We'll fry up some shrimp, shall we? And boil some noodles?" Mr. Walcott hums as he bustles around the kitchen. For such a large man, Jackson notes he is light on his feet. Bouncy. "Just a late-night snack."

Jackson rubs his temples. "Well, you should put air conditioning in, then. It's going to get hot this summer."

"*Farmer's Almanac?*"

"Pardon?"

"Just wondering where you get your information. Me, I like to read all kinds of things. Magazines, newspapers, biographies, fiction, poetry. I even read cereal boxes and recipe books. I'm always reading"—Mr. Walcott whistles a merry tune—"anything."

For a man who is a shut-in, who doesn't like to go out, Jackson thinks, Mr. Walcott is surprisingly friendly.

"A knowledgeable mind is a—"

"The radio," Jackson interrupts.

"Ah, you listen to the radio."

"That's where I heard about summer. About it being hot this year."

"Yes, well, that makes sense. It was hot last summer too. Hot, hot, hot." Mr. Walcott stirs the noodles boiling over in his pot. He licks his lips. "This is going to be good. Do you like spicy? Do you like hot? I can put some Cajun spice on these shrimp. I love spicy. I just sprinkle it on." Mr. Walcott shakes some spice onto the shrimp. Aroma fills the air. "You know, Jackson, it's funny we've never done this before."

"What do you mean?" Jackson says. The plate before him, topped with a huge mound of noodles and shrimp, makes him feel ill. Nauseous. The smell is tempting, but the sight makes him sick. He can't imagine putting all that food into his body. His head pounds.

"We've never just talked before, have we?" Mr. Walcott sits down, with great effort, across from Jackson. "I mean, we've never eaten together."

Jackson stares at his plate.

"Dig in, boy," Mr. Walcott says with his mouth bursting, noodles hanging out. Shrimp tails appearing on the table beside him like so many pink carcasses. "It's good."

Jackson takes a bite. A small one. The spice hits him. His eyes water. His stomach roils.

"I always wondered," Mr. Walcott says between bites. "My, it's spicy, isn't it? I always wondered about something and here you are to relieve my wondering."

Jackson says, "Can I have some water?"

Mr. Walcott points to the kitchen sink. "Can't get up, my boy. Not when the food is so tasty. Huge effort, you know. To get up. I'm not the man I used to be." Mr. Walcott stops eating and begins to giggle. "I was going to say I'm half the man I used to be, but look at me. I can say I'm double the man I used to be. Triple." He guffaws, his mouth open. Jackson can see food particles on the fat man's tongue. He gets up and gets water from the sink. He tries to swallow.

"Back to before, Jackson. I don't mean to pry. I don't mean to be a nosy-body, but I was just wondering something and maybe you could help me."

Silence. Jackson's ears are ringing. He is seeing shapes behind his eyes.

"You go out every night, don't you? Every single night. You go out in the truck. And I was wondering—"

Jackson turns suddenly, violently, and rushes toward the front door.

"Jackson, where are you going? Too spicy?"

He opens the door and the night breeze hits him. "I have to go. I have to take care of my mother." Jackson slams the door behind him and rushes down the stairs. He vomits water into Mr. Walcott's bushes. Retches.

Inside, Mr. Walcott says to himself, to his noodles, "Simple question, really. I was just wondering what the boy does when he goes out driving. Just wondering, that's all. It doesn't matter to me. Not one iota. Not one bit."

Outside, Jackson straightens and wipes his mouth. He waits until the pinpricks of light stop dancing behind his eyes, waits until he can steady himself on his thin, shaking legs, and then he walks home.

Inside, Mr. Walcott takes another bite of his shrimp. "What's not to like about this dish? Fish dish. Red fish. Blue fish," he whispers to himself. "It's delicious. Very, very good. Spicy, but good." He shovels the food into his mouth, and when he's finished with his plate, he forks Jackson's noodles and shrimp onto his plate and begins again. "But," he says, "shrimp aren't really fish, are they? They're crustaceans." He sucks a noodle up. That's a nice word, he thinks. *Crustaceans.*

Outside, the cicadas buzz.

A WEEK LATER. It is hot. The heat has hit the street, come down the hill behind the houses, enveloped the neighbourhood. It is hanging in the air. It is thick and humid.

Sunday morning and Nelson is tidying up his grass after cutting it. He is sweating. Holly is watching. She is standing in the air-conditioned house looking out at him from her side window.

Lindsay is inside painting her nails and talking on the phone to her ex-boyfriend who is now just a good friend.

Oliver sits on the top step of his porch and looks down the street at Nelson. Oliver would like to sit on the chairs on his porch but they are made of twigs and horribly uncomfortable.

Jill is inside staring at a magazine, trying to focus on the ads. She has had a fight with Oliver. About everything; about losing the Now perfume advertising campaign to a colleague, about how Kate won't talk to her without a snarl in her voice, about how Pearl is driving her crazy with her bossiness. About how Oliver never does all those odds and ends that need doing in the house. Like calling the plumber for the dripping tap, or calling the tiler for the chip on the kitchen floor. Jill is angry and fed up. She doesn't know what to do anymore, and Oliver doesn't want to hear about it. While Jill complained, Oliver's eyes wandered and he held himself as if on the edge of a cliff, ready to jump. "Oh," she says to the magazine. She looks closely at an ad for cheese: The Cheese Stands

Alone. Tragic but beautiful. "Oh, oh, oh. Why didn't I think of that?"

Oliver gets off the steps and walks down toward Nelson. At the same time Holly comes out of her house, gets knocked back from the heat, steadies herself, and begins to walk over to Nelson. When she sees Oliver walking, she thinks to go back into her house, see if the boys need her, but it's too late, it would look too obvious.

Nelson picks up cut grass with a rake and shovel. He puts it in a brown bag. The bag is limp from the heat.

"Hi, Nelson," Oliver says. "What are you doing?"

"What?"

"Well, cutting your grass. I can see that." Oliver looks back at his house. Standing on Nelson's front lawn and looking at his house makes him feel proud and secure.

"Hi," Holly says.

"I just cut the grass. Now I'm tidying."

"Just wanted to say hello," Holly says. "Nothing important." She looks at Nelson long and hard. It astonishes her how much she loves his appearance. She adores it. He is lovely. And, Holly reminds herself, in general, she's really mad at men. Oliver, for example, with his height, his thin nose, his reddish blond hair. She has no need for Oliver. But there's something about Nelson.

"Hi, Holly," Oliver says.

The three of them are awkward. Oliver and Holly watch Nelson fill the bag with grass clippings. Holly remembers that last summer this happened as well. All three of them converged somehow and stood stiffly and silently. And the summer before that, before Roger Smith, they stood together laughing about something the kids were doing. The street seemed fuller then. Expanded. Kids biking and running. Holly beginning to show, her stomach stretching forward. Joe playing something on the street with Gavin. Something like tag.

Holly can't remember. It seems so foreign now. The weight of the world on their shoulders, Holly thinks. Now the street is empty. It always is. Except for the teenagers with their bikes, it seems as if everyone comes and goes from their houses without ever running into one another. Odd. She looks over at her house and sees Joe standing in the window, staring out at her. Holly shrugs at him. He glares.

Nelson looks at Holly's legs. Is that hair on them? Lots of hair?

Oliver says, "So, the sniper—"

"Yes," Holly says, "the sniper." She shakes her head.

Nelson says nothing. He continues bagging the grass.

"Our gardener—" Oliver begins.

"He's the sniper?" Nelson laughs.

"No, but I could give you his name."

Holly has seen Oliver's gardener. She has seen the half-assed job he does, tossing green bags full of leaves into the back of his truck, most of them ripped open, driving down the street with leaves blowing everywhere. Once Holly saw him take a broken bag and toss it onto Mr. Walcott's front lawn.

Nelson straightens up. Lindsay would never let her leg hair get that thick, would she? Not that it would bother him if it were Lindsay, really, would it?

"I like taking care of my grass myself, Oliver." Nelson suppresses the urge to say that not everyone is as rich as Oliver, that Nelson's own low-end sales job won't afford him those luxuries, but there's no use starting an argument about something like that. There's only so much money to make when you have little more than a high school diploma.

"Oh, yeah. I guess," Oliver says, "it can be fun." For a minute he catches a glimpse of a woman walking past the window in Nelson's house. Is it Grace?

"I can't afford a gardener," Holly says. "But yours is doing a good job."

"Yes," Oliver says. "We're happy with him."

"What do you think?" Holly asks. She points toward the old house.

Oliver shrugs. Another nosy woman, he thinks. No wonder the guy doesn't want to introduce himself.

"Maybe he's the sniper," Nelson says. He laughs.

"We thought of that," Oliver says. "Well, Jill and Pearl thought of that."

"Anything out of the ordinary and women, well—" Nelson stops. He looks at Holly. "Sorry."

"I didn't think of that," Holly lies. The thought has crossed her mind many times. But then she thinks Jackson Kern could be the sniper too. Or any one of the people who call her every night and complain about their lives. For that matter, Holly thinks, any one of the men on the street here could be the highway murderer. Mr. Walcott even. Holly looks over at his house. Maybe he sneaks out at night. Galumphs down the street like the big friendly giant. She giggles to herself.

"I don't know," Oliver says. "He never goes out, does he? The man in the house."

"Do you think we should call the police?" Holly asks.

Oliver shrugs. "No reason to get involved if he's not causing any problems."

"But … what if?"

Nelson begins moving over a little with his bag. He moves farther from Holly and Oliver. Soon he is ten feet away and the space makes any attempt at conversation awkward.

Oliver says, "Let's just watch the situation. If we notice anything strange, then we should call the police."

"But isn't this strange?" Holly points at the house. "Just sitting in that house, looking out."

Oliver shrugs again. "Mr. Walcott does it."

Holly thinks that even Ivan could be the sniper. And then this thought grows in her mind. It starts as a seed, as a small joke to herself, but then begins to grow, take on roots. Holly shivers.

Eventually conversation dwindles and Oliver waves goodbye—"Have a nice day"—and trudges back up to his house. He sits again on his porch. He looks over at the empty house beside his and wonders if the man in there is dead or something. In this heat. It's stifling.

Holly stands outside with Nelson a moment longer. She sees Lindsay peeking out of the front-door window at her standing there. Holly stares at Nelson's arms as he shakes out a new bag. He stops and looks at her.

"How are your kids, Holly?" Nelson asks.

"Fine, just fine." Holly snaps out of it and rambles on about kindergarten and how exciting that will be for Joe and how he needs it and how she needs it, and Nelson watches her animated face and thinks to himself that Holly must have been as pretty as Lindsay when she was younger. He remembers she was pretty when she was pregnant with the smallest kid. Then Nelson catches himself wondering where his ex-wife might be and what she might be doing right now. And then he feels sad about all of that, about how it turned out for his kids, and he is glad they sleep in on Sunday mornings so he can be sure they are in the house, safe, where they should be.

"Nelson, honey, telephone," Lindsay calls out the front door. She is wearing shorts and a bikini top. She looks lovely. Even Holly thinks so.

"Oh, hello, Hillary," Lindsay says.

"Holly," Holly mumbles.

Nelson shrugs. "Well, see you."

Holly stands there, watching Nelson go into the house. She looks at his lawn-clipping bag, the rake he was using, touching, holding. What is wrong with her, she thinks. Ivan? The sniper? She would know if he was. Wouldn't she?

And then, from the empty house up the street, there is movement and Holly is suddenly made aware that she is being watched. A show. Her life has become a reality show for some guy who never shows his face. She feels a chill move up her spine.

Holly walks back to her house, straight into the air conditioning, which cools the sweat from her body.

"Mom?" Joe asks. Sweetpea is crying from his crib upstairs. The TV is on loud. The news. Holly notes a mangled car on the side of the highway.

"What?"

"What's a cereal killer?"

"What?"

"A cereal killer?" Joe holds up his bowl of Cheerios. "Cereal," he says. "Killer."

Holly has to laugh. She runs up the stairs toward Sweetpea's cry. "Oh, honey," she calls down. "It has nothing to do with your Cheerios."

The Highway Murderer

PEARL IS WATCHING TV.

It happened again. This time there was a baby in the back of the car. A baby in a car seat. Another one. Like the other two kids months ago. This time only two weeks have passed. The sniper is getting quicker. Pearl is horrified.

"A baby," she keeps saying to anyone who will listen. She shakes her head and fists at the TV. "My God, a baby."

The shooter aimed at the mother, who was driving, and shot her in the head. Pearl listens carefully to the news. The car swerved out of control. The baby died in the crash. The baby and the mother were going to the hospital. Late at night. Pearl can imagine the scenario. The baby had an ear infection and the mother was worried that the eardrums would burst. Pearl's heard of that before. Bursting eardrums. The mother put the baby in the car and told her tired husband she would call him from the hospital. She told her husband not to wake their four-year-old son. She ruffled her husband's hair and told him to get some sleep as the next day was important. Pearl imagines all of this. The hair ruffling. The news, she thinks, is so clinical. She has to pad it so she can see it. The husband had a job interview. Three months he had been without work. The mother drove toward the hospital. It was dark. Hot, humid. Dark, dark, dark. A row of street lights were out on the highway because of a brief thunderstorm. She drove carefully. Pearl can see her hands clutching the wheel at ten and two. Knuckles white. She was hoping to get a new prescription for antibiotics. She was hoping the doctor could cure the baby tonight so she could get some sleep. Her husband needed this new job and she needed some sleep. Doesn't Pearl know it. Her baby cried in the back seat. The baby wouldn't stop crying. Ear infections hurt, Pearl remembers. She had one a while ago and it hurt like crazy. The mother could probably feel the baby's pain.

A truck passed her. She was going the speed limit. Why would the truck need to pass her? People are always rushing, she must have thought. Pearl would have. I'm taking my kid to the hospital and that jerk is probably just going home to sleep.

But the truck began to slow down in front of her. The brake lights went on. The mother thought this was odd. Drunk driver, she thought, and she slowed down too. Tried to keep her distance. It was a two-lane highway, one lane each direction. The mother thought about passing the truck. The baby cried. There was no one out on the highway. A little farther ahead she could see the lights on the road appearing again, being turned on. It was three in the morning. The husband said later that the wife knew about the highway murderer. How could she not? She followed the news reports religiously. "It's just," he said, "that she forgot somehow. When your baby is crying," the husband said, "you forget the rest of the world."

The mother stayed behind the truck for a bit. The truck was erratic. Speeding up, slowing down. This is what Pearl thinks. Then the mother decided to pass the truck. As she passed, she looked over to see who was driving, to see if the person was drunk. She saw him holding something. She peered at it. She couldn't see what it was. Both windows in the car were open to the hot night breeze. Her baby suddenly stopped crying.

When the bullet hit the mother there was only a brief moment of pain. And there was a flash of white light. A loud sound. And then there was nothing.

Her hands were on ten and two when they pulled her out of the crumpled car.

Pearl opens her eyes to get rid of the flash of white light in her mind. She squeezes her hands into fists and stares straight ahead. Kate stares at her.

"That's crazy, Pearl," Kate says. "How can you know what she was thinking just from the news reports? How can you know if it hurt or not? How can you know the baby stopped crying or that there was a flash of white light? That's crazy."

"I," Pearl says, tapping her forefinger against her brow, "have imagination, Katie. I can see."

"I TOLD YOU," Esther Kern shrieks. "I told you he'd do it again. The last time was only two weeks ago. I told you, Jackson. You said no. You said wait a month. But I told you."

"He'll screw up soon," Shannon says, looking sideways at Jackson. Looking at his son from the corner of his eyes. Studying him. "Mark my words. He'll screw up soon. A baby. Another one. Jesus Christ, a baby."

"With an ear infection," Esther screams. "You used to have ear infections, Jackson. Do you remember?"

GAVIN WANTS TO BREAK into the house at the end of the street. Grace's joke about it has made him want to do it. In the evenings he sits in the tree behind the Raffertys' house, watching for any movement anywhere on the street. He wants to break in and confront the guy, tell him to get out of Mr. Smith's house, tell him to leave everything alone. Tell him to get off Blind Crescent, go back to where he belongs.

Gavin also wants to go back into the basement. If he goes back in there, faces it like a man, sees that Mr. Smith is not still hanging there, then maybe he'll stop having nightmares. Maybe next year at school he'll be tougher, able to ignore the comments, the names—"Piss-pants," "Scaredy-cat," that kind of thing.

"No way. I'm not going in there," Grace says. "It's dirty in there."

"But it was your idea," Gavin says.

"No, it wasn't. That was a joke, you idiot."

Gavin, Grace, and Kate are sitting on the front porch of the Quimbys' house. The heat hangs down upon them, thickens all around them. Grace is sweating and wants to go inside, into the air conditioning, but she thinks sweating may be good for her pores, open them up, clear out the few blackheads she has. She might sweat off some weight too. That'd be good. She is polishing her toenails bright pink and blowing the hair out of her face.

Kate is sullen. Grace keeps commenting on all her clothes and it isn't her fault she has so many. Her mom buys them. Kate wishes her mom would buy cool clothes, though, clothes like the stuff Grace wears—low-slung jeans that show her pierced belly button. Kate wishes she could get her belly button pierced. "No," her mom said. "Not while you're living in my house." Her house, Kate thinks. Shit. Kate doesn't want to be here, hanging out with Gavin and Grace. Well, she'd like to be hanging out with Grace because Grace is cool, but she really doesn't want to be with Gavin. She's sick of him. She's sick of how he looks at her, how his eyes follow every movement she makes. How he thinks it's hip or something to want to break into a house. A dumb house. A gross house. Kate thinks that trashy house beside hers ought to be bull-dozed. She'd like to see it come down. It'd be nice to be able to forget it ever existed. In fact, Kate thinks as she looks around the street, it would be nice to bulldoze most of these houses down. Clean up the neighbourhood.

Kate doesn't know why she's so angry lately, but most of the time she wants to hurt someone, she wants to punch and kick and scream at someone. It takes everything she has to hold these feelings inside.

"I'll go in without you, then. I just thought you might want to come."

"Why would we want to go into that house, Gavin? What's there for us?" Grace looks bored. She wants a cigarette, but her dad and Lindsay are in the house, probably arguing about something. Grace doesn't remember her mom and dad arguing. Seems they never even talked to each other. Didn't get close enough to each other to actually argue. But Lindsay and her dad argue all the time. And then they make up and that's even sicker. The noise that comes out of the bedroom is enough to make you want to cut your ears off, Grace thinks.

Gavin shrugs. "I don't know. I just want to go in."

"Boys," Kate says. She blows her bangs out of her face just like Grace did a minute ago.

Grace rolls her eyes. "Besides," she says, "there's someone living in there now."

Gavin looks up at the house. "Yeah, but...."

Lindsay comes out on the porch. "You kids," she says. "You kids are always just hanging out, bored. Don't you have anything better to do?"

Grace holds her feet up sweetly. She admires her long, tanned legs and her pink toenails. "They're wet," Grace says. "When my toes are dry, we'll go places."

"Do things," Kate says. She laughs.

Gavin smiles.

"You just don't get it, do you?" Lindsay huffs. "You're young once. Really do things. This is one of your last summers to actually do things."

"What do you mean, one of our last summers? We aren't going to die next summer," Grace says.

"Unless you're planning on getting rid of us," Gavin says. He pretends to have a gun in his hand. He pretends to shoot Grace.

"I mean that next summer, if I have anything to say about it—and I do—you will both be getting summer jobs." Lindsay turns around and walks back into the air-conditioned house.

"Fuck," Gavin says. He turns his fake gun on Lindsay's receding figure. "Bang."

"*She* won't be here next summer," Grace says. "There'll be someone else by then."

"I don't know, Grace. She's the one in control around here."

"Who cares?" Kate says. "That's a whole year away. What are we going to do this afternoon?"

BANG.

Lindsay shuts the door on the kids on the porch and fights the urge to lock it. This isn't her house, she reminds herself, but it almost is. She's been here enough months, she cleans it, she even painted the hallway, it's almost her house.

Nelson is in the kitchen reading the newspaper and drinking coffee. Lindsay looks at him.

"Another highway murder," he says.

Lindsay looks at Nelson's face, the way his jaw is beginning to sag slightly, the greying at his temples. She used to find all of this appealing, but those damn kids take any excitement out of life, any lust out of life, and turn it all into one endless nightmare of responsibility. And responsibility means Nelson's not such a fun time anymore. Lindsay admits that he is good in bed, that he enjoys pleasing her and is a gentleman and polite. She likes that in older guys. Young guys seem to have no manners. They just take, they don't give. But kids? She doesn't want kids. Lindsay wishes that Nelson's wife would appear from wherever she disappeared and take the kids off their hands. She doesn't know how long she can stand living here with them.

"Seems a baby got killed again."

"Any coffee left?"

Nelson signals with his head to the coffee pot. "A little."

"You should make your kids do something, Nelson."

Nelson looks up. "What do you mean?"

"I mean, they're always hanging around doing nothing."

"I'd rather they did nothing than did something bad."

"That's not the point."

Nelson shrugs. "What can I do?"

"You're asking me? I don't know how to be a parent. I didn't ask to be a mother."

Nelson studies Lindsay's long legs, her small waist and hips, her large breasts. Then he looks down at the paper again. He studies the picture of the car lying in the ditch at the side of the road. The windows were open, supposedly, so there is no broken, shattered glass in the front. Just shattered glass in the back, where they say the baby was strapped into a car seat.

"Sick," Nelson whispers.

"What? What did you say?"

"Sorry, I was just—" Nelson points to the paper.

"If you aren't listening, then what's the point of me talking?"

Good question, Nelson thinks. It's funny but his lust seems to have waned lately. All those romance-novel thoughts seem to have gotten stuck in the air with the heat. Ever since his kids have been home from school, he doesn't seem to see Lindsay in Technicolor anymore. Sure, he likes her. He might even love her, but, truth be told, he's actually getting tired of her.

"Nelson"—Lindsay sidles up to him, rubs against him—"come on. Let's go upstairs."

"I thought you were mad at me."

"I know, I'm just … I don't know. It's hot outside. I need some exercise."

"But Gavin and Grace."

"Who cares. We'll lock our door."

Nelson begins to follow Lindsay up the stairs. He can hear his kids on the front porch laughing about something. Gavin's low-pitched guffaw next to Grace's squeal. The Rafferty kid is out there too. He gets a glimpse of her blonde mane in the window of the door.

Lindsay can feel the sudden change in Nelson. There is something off, something not so attentive in his pose. He's paying attention to what's on the front porch, not her ass, as he follows her up to the bedroom.

Our door, Nelson thinks. She said "our door" like she owns the house. Suddenly Nelson doesn't feel like going upstairs to his bedroom anymore. Suddenly he feels like he wants to go outside, hang out with his kids. He thinks of that car crashed into the ditch, the poor baby, the dead mother. But then Lindsay pulls him inside the room and strips naked, and in a matter of seconds he's forgotten he even has children.

OLIVER CAN'T HELP HIMSELF. He is sitting in his den at the window on the second floor of his house and he is holding binoculars and looking through them, out the window, toward the Quimby house. He is watching Grace Quimby on the front porch as she bends in half to paint her toenails. God, she's lovely. He can see the colour she has chosen. A hot pink. He can see the little toes she has, pretty little toes. He can see her full breasts squish up against her tank top, pillow against her naked thighs, as she leans forward to brush on polish. Oliver can see a glimpse of red thong underwear coming out of the back of her cut-off jean shorts. Normally thong underwear does nothing for him. Normally (on TV or if a waitress in a bar is wearing it and Oliver catches a glimpse) all he can think about is how uncomfortable they must be to wear. But Grace....

Nelson's girlfriend comes out on the porch and Oliver drops the binoculars in surprise. Then she goes back in. Attractive, Oliver thinks, but nothing compared to Grace.

Every so often Oliver's binoculars look over at his daughter, Kate. Then they rush back to Grace again and Oliver pushes Kate out of his mind. She's his baby, his daughter, Kate is. Grace is nothing like her. They might be the same age, but they are completely different species. It's like fish and cats. Completely not the same.

Oliver can feel himself getting wildly turned on by Grace and he hates the feeling. He wonders if what he's doing is illegal—even though watching can't really be that bad, can it? He is, after all, just making sure his daughter is okay, not up to anything.... He reaches his hand into his tailored pants.

"Oliver?" Jill is knocking on his door. She opens it slightly and peeks in.

Oliver drops the binoculars into an open drawer on his desk and puts a three-ring binder in his lap. He turns toward Jill, his face flushed.

"Jesus," Oliver says. "Next time knock."

"I did knock."

"More than once."

"Why? What are you doing, Oliver?"

"Nothing. Just working. You scared me, that's all."

Jill crosses the room and looks out across the street. "God, I wish she wouldn't hang out with that Quimby girl."

"Who?"

"Kate. Isn't that who you were just looking at? Kate and Grace and Gavin. With those binoculars."

"No, I wasn't looking out. Just—"

"I've heard that Grace Quimby is already sexually active. Peggy at the school, Desirée's mother, said that Desirée says that Grace gives head to boys on the football team in the change room after school. For money. Can you believe it? Oral sex. At her age. She's much too young. I don't know if I believe Peggy, but I'm not sure Kate should be hanging around with her as much as she is. Maybe next summer we should put Kate in camp. Send her away for a bit."

Oliver can't talk. He can't say anything. He's lost his voice.

"I went to camp. I loved camp." Jill stares at Oliver.

Oliver looks down at the floor.

"Anyway, I just wondered if you'd like lunch. Or if you're too busy working."

Oliver nods.

"Come down when you're ready. Pearl's actually making something. She keeps talking about the new highway death and it's getting on my nerves. We've had enough dead people around here lately." Jill waves her hand toward Roger Smith's old house. "I wish, just for a moment, that people would talk about something else besides death. It's annoying. How are we supposed to live when everyone keeps talking about death?"

Oliver distinctly remembers Jill's mother saying that exact thing on her deathbed. Waving her arm in the air like the queen and saying, "Can't anyone talk about anything besides my death?"

Jill closes the door and stands for a moment in the hallway, thinking. Something strange is happening, but she doesn't know what. Jill looks at the photograph on the wall beside her. Oliver took it. It is a nice picture of Jill when she was in her early thirties. She is leaning on a fence, out in the open, the sky going on forever around her and her hair whipped forward and back in the wind. Jill touches the picture, traces her own face. It's hard to believe, she thinks, that this is me. It's hard for her to believe that Oliver took a picture that is so good, that shows her happy and trim and beautiful. Jill reaches up and takes the picture off the hook, takes it down from the wall. It's time something new went up there, Jill thinks. Maybe a painting or a mirror or a picture of Kate as she is now—proud and beautiful. Maybe Pearl is right for once. About pictures. Portraits. About having to look all the time at who you used to be.

MR. WALCOTT didn't used to be curious about the world outside his windows. But lately things have been getting interesting. There's that Quimby boy in the tree. And the same boy and those pretty girls on the porch across the street. Mr. Walcott remembers last summer when they would go off in the morning on their bicycles and come back in the early evening. Now, this year, they sit around some days on the front porch and stare at the street. Then there was Holly Wray and Oliver Rafferty talking to Nelson Quimby out front too. Seems the street is coming together again, like it used to. Mr. Walcott watched them as if he were watching an old movie. It made him feel warm inside to see the neighbours all together again. Friendship, no matter what flavour it is, is still exciting when it first begins to cook. There's something about it, a charged atmosphere perhaps, that Mr. Walcott finds tantalizing. And Jackson Kern coming for dinner. That was certainly a change of pace. Something new. Roger Smith's old house too. That person inside. And everyone always looking up there. Mr. Walcott watches the kids watching it, the adults watching it, Holly's little boy pointing over to it. It's all so mysterious.

Mr. Walcott finds the mystery man the most intriguing, more curious than television even, the shadowy figure stalking the insides of that house. It used to be he'd spend days thinking about the highway sniper, but now he spends days thinking about the man up the street. The lone man staring out at him staring in. Mr. Walcott is sure it is a man. It has to be. Mr. Walcott has begun to think of this man as his double. The skinny version of himself—because he assumes the man weighs less than he does. Most men do. The shadow is lean. Another man on Blind Crescent locking himself away in his house, peering out at those around him.

Well, Jackson Kern does peer out of his shed, and Shannon Kern does peer out of the front window, but they don't count.

Not since Roger Smith died has Mr. Walcott been so taken with life around him. He sometimes can't wait to get up in the morning. Even the news reports about more killings on the highways (babies dying!) don't bring him down as much as they did before. He can't wait to look out the window. These days he rushes through his breakfast even. Or stands before the curtains that he opens slightly, as if daring the world to look in on him. There's something cathartic about the man in that house. Pulling him out, pulling him toward something. Mr. Walcott doesn't know what. Maybe he'll venture out someday and introduce himself to the man. He'll climb up those rundown stairs, knock on the big front door, and say hello. He'll tell the man that they have much in common, that maybe they can share their fears of the world and, in doing so, rid themselves of all their worries.

Maybe.

Maybe not.

Mr. Walcott laughs at this idea. It's intriguing, but he still can't fathom actually doing it. In fact, Mr. Walcott can't actually fathom doing anything but peeking occasionally out his front window. That's courageous enough for him at the moment. It has given his life new meaning. All this spying. He laughs to himself.

Day in, day out, he watches TV and reads the paper. He listens to the radio. He works at satisfying his itch. He reads the magazines Judy ordered: *The New Yorker, Harper's, Chatelaine, This Century's Home*. He learns about politics, new fiction, movie stars, and redecorating. He wonders about his house, the colours are old fashioned—browns and greens and oranges—but what can he do about it? He hasn't the energy to paint. He wonders about the house up the street, what it looks like inside now. He hasn't been near it since Roger Smith ... since the event.

He eats. Mr. Walcott learns new words, interesting words, from a column in the local paper called "Word Watch." He learns the word *dwarfsploitation*, which is the exploitation of little actors in film. He gets Jackson to rent him *The Wizard of Oz* from the video store— Jackson looked oddly at him when he requested it, didn't he? Mr.

Walcott wonders why. He feels a stab of pain and sorrow for the Munchkins because he knows they were paid less than Toto, the dog. "That sure is dwarfsploitation," he says to himself, trying the word out in his big, thick mouth. Mr. Walcott learns new sayings from the same paper, things like, "If today were a fish, I'd throw it back in the river," and "She's so slow she can't get out of her own way." He thinks these are funny. "When the chips are down, the buffalo is empty." He doesn't know what that means but he likes the ring of it.

Jackson Kern comes by with his food. He takes his videos back to the store and takes out his garbage. Jackson hasn't stayed for dinner again, although Mr. Walcott has asked. Jackson wakes Mr. Walcott every night when he leaves in his truck. But this doesn't seem to bother him as much anymore. There's something about sharing a disability with that someone up the street that makes him feel almost normal. Since the reclusive man moved into that house Mr. Walcott has been happy. Nothing—not Jackson in the middle of the night starting up his truck, not that damn boy with the basketball, not his overactive summer synesthesia, his taste for shapes, not his insatiable itch, or the highway murderer—nothing could take Mr. Walcott's mood down.

If he were one hundred pounds thinner, Mr. Walcott thinks, then perhaps he could dance.

LATE ONE NIGHT, Gavin is in his tree spying on Kate who is reading in her bedroom—pretty boring—when he sees movement behind the Smiths' old house. A figure emerges from the back door. It is the man. He moves out a bit into the yard and then scales some of the hill. He stands on the side of the hill, balancing himself unsteadily, and stares up the hill into the trees. He breathes deeply— Gavin can see his chest rising and falling. Gavin tries not to move.

The man then bends to the ground and begins to retch. He coughs dryly and heaves. Nothing comes out. Then the man moves back toward the house, leans over the old rain barrel still left there, dips his hands in, and begins to drink. Gavin watches.

A car door slams out front. Gavin hears voices on the street. The man looks up from his drinking and then moves swiftly, silently, back into the house. Like a shadow, Gavin thinks. He slides.

Gavin thinks that it is now impossible for anyone to knock on this man's front door. It has been too long. It wouldn't make sense. Everyone in the neighbourhood has to just ignore it now. No matter if he's a squatter in there illegally, or if he's bought the house, or if he's dying in there. No matter that he's drinking from the rain barrel and obviously sick. There's a time limit for being neighbourly, Gavin realizes, and Blind Crescent has passed its limit. It wouldn't even help to tell anyone about him. In fact, it might make matters worse. Gavin can imagine the police coming in and kicking the guy out on the street. It's too bad, Gavin says to himself, it's too bad no one went over right away. Helped him out. But the man obviously wants to be left alone. If Gavin really thinks about it, it's probably for the best that no one has bothered him. There are reasons people do the things they do. Gavin knows this. Even though some reasons, like any reason his stupid mom had, don't make any sense at all.

OUT FRONT, Oliver is getting out of his car. A late night at the office. An important case. He is tired and grumpy. Craving that drink he knows is coming. But there's Grace—sitting on the curb near his driveway, smoking a cigarette. Or hiding a cigarette. Under her legs, the smoke making a thin line up by her knee. She shrugs at Oliver and grins sheepishly.

"Hi, Grace."

"Hi, Mr. Rafferty."

"What are you doing out here?"

"Just hanging out," Grace says. "There's nothing to do inside the house. Lindsay's hogged the TV."

"Should you be smoking?" Oliver says.

Grace blushes. "They don't know I smoke."

Oliver starts to go up the stairs into his house, he starts to head into the bright light and air conditioning, up toward his wife and the nanny and his teenage daughter, but then he stops and comes back down and walks over to Grace. She leans back a bit and stretches her legs out in front of her. He doesn't know why he's turned from his house, why he's come close to her. She is wearing something, Oliver doesn't know what—it's not important—that reveals her stomach and it is taut and tanned, her belly button pierced. Oliver clears his throat. He looks away.

"Why don't you sit down?" Grace says. "You won't tell on me, will you?" She holds up her cigarette. She takes a daring puff and blows smoke toward Oliver. Usually, Oliver can't stand people who smoke, especially women. Usually, it turns him off.

"Well, you shouldn't be smoking," Oliver says. He puts his briefcase on the grass and crouches down and sits on the curb beside her. "But I won't tell."

"Yeah, well, it's not as if it's going to stunt my growth. Look at my legs. My dad says I'm like a horse." Grace holds up one long leg and moves it over toward Oliver. Almost touching him. He leans away.

"Yes," Oliver says. "You do have long legs."

"I run a lot," Grace says. "In gym class. All the girls run. We get so sweaty and then all the showers are hogged and sometimes I have to skip class to come home and shower." Grace laughs. "I guess I shouldn't tell you that."

"No, that's fine. I used to skip classes too." Oliver is imagining sweaty girls in the shower, Grace in the shower. Of course he is. She did that on purpose, he thinks. Or did she? Oliver isn't sure right at this moment if Grace knows what effect she's having on him. He isn't sure how old she really is inside that mature body.

"You're pretty cool for a dad, Mr. Rafferty," Grace says. She smiles at him. "Most dads would tell on me for smoking."

Oliver nods. He should tell on her, he thinks. But he won't. What good would it do?

"Kate doesn't smoke, does she?" he asks.

Grace shakes her head. "No, she thinks it's gross."

Oliver's breath steadies.

Grace finishes her cigarette, stubs it out, and leans back again. Oliver glimpses her belly button again, the jewel shining, he looks sideways at her breasts which seem to him as if they are forcing themselves out of her top. He studies her legs and notices a thin, silver ankle bracelet, a toe ring.

This is insane, Oliver thinks.

"Can you keep another secret?" Grace whispers. All the high-pitched, teenage shyness is gone from her tone. Suddenly it is thick and full and deep and practised, her voice. Her voice has turned her into an adult, into someone Oliver would have sex with.

Fuck, Oliver thinks. What am I doing out here? He begins to get up from the ground. He begins to try to move away.

"I know you've been watching me, Mr. Rafferty."

"Well, I—no." Oliver sits down again.

"It doesn't matter." Grace pulls her legs up and leans forward on her thighs. Again, the thong underwear. Oliver is stuck there on the curb. He can't move. He'll have to wait until she leaves. He feels like a teenager again, as if he's in high school. No control.

"You—" he begins, but he can't say anything. He wants to defend himself, say that she hangs out with his daughter, of course he's watching out for his daughter. But he can't say anything.

Is this my mid-life crisis, Oliver wonders. If he were a religious man, Oliver would think he was being tested. As it is, he's wishing he had bought a new sportscar for his mid-life crisis. Anything but this feeling he's having. This fear mixed with lust mixed with anger mixed with shyness. Fear. Fear. Fear. More fear than anything else.

"I just wanted you to know," Grace says, "that I've been watching you too. And that's okay, Mr. Rafferty. I think you're pretty cute."

"Cute?" Oliver's voice cracks.

"Well, handsome."

Oliver runs his hand over his slightly balding scalp.

"Handsome," he echoes. He can barely force the word out.

"I know a lot of girls who go out with older men," Grace whispers, almost to herself.

"You do?"

"Yeah."

"Oh."

"It's cool. I just thought I'd tell you that." Grace stands up in front of Oliver. She stretches high. "It's hot out, isn't it?"

Oliver can see wet marks just under her armpits, on her tank top. And a wet mark between the wings on her back when she turns to walk away. She walks slowly, as if she has nothing better to do than walk away from him oozing sex appeal. She swings her hips slightly, but not overtly. Nothing is overblown. Nothing is young. Nothing reminds him that this is a child. And she turns, when she's just in the middle of the street, and flashes him a grin. "Good night, Mr. Rafferty," she says. "Sleep tight."

He waves at her awkwardly. A flimsy, little wave. What else can he do?

"You look like the cat who ate the canary," Lindsay says to Grace when she comes back inside.

"Well," Grace smiles, "it sure tasted good." She wishes Kate had been there with her, with her dad. That would have been hilarious. She could have played them both. Although Kate probably would have blown a gasket and Grace doesn't really want Kate angry at her. Not really. She wants to push some buttons, sure, but not lose out on the rest of the summer with Kate. Even though Kate's a rich girl, she's still fun to hang with.

"Ha, ha," Lindsay says. She watches the girl walk away from her, up the stairs. She pokes Nelson, beside her on the couch, watching TV. "She's up to something, Nelson. You better find out what."

"What?" Nelson says.

"Drugs or something, I bet. She smells of cigarettes, that's for sure."

Nelson looks up at the stairs that lead to his daughter's room. Lindsay, looking at him, could swear he is scared. There is fear in Nelson's face. She snorts.

Slap

SOMETHING IS UP with Oliver.

Jill is perched awkwardly on her uncomfortable stick furniture on the front porch. The day is hot and humid. It is Saturday. Jill's shirt is open at the neck, her skirt is airy and light, her naked legs jut out from the front.

Something. Oliver is up to something.

Jill's toenails are blood-red. She had her hair done yesterday before she came home from work and it is lighter than it has ever been. A white blonde, almost transparent. From a distance her hair disappears. There is just a glow around her head.

Kate left early this morning for the beach with Gavin and Grace. Pearl is in the basement watching TV. Oliver is at work (of course). Jill is cloudy-minded in the heat. Now that the Now perfume campaign failed and her salary has decreased by half, she spends her days at work watching Harry, the new intern, line up photo shoots and TV commercials. Harry got Now. He's filming in Barbados.

There is absolutely nothing that needs to be done today. Nothing she can do. Jill twiddles her fingers together, trying to look comfortable. The heat. The chair. Her job. Her husband. Her life. Everything makes her ornery. But she doesn't want to go inside. Pearl is inside.

Jill waves her hands in front of her face. Fanning herself.

Last night Oliver tossed and turned in bed beside her. She lay still, listening to his movements in the dark. He couldn't sleep either and she can't figure out why.

Jill looks out on the neighbourhood. It's strangely silent out here this morning. Because Gavin is at the beach, there isn't the sound of his basketball. She can hear the whirr of air-conditioning units. Jill notes that Mr. Walcott doesn't have an air conditioner and she wonders if he's dead in there. Drowned in the sweat from his fat.

Jill tries leaning into the chair. Back cushions. That's what she needs. Lots of funky back cushions. Then, maybe, these chairs would be comfortable. The butt cushion is okay, but not perfect. A twig sticks into her shoulder blade. Why ever would her designer have suggested these chairs? Rustic, twig chairs—modernity mixed with old-fashioned country. What about comfort? Where did that go in the mix? Although, come to think of it, everything stylish is uncomfortable. Clothes, shoes, makeup. She remembers that peel she had on her face last year. Now that was stylish (and did wonders for her complexion), but it certainly was not comfortable. Neither was the Botox. Or the pedicures—someone scraping at her feet with a cheese grater.

Before Oliver came to bed last night he locked himself away in his den, like all the nights lately, to work. Locked himself in—"Secret case," he said, "confidential." Whatever could a corporate lawyer be doing that is confidential to his wife? Maybe lots, Jill really isn't sure what Oliver does, but he's never kept his work from her before. Not like this. Usually he just doesn't talk about it. And she doesn't ask him about it—what could she want to know about being a lawyer? Ha. But last night he even locked the door of his den from the outside after he came out. Pocketed the key. Jill caught him doing it when she passed him in the hall. Strange.

Jill feels lately that she doesn't know much about anything. She knows nothing about how to sell disgusting perfume, obviously. Nothing about what Oliver is up to. Nothing about Kate and her friends, or about where her daughter goes all day. The beach. What beach? Or the highway murderer. She didn't know about him until Kate told her. Now, of course, she knows more about him. She has been trying to watch the news, trying not to fall asleep during the incessant babble. But she really couldn't care less about him. She doesn't drive on the highway. Oliver doesn't. Kate doesn't drive yet. So it's really no concern to her. She has as much chance of getting killed by a sniper as she does of getting hit by lightning.

Jill sees Jackson come out the front door of his house and walk down the stairs and go into his shed. She looks away quickly. No eye contact. Creepy man, she thinks. What Jill would give to move away from this dead-end street. There are too many undesirables here. Ever since Roger Smith—well, she doesn't like to think about that, but ever since he did himself in, it seems this neighbourhood has effectively gone sour. The cause is the empty house on the street. An empty house where the last person who lived in it was found hanging in the basement. Yes, Jill thinks, that could certainly force a neighbourhood to go downhill. Cause and effect. Jill shuffles on her chair. She swivels in her seat and tries to pull out the damn twig that is sticking in her back.

When she turns back, that little snot-nosed kid, Holly's kid, is standing right in front of her. She jumps. She didn't even see him coming.

"God, you scared me." She puts her hand on her chest. Her heart is beating like mad.

Jill sees Holly and the baby huffing and puffing toward her, up her stairs.

"Oh, no," Jill groans.

"Hello," Holly says. "Good morning. I'm sorry.... Joe just came over. I turned and he was gone."

"He scared me," Jill says. "I didn't see anyone outside. The street was empty."

"Joe, apologize to Mrs. Rafferty. You frightened her."

"Ms. McCallan, Joe," Jill says. "Not Rafferty." Jill laughs. "Mrs. Rafferty is my mother-in-law's name. And she lives in Florida and wears horrid polyester leisure suits."

Joe smiles. This little boy reminds Jill of all those strange little boys in scary movies. The little boys who are too smart for their own good. Smart and kind of cute, but with a devilish grin and hard evil inside that will suck the blood from you. He gives Jill the shivers. She studies her nail polish while waiting for his apology. She thinks of his clown comment from a while back and wonders if her lipstick is bleeding outside her lips.

But Joe just walks closer to her and then, quite annoyingly, sits in the chair right beside her.

"These chairs hurt," he says.

"Yes, well, they aren't made for little boys."

"Joe, come home," Holly says. She is trying to be firm with Joe these days, order him about with a tough father-like voice, deeper, stronger—but now Sweetpea has toddled off and is heading for the road. No cars in sight, but you never know. Holly holds her hand up to Joe. One finger. Threatening him. Then she rushes off to get Sweetpea, his diaper drooping.

Jill sighs. The little one is not wearing anything but a stinky, drooping diaper. This neighbourhood, she thinks. Down, down, down.

"What are you doing with your thumb?" Joe asks.

"What?" Jill had forgotten for a brief second that the little brat was still there. She looks at her hand. She is making the thumbs-down sign. Jill clutches her hands together. "Your mother wants you. Why don't you go home?"

"Because."

"Because why?"

"Because."

Jill scowls. The boy has given her an instant headache.

"Go home," she hisses. "I don't want you here."

"Here we are," Holly says, coming up the stairs again, Sweetpea in her arms squirming and kicking. "I got him. You're a slippery little boy, aren't you? Like a snake, aren't you? Yes, you are. Yes, you are."

"Because I have something to tell you," Joe says.

"What?"

"What, honey?" Holly says. "What did you say? You were whispering. Sweetpea, stop kicking."

"What do you have to tell me?" Jill says, suddenly curious. He is just like those horror-movie kids. He's going to say something spellbinding, something that has "meaning," something that will hang over her for the rest of her days. He will tell her the future. Jill sits forward in her chair. She wants to ask so many questions suddenly: Will she be married to Oliver in ten years' time? Will Kate go to Harvard or Oxford? Will she be a wildly successful advertiser?

The heat is palpable. Holly wipes at her face. Her armpits are wet.

Or, Jill thinks sullenly, will she end up dying of cancer like her mother did? Alone and grumbling.

Sweetpea escapes and begins to pick the flowers out of Jill's carefully tended flower patch.

"No," Holly growls. She's had it. Another postcard from Ivan this morning. Nothing on it this time. No stamp, no postmark, no message. Nothing. Just the women on the beach. This time they were lying on their backs, with their bathing-suit tops on. So brightly coloured. So tanned and beautiful. They all had sunglasses on and pink lipstick.

Sweetpea begins to cry.

"Oh, for Pete's sake," Jill says loudly. "What do you want to tell me, little boy?"

"It's about your neighbour."

"Which one?" Jill looks frantically at Mr. Walcott's house and then at the rundown house next door. "That one?"

"Sweetpea, leave the flowers alone. Oh, God, I'm sorry, Jill. He just picked—"

"What about him? What do you know?"

"You have to pay me first," Joe says. He holds out his hand. Jill wants to smack it.

The hollering Sweetpea stops crying.

"Pay you?"

"Fifty."

"Fifty cents?"

Joe laughs.

"Little boy," Jill says. "I don't know what you are on about. You think I'm going to pay you fifty dollars to tell me something about my neighbour? That's obscene."

"What does 'obscene' mean?" Joe says.

"Joe," Holly says, "what are you talking about? Leave Ms. McCallan alone. It's time to go home. Oh, Sweetpea. Come back."

Jill sits back in her chair and then sits forward quickly because the twig pokes her. "How about," she hisses, waving her arms,

"I don't charge your mother for the damage her stupid child has just done to my flowers."

Joe laughs and points to his brother.

Jill looks down her steps and watches in horror as Holly pulls Sweetpea away from her garden and Sweetpea heads quickly back into it, trampling the flowers, squashing bushes, pulling everything in his path.

"Get him out of there," Jill screams.

"I'm trying. He's like butter. He's so wet from the heat. He slips—" Holly lunges for her son again. She is caked in mud from the garden, her hair falling into her face. She has a cold sore on her lip from stress. She swears she has gained ten pounds in the last two weeks. She just eats and watches out the window for any sign of Nelson Quimby, any sign of Ivan. She sits all night on the phone talking to people, women mostly, who are afraid their children will get shot by the sniper if they go out for groceries.

Holly grabs Sweetpea. Holds him. Says, "NO," very loudly. Sweetpea laughs and slides out somehow.

Holly sits down on the grass. She puts her head in her hands. "I can't do this anymore," she whispers.

Jill is standing. "You can't just sit there. Get up. Get out of my garden. Get out. Now. Doesn't he speak English? Can't he hear me? Is he deaf?" Jill surveys the disaster. "Holly Wray, get a hold of yourself. Get hold of your son. What's gotten into you?"

Holly has begun to cry. She is sobbing. She is blubbering away there on the front lawn, cross-legged. Her small child is rollicking in the flowers, smushing them to his mouth. Laughing. Her older child is perched on the twig chair on the rich lady's porch and he's giving his mother a look that she knows is pure contempt. She's seen it before. One too many times. On Ivan. And Jill McCallan is standing there in her rich-lady clothes, clothes that probably cost more than Holly's grocery budget for the entire month, standing there screeching at her when—can't she see?—when there is nothing, absolutely nothing, Holly can do.

And, Holly thinks through her tears, today started out just fine. The morning was peaceful, in fact. New cartoons on TV. The kids were transfixed.

What happened? Everything turned so quickly.

The postcard.

Jill storms down the steps. She storms down toward the child and grabs his arm and yanks him out of her garden. She doesn't want to touch him, but she must in order to get him out. She pulls him forcefully toward her and then she goes down on one knee, bends the other knee, and puts the little boy over it, face down. Then she spanks him. She smacks his dirty diaper hard. Once. There is a squelching sound.

"Jesus," Jill screams. "There's shit on my hand." She drops the stunned little boy, who begins to wail.

"You hit my son," Holly shouts. "You hit him."

"Get up," Jill says. "Get up."

"How dare you hit my son." Holly rises off the ground and swells up with air and anger. She looks huge suddenly. Jill shrinks.

Jill holds out her hand, which is covered in shit. "Look what he did to me. If you just spanked them every once in a while, Holly Wray, you wouldn't have such horrid children."

Holly steps up to Jill, moves right in front of her, and raises her arm. She smacks Jill across the cheek.

"I don't hit my sons," Holly shouts.

Jill squeaks. She raises her hand up to touch her cheek and ends up with shit on her face. She begins to gag.

"You hit me."

"You hit my son."

Joe walks down the steps. He pulls his little brother up from the ground and tugs him toward their house.

Holly storms off after them.

Jill stands at the bottom of her stairs, her garden a mess of trampled plants, her hand and face covered in baby shit. She stands there and begins to cry. She sobs. Wails. Lets it all out. Oliver. Kate. Pearl. Her mother. Her father. Her job. Everything. Lets it all flow. And then, just when she's released almost everything, she looks up and sees Nelson Quimby leaving his house. He looks over at her.

"Everything okay?"

"Not really," Jill says.

Nelson looks at his car keys, then he looks at Jill. He studies her. She is crying. Nelson puts his car keys in his jean pocket and starts walking across the street toward her. Neighbourly, he thinks, sighing, sometimes we have to be neighbourly. It's why we're human, Nelson guesses. That and opposable thumbs.

"Can I help?"

JACKSON IS IN HIS SHED, getting his roses ready to deliver to the florist.

Weddings in the summer and lately the craze has been for dried-flower arrangements as centrepieces on every table. Jackson doesn't know why. The humidity in the air wilts the centrepieces in a flash, plus the dried flowers are so fragile they probably end up as potpourri if someone takes them home. But Jackson doesn't question this strange fad. It brings in some money. If everyone wants to put on black tuxes and heavy satin wedding gowns and go out into that heat, if they want to spend twice as much money on his dried flowers, that's their problem. And they all want roses. It baffles him. If he were ever to get married, he'd get married in the fall. All the wonderful colours and the heat gone south. He'd do something with fallen leaves and pine cones. *If he were to get married.* Funny. If Jackson were the type of man to laugh at himself, he would. As it is, Jackson places the dried rosebuds into boxes of matching colours. He labels the boxes. "Red," "Burgundy," "Blue"—on and on. When he first began doing this he would use exotic words to describe colours, "Tropical Sunset," or "Sea Foam," but the women at the shop he delivered to used to laugh at him. They would natter to each other and then laugh at him. Turn, with mouths open wide, and laugh. Sometimes point. "We don't understand," the owner told him. "Why not just 'Red'? Why not just 'Blue'? Why these fancy words?" So Jackson modified his language, toned it down, made it ordinary, and hoped that his flowers would speak for themselves.

They also laugh at him for using the sand-drying method when a freeze-dry machine would do the job. But Jackson is a traditionalist, he likes the feel of the sand between his fingers, he likes to take time on things in order to make things perfect. He likes to know what he'll get at the end of the process.

Now he is standing in the coolness of the shed, in the darkness. In the background he can hear the low murmur of voices from the end of the street. Suddenly the sounds shift and he can hear loud fighting. Women fighting. He hears a child crying.

Jackson peeks his head out the shed door and looks toward the sound. He sees Jill with one hand on her hip, the other hand, dirt covered, raised high. Holly's little boy is standing near the flowers. He has crushed them all, destroyed the Raffertys' beautiful garden, a garden Jackson admires from afar. And Holly is screaming something and rushing away now after her two children who have marched off together. Joe looks up at Jackson as he passes the shed and he waves. A salute almost. A nice, clean wave. Jackson waves back. He can't help himself. Joe, holding his brother's hand and looking both ways, then crosses the street in front of Jackson's house and heads up the front walk of his own. Holly comes quickly after them. She doesn't see Jackson.

"Watch for cars," she screams. "Wait for me."

Jackson shuts the shed door and disappears back within. He shakes his head. Thinks a bit. Then checks his watch. He'll be late on delivery if he doesn't hurry.

While boxing the roses, he can't help but wonder what happened. It must have been a fight over the damage the boy did, that would make sense.

Everyone is becoming more and more violent these days, Jackson thinks. His parents are just the tip of the iceberg. Steeped in anger.

Lately everything makes him worried. Even Mr. Walcott's health. Jackson doesn't really care about Mr. Walcott in general, but the man is too happy these days. Lumbering around his house like a jolly cartoon beluga whale, smiling even, talking to him, inviting him to eat, eat, eat. Jackson doesn't want to talk. He doesn't want to eat. He preferred when Mr. Walcott just took the groceries from him and said good night. And Mr. Walcott keeps talking about the man in the house at the end of the street, going on about coincidences, about how bizarre it is that there are two such people, "inmates," he calls them, living on one cul-de-sac. Jackson boxes the daffodils and lilacs. He strokes the pink rose petals.

His headaches. They won't go away. Every day they get worse. A pounding at the base of his head, near his neck. Everything is stiff. His arms, his back. There's a ringing in his ears. His vision is often blurry. His balance is off. Jackson knows he should see someone. But he certainly does not want to be touched. Not by anyone. So, for now, Jackson has moved on to Advil from Tylenol. He's taking about ten a day and each two capsules are supposed to last eight hours. Essentially, he is overdosing. But he doesn't really care as long as the headaches become numb.

Jackson pricks his finger with a thorn. He sucks at the blood.

His mother's screams slice through his mind like knives. Even when he's in his shed he can't get away from them. It seems they have a long life, longer than the second they take to move into the air and dissipate. Her screams follow him around, echo in his mind. The ringing he has in his ears—he thinks it might be his mother's voice stuck there in his ear canal, knocking around in there with no way out. Jackson, for one brief moment the other night, contemplated sticking a meat skewer in his ear and poking her voice out. The relief would have been sweet, he thinks. Much sweeter, however, if he stuck the skewer in his mother. He thought about that too.

There's violence everywhere, Jackson thinks.

Jackson leaves the shed and goes out into the blinding heat, still sucking on his finger. He is struck by it, as he always is. The day. The sun. The light all around him. Little jagged slivers of pain stick to his eyes. He stands and squints, willing his eyes to get used to it. Then he walks into his garage and starts up the truck. He backs it out, and leaving the engine running, he begins to load his rose and daffodil and lilac boxes from the shed into the back. It seems lately that although the days are longer, there isn't as much time for everything.

When every box is loaded Jackson walks slowly up the stairs to the front door and opens it carefully. He listens. The dull hum of the TV, but other than that, nothing.

"I'm off now," he says.

Nothing.

"I'm off." Louder.

Still nothing.

Jackson closes the door and walks down the steps to his truck. He knows they are just inside. They are sulking. His father in front of the TV, angry at the world, his mother angry at Jackson for leaving her and going out. He can fantasize that they are both dead inside, multiple heart attacks. Quick, silent killers. But, no, he can see them in his mind's eye as they sit sullenly in front of the TV in the living room, his father's hand on the remote, his mother's face permanently set in a scowl.

"I'm gone," he says to his truck. Jackson climbs inside and puts the truck in reverse. A quiet Saturday morning. The florists are waiting for the dried flowers. He has things to do. Fresh flowers to pick up from the wholesaler who gets them from a woman who runs a farm somewhere and has no use for the flowers she loves to grow. Around the cul-de-sac once, and then down the street. A right on Edgerow Boulevard and Jackson feels the weight of his world leaving his shoulders. He feels lighter, his recent weight loss obvious, his headache dulls to a small roar in his ear. The wind streams in through the side windows. Jackson Kern goes about his day. Gets things done. Carries on.

MR. WALCOTT IS WAVING at Jackson through a crack in the curtains of his front window but Jackson isn't paying attention. Mr. Walcott pounds on the window. Again—harder. Jackson drives off.

"Shoot," Mr. Walcott says. He backs up heavily and collapses on his couch. "Point-blank."

It is hot in his house. The smell of his garbage, his body, the stench coming off him, the stink is everywhere. Mr. Walcott feels nauseous. He knows there is the chance of dehydration but he can't drink any more water. He's sick of water. Gallons of the stuff. It's coming out of him. He's soaking wet. His couch is wet. His fat feet leave footprints on the rug, on the floor.

Mr. Walcott had his back door open for ventilation. Just for a minute. But then he got nervous about somebody walking in. The little boy from across the street walked past earlier, trespassing in his backyard, and Mr. Walcott quickly closed the door and burrowed back inside. The bathroom window is open but there is no relief from outside. There is no wind. As Jackson drove down the street Mr. Walcott could see the wind blow his hair, but standing still inside is just that—still. No wind. No movement in the air. Stifling.

Maybe he should get an air conditioner.

Mr. Walcott woke early this morning with the heat. It fell upon the city like snow. Suddenly it was hot. Humid. Yesterday it wasn't. Today it is. Last week it was. Jackson should come by later for the grocery order, but Mr. Walcott wonders if he'll survive until "later," whenever that may be. Sometimes it's just after lunch, sometimes it's toward the evening. He's really not all that dependable. Dependable people come the same time every week. People you can't trust come irregularly.

Mr. Walcott groans. If only Jackson had seen him. Taken his order earlier. Done something about this heat.

He's not even interested in the big house today. Not interested in the article that captivated him yesterday about the cab driver in Los Angeles who eats twelve iceberg lettuces a day smothered in chocolate sauce. Or the article he was reading two days ago about the L.A. county fair that is selling deep-fried Snickers bars on a stick—as if, Mr. Walcott thought, anyone could improve on Snickers bars. Not interested in anything but the sweat pouring out of his body. It is leaking out of him. His soul—a big, wet puddle lying on the living-room rug. In fact, Mr. Walcott hasn't even eaten yet. He's not even interested in food. The thought is mind-boggling. It's as if his synesthesia has turned off in the hot weather. *Click.* He can't taste anything.

Mr. Walcott sits up with great force. He pulls himself up using the back of the couch. He looks around. The picture frame there. He looks at it. Studies its shape. Okay, yes, peanut butter, but he doesn't feel like eating peanut butter. The shape of the coffee table, the chairs. Each item in his living room still lets out a flavour, yes, but the will to do something about it, the will to move toward the kitchen, is gone. Mr. Walcott wonders for a minute if he were to live in a tropical climate, would he then be skinny? Would he then be free of his shape addiction? The thought entices him. The thought suddenly consumes him. He imagines himself on a beach, walking up and down, his toes in the sand, his body free of its weight. But then in the shape of the waves in his mind he tastes peppermint, in the cut of his swim trunks he tastes liver and onions.

"Ah," Mr. Walcott says, clearing the phlegm from his throat. "I wouldn't be me without it." And no matter what anyone else may think about him, Mr. Walcott does quite like himself. He's read many books about loving oneself and how beneficial that is toward living a full and healthy life. Yes, Mr. Walcott loves who he is, although, truthfully, he would change some things if he could. Only to make life a tad more interesting. Go outside occasionally. Yes, he would like to do that. Even to the front yard. Just to the middle of the cul-de-sac maybe. And he would love to get into Judy's Impala. Especially today. Let the heat move through the car, through his thin hair and out the side window. It's not himself he would change, particularly, it's just the way he would like to run his life if he could. He can love his jolliness (the books tell him to call himself that) but still want to change a few things.

Ah, his mind's a whirring, buzzing thing today. He can't keep thoughts still. He can't concentrate. Heat will do that to a person. No wonder they're fighting wars in Africa, they can't think straight in the heat. Discombobulated. That's what he is. A wonderful word. *Dis-com-bob-u-lat-ed.* Six syllables. Mr. Walcott rolls the word on his tongue. He lies down again on the couch and studies the ceiling. Are they fighting wars in Africa? He really isn't all that sure. The Middle East. He's sure of that. Wars there all the time. Is it always hot in the Middle East? He must be dehydrated now. He must be insane, reaching a point of no return. He watches a small spider scurry across his ceiling and thinks of the Maltese proverb from his *Book of International Proverbs:* "To destroy the cobweb, destroy the spider." Simple, yes, but direct. Good approach. Makes sense to Mr. Walcott.

He sits up again. All this up and down, this exercise, is killing him. Sitting up is not a simple matter. It requires great arm strength and stomach muscles—both of which he does not have. Mr. Walcott huffs and puffs and sweats. He almost falls upon standing up. He catches himself and heads heavily toward his bookshelf. He pulls out the proverb book and lets it fall open. With one fat finger he pokes at the centre of the page.

"Ah," he says, and reads: "If the timid sees a glowworm, he shouts, 'Fire!'" Mr. Walcott sighs. Armenian saying. Perfectly lovely.

He stares out at nothing in particular. He must not be dehydrated, he reasons, as he's suddenly interested again in everything. He's hungry. Taking his book with him, he rolls his legs toward the kitchen. He'll eat while reading. That's always nice. He'll drink more water. Maybe make a pot of dark-roasted coffee and then cool it off with ice cream, make an ice-cream coffee shake.

Mr. Walcott chuckles to himself as he begins preparations for a meal. It really does amaze him how adaptable he is. Nothing really takes him down, makes him depressed, for long. He has the great capacity to be able to cheer himself up. Even in this heat. Even without air conditioning and without Jackson. Simple proverbs, simple learning, reading, these are the things that make him complete. That's another thing he loves about himself, he thinks, his capacity. He has great capacity.

"One beetle knows another," Mr. Walcott reads. Irish. He laughs. He reaches around to his back to scratch.

"Into a closed mouth no fly will enter." Moroccan.

"The hinge of a door is never crowded with insects." Chinese. That one stops him for a minute as he's blending his coffee/ice-cream shake. Of course, he thinks, because they would be squished. So, he reasons, that must mean you should live in dangerous situations if you want to be left alone. Something like that. Mr. Walcott continues blending the drink. He pours it into a cup and drinks it quickly. He continues on. Living his life.

NELSON IS BACK at the house. He helped Jill wash her hands, comforted her as much as he could (although the whole thing made him very sad for some reason), and then he went back inside his house and sat on the sofa in the air conditioning. He couldn't remember where he was initially going. So now he sits on the sofa and thinks about things. About his kids, off at the beach somewhere. A hot summer day. And thinking of them makes him horribly sad, makes waves of sadness and despair wash over him. He misses his children. He misses his wife, even though he doesn't think he ever really loved her. He misses everything suddenly: his own childhood, his mother and father, his sister—all living elsewhere— his friends, the boy who lived on his street and rode bikes with him. Jerome.

Nelson wants so much all of a sudden. He wants more than he's ever wanted before. He wants long life and happiness and world peace and kindness. He wants everyone around him to smile. He wants to say he's sorry to Anna. He's sorry that he treated her so poorly, he didn't respect her, he took her for granted. Because now he wouldn't take her for granted. Now he's seen what being a mother is all about and he wants desperately for his children to have a mother.

"What are you doing?" Lindsay is standing in the doorway watching Nelson. "I thought I told you I needed more bottled water. Did you get the bottled water?"

"Bottled water?" Nelson stands. "I forgot."

"What's going on? Are you hurt?"

Nelson shrugs. There is nothing he can say. There is nothing he wants to say. All he wants, immediately, now, is his children. His little Grace. His Gavin. He wants to hold them in his arms. Violently. Hug them hard. When he passes by the fridge these days and sees the pictures up there of them as babies, he feels as if he has been punched in the stomach. All the air goes out of him. Whoosh.

"Is this about that argument this morning?" Lindsay asks. She shuffles from one bare foot to the other, her hands on her hips. "Because I'm not mad anymore."

"No, that's not it," Nelson says. "It's nothing." Nelson composes himself. Reaches in his back pocket for his wallet. Checks to see if he has money for the bottled water. Clears his throat. "I just want everyone to be happy," Nelson says. He laughs.

"*Happy?*" Lindsay says. "I don't get it."

"Just that everyone"—Nelson wipes at the air in front of him, suggesting the world—"is unhappy all the time."

"You shouldn't read the paper. That sniper stuff always depresses you."

"It's not the sniper, it's just—"

"What?"

"I don't know."

"Well," Lindsay says. She crosses her arms in front of her chest. "Well … I'll get the bottled water. Just give me the car keys." She holds out her long fingers, reaching for his keys, and Nelson stares at them. Her long, shapely fingers. The nails painted silver. He reaches into his pocket to get the car keys. He gives her the money he is holding.

"You don't understand," Nelson says.

"Must have something to do with old age," Lindsay says. She tries to laugh.

"You're no spring chicken yourself." Nelson looks at her.

"You know, Nelson," Lindsay says, "you're pretty lucky to have me. Most women wouldn't want this." She flips her hand, jingling the car keys, at Nelson. "This sad, sorry person. It's depressing." She leaves the room.

Maybe she's right, Nelson thinks. Maybe he is lucky. Maybe he just doesn't take advantage of his luck, doesn't use it to its full potential, doesn't acknowledge it. Luck, Nelson thinks. That's what it's all about. Good luck. Bad luck. Nelson thinks you can turn certain kinds of luck around. He's sure you can. If you try hard enough.

"I can't believe it, I can't believe it, I can't believe it."

Holly is stamping her foot on her living-room rug and peering out the window toward the Raffertys' house.

"He's with her. I can't believe it. What a whore. She has a husband. What does she need with someone else's too?"

"What's a whore?" Joe asks from his position on the couch. He's watching *Sesame Street*. He's interested in the letter *Q*. "What's a quail?"

"She just beckons him into her house. My God, the woman hit my child. She spanked him. Bitch." Holly stomps around. Her face is red. She smacks her hands together like a boxer.

"What's a bitch?"

"Joe, don't say that word."

"Quail?"

"A bird."

"Why can't I say 'quail'?"

"No, you can say 'quail.' Don't say 'bitch.'"

"Why can't I say 'bitch'?" Joe likes how the word feels on his tongue. It feels like spitting. "What's a bitch?"

"Joe, I said." Holly puts her hands on her hips. "A bitch is a female dog."

"Oh," Joe says. He's curious. He gets up from the couch and moves over to the window. He looks out. "I don't see any dog."

"What dog?"

"The bitch."

"Right there," Holly says. She stamps her foot again and points at Jill McCallan, who is going into her house, crying, holding her poopy hand out in front of her, Nelson Quimby right behind her. She watches Jill's butt in the silky skirt she's wearing and Holly can practically smell the sex smell coming off her. "It's like she's in heat," she cries.

"Well," Joe says, sitting back down and watching the queen quail sing to the twelve little quails. Twelve is today's number. "It *is* hot." He is disappointed that he didn't see the dog. "Can we get a dog?"

Sweetpea is sucking his thumb. His diaper has been changed. The mean lady is gone. His bum hurts where she hit him. He has a rash there. But twelve baby birds are dancing to a song their pretty mama is singing. The whole thing makes him feel content and tired. Tired and content. Sleepy. His thumb tastes great. Like dirt.

"Why," Holly says, "can't I ever get anything I want?"

Joe ignores his mother. He's on to better things. Quacking quakers. Whatever quakers are. He doesn't know what a whore is and he still hasn't figured out really what a quail is, it just looks like a pigeon, so he's not about to ask what a quaker is. Someone in a hat. Twelve someone's in twelve hats quacking like ducks. His mother says, "Why can't I ever get anything I want?" about ten times a day, maybe even twelve times a day. The question doesn't interest him. Because he is slightly bored, he reaches over and punches his little brother on the arm. Sweetpea begins to cry.

"What? What? What?" Holly shouts. "What do you want from me?"

Joe shrugs. "A bowl of ice cream, please," he says over the noise of his brother's wail.

Holly begins to cry.

"What?" Joe asks. "I said *please.*"

Numb

WHAT WAS ORIGINALLY THRILLING, a long, hot summer, is now endless, stretched out farther than Gavin could ever imagine. With no school work to occupy his mind and with the heat making it too uncomfortable to bounce his basketball, Gavin spends his days bored and his nights tossing and turning. He spends his days staring at Kate's breasts in her bathing suit and wondering about the man in the house. He thinks about the highway sniper as he's riding his bike to the beach and he worries about his mom out there somewhere, he worries she may be driving. He worries about her safety. Some evenings, if he feels up to it, Gavin sits in the tree and waits for the man to come out, but he hasn't seen him again.

And to make things worse, the other day Gavin and Grace came home from the beach slightly drunk (Kate made shit mix in a jam jar from her father's liquor cabinet), falling off their bikes and laughing, only to find their father sitting in the darkened living room, staring at a blank TV screen. He looked so sad. Grace said it was because he doesn't like Lindsay and doesn't know how to get rid of her, but Gavin felt it was something deeper, something less tangible. As if he were being haunted by something.

There was something sunk deep in his eyes that Gavin hadn't seen in a while.

Gavin mentions this to Grace. Wonders if it has anything to do with Roger Smith.

"Don't be so melodramatic," Grace said as she stormed into her room. "Haunted? That's ridiculous. No one even remembers Roger Smith anymore. Give it a rest, Gavin."

Gavin wonders if she is right. Maybe no one else does remember Mr. Smith. Certainly, no one ever mentions him. One minute he was there, with his family, the next minute he was gone and his family left too. Quickly. Moved out their furniture, erased themselves from Blind Crescent memory.

Gavin sometimes wonders if the man in the house now is Mr. Smith. His ghost. Just sitting in there waiting for someone to remember him.

Gavin wishes the kids at school would forget, though. Forget the story of him pissing his pants out of fear. Maybe when school starts again in September there'll be other stories, something new to overshadow his humiliation. It was two Christmases ago, and if the laughing didn't stop last year, it certainly won't stop this year. It seems "Piss-pants" will always be his name. It's stuck on him. There's nothing he can do but graduate and get out. Take off.

So Gavin sits on his bike in the middle of the cul-de-sac, or in the tree behind the Raffertys' house, and he thinks about how he'd like to break into Roger Smith's house and put an end to his suffering. He'd like to confront the guy in the house, find out what he's doing there, see if he's okay, and then he'd like to go down into the basement and look at that beam and prove to himself that Mr. Smith isn't hanging there anymore. Gavin would like to make Mr. Smith stop haunting him. He would like to bury him, once and for all.

He wants Kate and Grace to come with him. But they won't. They refuse. They giggle and say "gross" and they won't do it.

And Gavin doesn't want to go in alone. He can't imagine it. Not right now, at least.

EVENTUALLY THIS HAS TO END, Oliver Rafferty thinks to himself. Eventually he'll just have to stop watching her, stop thinking about her. Ignore her when she approaches.

Eventually.

He knows this is wrong. So wrong.

His garbage can is full of sticky Kleenexes.

His marriage sucks.

"Oliver," Jill calls. She taps at his door.

Oliver jumps.

"Aren't you going to come down for dinner? What are you doing?"

Oliver unlocks the door for Jill. "I'm just working. I've got some things to finish. I'll be there in a minute."

"Good. Kate's friend is here too. Grace."

"Grace?"

"Yes, for dinner. Are you all right? You sound funny."

"Yes, I'll be there in a minute. Let me save this file."

Jill looks at Oliver's computer. It's off.

"Whenever it's convenient for you," she says.

"I'll be there. Wait."

"I've started without you." Jill holds up a glass of red wine and tilts it a bit. "Done it before. In fact, I've done it a lot lately."

"I've been busy, Jill. You know that."

Oliver and Jill look at each other. They read each other's faces. The eyes. And then Jill turns and leaves Oliver's den. She goes into their bedroom, crosses over to the bathroom mirror, and stands before it. She flicks on the light and begins to study herself. "What's wrong with me?" she whispers. Jill can hear the girls laughing downstairs and Oliver clearing his throat in his office. Her teeth, her hair, her mouth, her makeup, her clothes. Jill puts her wineglass on the counter and lifts up her top. She stares at her breasts. What's going on? First she looks at her breasts in the bra and then she lifts her bra and looks at her nipples. She lowers the elastic on her skirt and stares at her belly. At her belly button, sunk deep. She turns. Jill tries to remember why she fell in love with Oliver in the first place. Was it only to get back at her mother and father? She married a man who came from nothing. But then her father took him and made him into something. And now, like this mirror image before her, she's become her mother, everything has reflected back on her, everything she tried to get away from. She is her mother. Oliver is her father. Oh, God. Jill looks at her back, then her facial profile. She checks her neck for sags. Then she picks up her wineglass again, turns off the light, and walks out of the room. Her gait is slightly altered. A few more glasses of wine, perhaps the whole bottle, and she'll be numb. Maybe, Jill thinks, looking at her wineglass. Maybe she is a drunk. That would seal the deal, wouldn't it? That would make her exactly like her mom.

In the kitchen Jill watches Kate—over in the corner, laughing with Grace, drinking pop—and she thinks how much she loves Kate. And then she remembers that there were many moments in her childhood where she loved her mother so much it hurt.

DURING DINNER, takeout Chinese food (Pearl has the night off), Jill watches as Oliver completely ignores Kate's friend. He dotes on Jill, refilling her wine, complimenting her clothes and hair. So Jill realizes what has been wrong with him. Even with all the wine, she figures it out. It's not about her. It has almost nothing to do with her, in fact. Oliver is lusting after Grace Quimby. A teenager. And Grace Quimby is doing a good job of trying to get Jill's husband into bed.

Jill almost wants to laugh. If it wasn't so sad, she would laugh. But it is sad. Very sad. She watches her daughter and is relieved to see that Kate is oblivious to all of this. In fact, Jill thinks that Kate may be a little in love with Grace Quimby herself. And why not? The girl exudes sex. It leaks from her pores. She's dripping with it.

Immediately angry and obviously drunk, Jill's first thought is that if it weren't for Kate, for her daughter, then Grace could have Oliver. Just take him away. The girl would notice soon enough that life wasn't all peaches and cream with that man. She'd find so much lacking that Jill gives her twenty days maximum before she'd come crawling home again, sick with the sight of Oliver standing there, looking lost, rubbing his balding head.

When Grace leans forward her breasts curve out of her top slightly. When she helps clear the table it is apparent she is wearing no underwear under her tight miniskirt. Jill feels disgust and despair. She feels sadness for Grace. The girl is a teenager. But she has no mother. And her father, well, he's doing his best but he's certainly no example. A different girlfriend every couple of months.

Oliver clears his throat over and over.

With more wine, the anger in Jill lessens. Now the situation is almost comedic. Laughable. Silly even. In a sense, Jill is relieved that this is the problem. Grace is not as threatening as someone else might be—a woman Oliver works with, say, or a client. Grace is a young girl and young girls are fickle. She will soon stop flirting with Oliver and Oliver will stop wanting her. It's a mid-life thing. Oliver is going through a crisis. Most men go through this. Jill's heard about it from other women at work, read about it in magazines. It's natural. And Jill can remember being in love with some of her father's friends. Teasing them. Dunking them in their pool. There was even one colleague of her father's who used to place his hand on her ass every time he passed her in the hall. He used to stroke her. She remembers how good it felt. How proud she was of herself for attracting older men. Men like her father. Powerful men. The mothers though, with their gin martinis in hand, lounging beside the pool out back of their house, slapped her with their eyes.... Jill's mother shouting, "Come out of the pool now, Jilly. Cover up. Your bathing suit is indecent." Jill never really understood what was wrong back then. Innocent, really. A little flirting. Grace is just trying to put two and two together. Just trying to get used to her power, see what she can do with it.

Although, Jill remembers, Peggy did say she gives head to the football team.

Jill taps her long nails on the dining-room table, pours herself more wine, and then turns and tries to smile at Oliver's attentions to her across the table. Might as well play the game, she thinks. See what happens.

There is not much else she can do right now.

LATER, WHEN JILL FALLS ASLEEP in front of the TV, an empty wine bottle overturned on the table beside her, when Kate is in the bathroom getting ready to go over to Grace's for a sleepover, Grace finds Oliver in the kitchen doing dishes. She sidles up to him and puts her hand on his forearm and he can suddenly feel the muscles he has, muscles he didn't even know he had. They are bulging out of his arm under her fingers. Oliver pulls away quickly, soapy water sloshing on the floor.

"No," he says. His voice cracks. But for some reason he doesn't turn toward her. He stays with his back to her, his waist pushed up against the wet sink.

"Mr. Rafferty," Grace whispers. Then she puts her other hand on his waist, she is standing behind him quietly, and Oliver can feel the tightness of his waist, a waist with no love handles, just taut skin and bone and muscle. With the touch of Grace's fingers, he feels like he did in high school. "There's nothing wrong with this."

"I really don't think so," Oliver whispers. "No."

Grace moves up close to Oliver's back—one hand on his forearm, one hand on his waist—and she presses her whole body to his. And Oliver can feel her chin and then her soft breasts, and her tight stomach and her hips, her groin, her thighs, her knees press into him, press him up to the counter. He thinks he can feel her belly-button ring. He drops the knife he was washing into the soapy water and it makes no sound, just disappears beneath the bubbles. He stares at his reflection in the window, and other than Grace's two hands, her long fingers (pink-polished chipped nails), he can see nothing of her. She is completely hidden behind him.

"I'm afraid," Oliver says. He meant to say, "I'm afraid this is a bad idea," but the whole sentence stops with the first two words.

Grace moves suddenly, quickly disappears, and Oliver turns and watches her walk out of the kitchen to meet Kate in the hallway. Kate is smiling and laughing at something Grace has just said. "Bye, Dad," Kate says, coming into the kitchen to kiss him goodbye. "See you tomorrow." She stops then and looks closely at him. "Are you okay?" Grace giggles in the background.

It's a game, Oliver thinks. A game.

"Yes, I'm fine. Have fun," Oliver says.

Kate looks at Grace. She looks at her father. "Good night then." She leaves. Oliver notices that she looks exactly like Jill when she says it. She looks angry and aware. Her mouth a thin line.

Oliver remains pressed against the sink, his whole body alive and aching. He can hear his heart, his blood coursing through his veins. He can hear his lungs working, his whole being is vibrating.

Oliver looks again to his reflection in the window. "Oh, shit."

OUTSIDE, GAVIN IS IN THE TREE looking directly into the Rafferty kitchen. He is drinking out of the shit-mix jar Kate prepared for her little sleepover with Grace. He stole it from Grace's room. He is tired and warm. He doesn't gag with every sip now.

There. He sees them.

Grace and Mr. Rafferty. Mr. Rafferty looking directly at him through the window and his sister touching the old guy.

"Shit," Gavin whispers to himself. He looks at his jam jar and then back at the window and Grace is gone.

OH, GOD, Oliver thinks, what will he do when Jill finds out he's in love with Grace Quimby?

Jill will find out, Oliver thinks. He's sitting on the front porch, nursing a gin and tonic. It's inevitable. She has a sixth sense for this kind of thing. Always knows when her co-workers are having affairs. Sometimes knows before they even know.

The night is still hot. Oliver is perspiring. He loosens his tie, which he is amazed to see he is still wearing. From air-conditioned office to air-conditioned car to air-conditioned house, Oliver hasn't even noticed the heat until now. Oliver shakes his head. Sucks his breath through his teeth.

But he's not going to have an affair. What is he thinking? He's never had an affair on Jill. Never.

He stands, stretches, looks once over at Grace Quimby's house (but there is no light coming from her bedroom), and then starts to go inside. He stops.

No one has ever asked him to have an affair though, have they? He enters the house.

The cool air is a wall. He walks straight through it.

GAVIN CLIMBS OUT of the tree. He walks over to a basement window of the empty house. He bends down and peers inside. It's dark. He can't see anything. Gavin wants so badly to see something. Anything. But all he can see is his own reflection looking back at him. He looks like his father and he rubs his face a bit, messes up his hair so that he'll look less like him. Gavin is numb from the alcohol. He stares at his reflection and then he touches his lips with his fingers. They feel puffy and warm, slightly swollen. Weird. Then Gavin leans into the window and puckers up. He kisses it. Kisses the dirty basement window. A big kiss. A long one. He smears the dirt on the window. It gets on his lips.

And then he hears a noise. A howling noise. Like a dog. And as suddenly as it started, it stops. Gavin runs. Home. His heart beating heavy in his chest.

What if the man in the house had chosen that moment to look out the basement window at him? Gavin feels sick. What if the man was there, crouching in the dark, looking out at him looking in?

Gavin knows he'll have nightmares tonight. There's no doubt about it.

In bed, he hovers under the comforter. He is sweating. Scared.

Part Four

Howl

HE IS ALL ALONE. He is hungry. His food is running out.

His skin is pale and glows in the moonlight. There are rashes developing under his arms and his finger is infected from cutting it on a rusty wire in the basement.

He knows he is falling apart, that he has already fallen apart. He can't seem to close up the seams. And he doesn't really want to do anything to stop. It hurts too much to stop unravelling. He's hurting. It's easier to collapse. He wants everything to stop.

He moves toward the back door. He needs water from the rain barrel. The water is low, the heat of the day evaporating it. Soon there will be none left.

That boy is in the tree. He wants to throw something at him. Shoo him away, hiss at him.

Leave me alone.

Water.

The heat makes him sluggish. Everything is slow motion. He sinks up against the back door. Slides down onto the floor, his legs splayed out in front. He feels violently ill, hot, the air is stiff. Nothing moves. He can't breathe. Sweat on his forehead, on his top lip.

"I give up," he whispers. "I give up."

Who is he anyway? Who does he think he is?

What good does this all do? It won't bring The Others back.

Once in his life he was in control, he had control of many things, he was able to make a move and people would follow. Once in his life.

Now there is nothing for him. He can do nothing.

He puts his head in his hands and moans. The sound is like the crying of a dog, a wolf howling at the moon. An animal in pain. And then he stops.

Postcard from Ivan

EACH POSTCARD TAKES HOLLY BY SURPRISE. On the front are the same sort of women that were on the front of the last two, but this time they are running down the beach, their bikini tops and bottoms on. Holly can see their faces as they laugh and run and jump. Where are the hyenas at the zoo? Holly thinks. Why the women? The caption on this postcard reads, "Care to join us?" Holly wonders where he's getting these postcards from. She's sure they are the same women. Is he making them himself?

Holly turns it over. Again, no postmark, no stamp. A smudged fingerprint in the corner. It looks as if Ivan's pen is leaking. This time he's written something.

"Damn," Holly hisses as she looks at what is written there. Simple, really, just the word "HI," in capital letters. And a drawing. It is a sketch of the cul-de-sac, of Blind Crescent. From above. A shaky circle with the houses spread out around the centre. The tops of the houses. And in Holly's front yard, Ivan has sketched stick figures on the grass. Two little kids and a woman in a dress. He has the perspective wrong so the figures look as if they are lying on the grass, looking up at the sky. Holly thinks it

181

looks as if they are dead. As if she, Joe, and Sweetpea are dead in the front yard.

Holly reaches up and puts this postcard with the other three, high on the shelf. Then she says to herself—out loud so she can't take it back—"One more and I call the police."

Shazam

ANOTHER HIGHWAY MURDER. Again, it hasn't been a month. Esther and Shannon are debating it over breakfast. The window air conditioner hums. They speak loudly.

"I heard it was two shots this time," Esther says.

"Two people?"

"No, two shots."

"Ah," says Shannon, "the shooter is getting clumsy."

"Took two shots to kill him, I heard," Esther says, ignoring Shannon. "Two in the side of the head."

"In the head?"

"In the head."

Jackson is buttering their toast. He is cutting the crusts off his father's toast and putting marmalade on his mother's. He licks his finger. The taste is bitter. Orange marmalade, pieces of orange rind floating in it like fingernail clippings.

"Doesn't Jackson look tired?" Shannon says. "Jackson, you look tired."

"I am tired."

"Nonsense," his mother says. "What would you be tired for? It's not as if you're old like us and can't get a moment's rest without some ache or pain making you sit up in bed and cry out. Besides, you go to sleep early every night."

"That's true," Shannon says sadly. "The aches and pains. Everything always hurts."

"You just wait," Esther says. "You've got nothing to look forward to. This"—she taps the table hard with her finger—"this is heaven now. I know. I remember. From this point on, Jackson, it's downhill. It's all downhill."

Shannon stares at his plate.

Jackson rubs at his temples. His headache flares up. Hot, flashing pain. It's creeping around his skull, moving from place to place— behind his ears, down his neck, on his forehead. Something is different, though. It's more intense than usual. Hotter, somehow. And his hand is hurting again. Aching.

"Good for nothing," Esther mumbles.

"Marmalade?" Jackson says to his father.

Shannon grunts. "This guy's going to get caught soon," he says. "I can feel it in my bones."

"Hasn't even been a month. Again, two weeks only between shootings," Esther says. "Two shots. He's going against everything he's ever done before. First those two kids, then the baby. Now this. Two shots."

"Running scared, I think," Shannon says.

"I think he's scared," Esther says.

"That's what I said."

"He's scared the police will catch him before he gets to kill someone else. That's why he's upping the … upping the … upping the what? I can't think of the word."

"Speed?" Shannon says. "The speed of the killing?"

Esther nods. "Or ante—upping the ante. Isn't that what you say, Jackson? Jackson?"

Jackson is drifting in and out of reality. He sees the pain in his head like a cartoon lightning flash. The word *Shazam* above it. All red with black outline. A bit of gold shining through. He sees the flash moving around and around his head rapidly. Lightning striking. He swears he can actually hear thunder. He's so hot.

"Shazam," Jackson mumbles.

"He's your son, Shannon," Esther says. "Never paying attention. Thinks he's got better things to do than listen to some old people natter."

"Ha," Shannon says. "You're old."

"What time did it happen last night?" Jackson suddenly asks.

"What?"

"The shooting."

"Why?" Esther says. "Why are you so interested?"

"I just want to know."

Esther shrugs. "Beats me. They didn't say on the news, did they, Shannon? Did you hear anything about the time?"

"I didn't want marmalade," Shannon says. "The stuff is disgusting. It's too bitter. There are chunks in it. Chunks of things."

"Shannon, listen," Esther shouts. "Did they say anything on the news about the time of the shooting?"

"Who cares," Shannon says, looking angrily at his toast. "Who the hell cares what time it happened? It was last night. Jackson, get me another piece of toast. Last night, for God's sake. No marmalade this time. Your mother likes this stuff, not me. You know that. What's gotten into you?"

Jackson stands and moves over to the toaster. Lightning. Lightning. Crashing lightning. His head is going to rip apart. It'll rip apart and burst like fireworks over all of them. The police will come to their house and his brains will be splattered everywhere, still lit up like the sun. Shining in their gore.

"Damn boy," Shannon grumbles. "Marmalade. What's wrong with you?"

"After midnight," Esther says, digging into her toast. "I'm sure it was after midnight."

"I hate marmalade. You know that."

"He never pays attention," Esther says. "Always thinking about himself and his flowers. He doesn't care about us."

There it goes, Jackson thinks, there goes my head.

Roughly, and with little grace, little flexibility, and little motion, Jackson slides down to the floor and passes out.

It takes approximately two minutes before either Shannon or Esther notice their boy is missing from his stiff upright position at the counter.

"Where's my toast?" Shannon says, looking around.

"Get up, Jackson," Esther says. She prods him with her toe. "Get up."

"Dreaming," Shannon says. "He's always just dreaming. What's he good for anyway?"

"Nothing," Esther says. "Didn't you hear me? I said he's good for nothing."

"What do you know anyway," Shannon complains. "I didn't get my toast. I'm hungry."

"I guess we'd better call an ambulance," Esther says. "He's always ruining my day."

"Probably just drank too much."

"For breakfast? He doesn't even drink."

"You never know. What do we really know about him anyway?"

"Call an ambulance, Shannon. He's sick. Rundown, I guess. Dehydrated maybe? Too much time with the flowers." Esther stands stiffly and looks down on her son. "I mean, really. What a scene. He's always been such a sensitive boy. Just wish he'd made coffee before he passed out."

Nodding, Shannon goes to the phone and places the call. "That's right," he says. "Number one, Blind Crescent. That's where we are."

MR. WALCOTT IS LOOKING at Roger Smith's house from his front window when he sees and hears the ambulance pull up.

Soon the street begins to fill. Everyone stands outside and watches the ambulance drivers as they manoeuvre the stretcher up the Kerns' front steps. Holly Wray and her children are standing out in front of their house.

"Is there anything I can do?" Holly calls across the street to the ambulance men, but they ignore her and go about their business.

Gavin, Grace, and Kate slouch in front of the Raffertys' house. They are holding backpacks with beach towels and alcohol-full jam jars in them.

Nelson comes out of his house with a towel around his waist. He stepped quickly out of the shower when he heard the ambulance come. The first thing he sees is Holly Wray next door, waving frantically at him. He waves back nervously.

Jill walks down her steps to join the teens in the front of her house. She sees Nelson in his towel, Holly and the kids down the street. She feels like going inside and putting an ice pack on her forehead.

"What happened?" she asks Grace and Gavin.

They shrug.

Holly Wray notes that Jill is wearing a silk bathrobe. Does the woman never wear anything polyester? Holly bets the robe stinks—

like coffee and toast and sweat and age. No one can wear a robe like that without it stinking. She's sure of it. And a robe like that must have to be dry cleaned, you couldn't just throw it in with your underwear. It's pure silk. Last night on TV Holly learned that you can put a down duvet in the dryer if you want. Just put it in with tennis balls. Something about the balls makes the duvet keep its form, stay fluffed. Last time Sweetpea vomited on her duvet it cost forty dollars to clean. Holly wants to try washing it with the balls next time and so she makes a mental note to buy tennis balls when she's out shopping. Dry cleaning is very expensive.

Kate is shaking her head slightly. She's turning red. Why is her mother standing here with them?

"What do you want, Mom?" she asks.

Pearl comes out of the house, drying her hands on her apron.

"What's going on?" she shouts down at Kate.

"Your servant wants you," Grace says.

Gavin laughs nervously.

"She's not a servant, Grace, she's our employee," Jill says.

"Ah," Grace says. "Is there a difference? I've always been curious."

"Mom."

"What, Kate?" Jill says. "And, Grace, you really shouldn't be so cheeky. It's rude. Respectful—that's what you should be."

"Mom," Kate says, under her breath.

Her mother ignores her.

"Come down, Pearl. Join us. It seems someone has been hurt at the Kerns' house." Jill hopes it's one of the older people. She hopes that they have to sell the house, move to a rest home, maybe. Jill would like someone to buy up that property and tear down the house. She might even do it herself. Put in a nice new home, some-thing with three levels. No car park or front garage. In fact, looking around, she could buy up the whole neighbourhood as an investment. Turn it around.

Pearl comes down the steps and stands with the others. She looks disapprovingly at Jill's bathrobe. "You're not dressed yet?" she says.

They all watch the Kerns' house.

Holly stares miserably at Jill as her mouth opens in a wide laugh. It's like a cavern, her mouth. Holly looks down at her kids but they aren't there anymore. They aren't where she put them, at her feet. In fact, she can't see them anywhere.

Joe and Sweetpea have crossed the street and are climbing into the back of the ambulance.

"*No*," Holly screeches. How did they cross the road without her noticing? She's become such a sad mother. A sad, bad mother.

"Oh, God, that woman again," Jill hisses. "Her children are completely out of hand."

"That's what happens when you're not being respectful to your mother, I guess," Grace says.

"Yes, exactly." Jill nods thoughtfully and then realizes Grace is mocking her. "Well, they aren't respectful, those kids. They aren't. They don't respect anyone, let alone their mother."

Grace laughs. "I don't have that problem, Ms. McCallan. I don't have a mother."

"Of course you have a mother," Jill starts.

"Come on," Kate says. "Let's go to the beach. This is boring,"

"Just a minute," Grace says. "I want to see if those kids can start up the ambulance and drive away."

Gavin smiles. He'd like to drive off in the ambulance. He'd even just like to stand up close to it and look at it. But he doesn't want to look like a baby so he stays his distance and pretends he's not impressed. Why is it that when you get to a certain age you have to pretend that nothing thrills you anymore? Ambulances are great, Gavin thinks. They are noisy and fast. They are colourful. Gavin sighs. He pretends to be bored. And then he remembers the last time he saw an ambulance on Blind Crescent and he quickly holds his backpack up against his stomach.

"Oh, my God, she's running," Jill says. "She shouldn't run wearing that flimsy top and no brassiere. Oh, my God, would you look at that."

Gavin is looking.

Grace is looking.

Kate is looking at the ground.

"Where is Oliver when exciting things happen?" Jill says. "He's always working. He misses all the fun."

"Yes, where is Mr. Rafferty?" Grace says.

Jill looks over at the girl.

Nelson Quimby watches Holly run across the street. He wants to run toward her and help her get her kids out of the ambulance. He has this sudden feeling that she's going to injure herself, that something bad is going to happen. Her large breasts sway violently up and down as she runs. Maybe she'll hurt herself with her breasts. Knock a tooth out. Sweetpea and Joe are in the back of the ambulance now. Nelson can't see them anymore. For all he knows, they could be injecting themselves with needles back there. Nelson holds his towel tighter. If he runs to help, his towel will fall off. Holly will gain control of her children, won't she? They don't have needles in the backs of ambulances, do they?

Lindsay comes out onto the porch.

"What's going on?" she says. "Oh, my God, look at her run."

Holly gets to the back of the ambulance and climbs in.

The neighbours all watch.

Mr. Walcott is chuckling from behind his curtain. The whole thing is quite funny. The boxy shape of the ambulance brings on the taste of curried lamb. Then he sobers up when he thinks of Esther or Shannon, when he remembers the seriousness of the situation. He hopes whatever happened to whichever one of them, whatever it was, it happened quickly. Silently. Painlessly.

The ambulance drivers carry the stretcher out the Kerns' front door and down the steps. Everyone holds their breath.

"It's Jackson," Gavin says.

"Oh, God," Mr. Walcott mouths. He's lost his voice suddenly.

Holly comes bursting out of the back of the ambulance just when the drivers get near. She has each kid by an arm and is looking down at them. They are both howling. The commotion seems unreal for a moment. Jill holds Pearl's arm. Kate watches, open-mouthed.

"Christ," Nelson says, almost dropping his towel. Lindsay looks at him. Looks at his towel. Smiles conspiratorially. The excitement has given him a slight erection. He starts to back into his house.

"You can't leave now," Lindsay whispers. She holds his arm. "It's just getting exciting."

Holly crashes into one of the drivers who stumbles with the stretcher. The stretcher is on wheels but, for an instant, it tips to one side and almost falls.

"Hold it," the driver shouts.

"Shit," the other one says. "What's she doing in there?"

They work together to balance the stretcher but Jackson's weight is too much.

"Oh, dear," Mr. Walcott murmurs, his voice now a whisper. "He's going to fall."

Jackson tilts, precariously angled, he tilts more, then the stretcher is sideways on the ground, Jackson strapped to it.

"I'm so sorry," Holly says. She begins to cry.

"This," Jill says, "this is like something out of the movies."

"A freak show," Grace says.

"Yeah," Gavin says.

"I feel sorry for her," Kate says, and Jill looks at her daughter, moves toward her and tries to put her arm around her. Kate shrugs her mother off.

"I guess I do too, Kate," Jill says. "She has a lot to deal with, doesn't she?"

Nelson clutches his towel in front of him. Lindsay moves closer and puts her cool hand around his waist.

"What's turning you on?" she whispers.

"I don't know." Nelson is trying to hold down his ever-growing erection.

The drivers bend to right Jackson Kern. Esther is standing in the front window of her house shouting something.

"Look at the old lady," Grace says.

Esther is shaking her hands. Her mouth is moving quickly.

"She's going to have a heart attack," Pearl says. "You watch. They should call for another ambulance right now."

Jackson looks none the worse for wear when they bring him back up to a level position. The drivers wave to Esther and then roll the stretcher into the back of the ambulance.

"I'm so sorry," Holly says. "My children. They were in the ambulance."

"Listen, lady," one driver says. "If anybody sues us, you're to blame. Look around. The entire neighbourhood saw it. We have witnesses." He gets into the back with Jackson Kern. The ambulance drives off, the lights flashing.

"Lights," Sweetpea says.

"Mom, he talked," Joe says. "Sweetpea said 'lights.'"

"Oh, my God," Holly says. "I might get sued." She looks over at Nelson Quimby on the front porch of his house, standing there with Lindsay. She looks over at Jill and the kids. She looks at Esther Kern in her front window, still angry. Holly takes each of her children by their hands and leads them across the street to her house. She slams the front door behind them.

"I was hoping the kids would drive away in the ambulance," Grace says. "Boring." She yawns.

Gavin imitates the sound of the ambulance. "Whoooo, whoooo."

Gavin, Grace, and Kate move off. They get their bikes and cycle down Blind Crescent, toward Edgerow Boulevard.

"Don't you want to know what happened to him?" Jill calls out. "Where are you three going?"

"Gavin … Grace," Nelson calls at them as they pass. Lindsay is pulling him into the house. "Come back here. I thought we'd do something together today."

"Let's go, Nelson. Come on. Let's not waste this." Lindsay points to his towel. Nelson's face turns red. The kids bicycle away.

Pearl silently climbs back up the front porch of the Raffertys' and goes into the house. She'll finish cleaning the kitchen from breakfast and then call her mother. Another story to add to the pile.

Mr. Walcott looks at his hands. He looks at his floor. He takes up a handful of his stomach and looks carefully at it. He studies it. He moves away from the window.

"What am I going to do now?" he says, his voice so loud it startles him.

No Movement

A RAT SCURRIES OUT of the empty can of beans lying beside him on the floor.

He is making his lists. Trying to ignore the rats. Trying to ignore the heat.

The squashed bristles on the toothbrush, a comb and brush, perfumes, nail polishes and eye makeup and lipsticks, earrings and jewellery, clothing, boxes of it, shoes, small pointy-toed, high, low, sneakers, Keds, slip-on sandals, silver sandals, low-backs, high-backs, glittery, plain, a watch, lingerie and underwear, push-up bras, sports bras, and maternity bras, thongs and jockeys, and bikinis, and high-cuts, nightgowns and pyjamas, bathrobes and winter coats, hair bands and clips, a mouth guard (teeth caught forever in a plastic mould), gardening gloves, shampoos and hair-straightening creams and gels and hairspray, a computer with its emails and endless files of letters, books, videotapes, phone numbers crossed out over and over in an address book, photographs stuck to the fridge, purses, a recipe book with clip-outs from magazines, letters, a doll, an annotated version of *Alice's Adventures in Wonderland* bound in leather, an old, broken ghetto blaster, files of receipts all carefully organized, notes: "defrost freezer," "call Jane," "dinner with Randall Friday?" "milk—basement fridge," "T's art class—wed.," "S pulling ear—infection?"

He cannot move.

He is lying on the floor now. He opens his eyes only to watch the rat when it leaves the empty can of beans and scurries out of the room.

There is the familiar ache in his belly. Hunger. Thirst. The rain barrel is almost empty.

It angers him that his body has needs, wants, demands, requirements.

"Fuck," he screams. His voice cracks. His throat is raw. The sound comes out full-bodied, though, and sails out through the slightly open window.

Scream

JILL IS ON THE PHONE to Oliver, telling him about Jackson Kern, when she hears the scream. She says, "Shush a minute," and holds the phone out from her ear. She listens out the open window but doesn't hear anything again and has to assume it was her imagination. Because *fuck* would be exactly what she would be thinking right now. Right this minute. Oliver is being sweet, saying he loves her and wants to start spending more time with her. He's more serious about this little girl than she thought. *Fuck*—that's the perfect swear word. She must have said it herself, although the sound was a deeper sound, a richer sound, a more desperate sound, than one she could make.

Pearl is on the phone to her mother. She is in the basement, the windows are closed, her air conditioning on full blast, her mother is laughing hard in her ear—"They dropped the stretcher? No. Oh, Pearl, you live in such a funny place"—and so Pearl does not hear the scream.

Nelson is lying under Lindsay and thinking that his hair will stand up if it dries this way. And then he wonders why he's thinking about his hair when beautiful Lindsay is above him, her eyes closed, making lovely moaning sounds, soft and delicate. And then he thinks about his kids on their bikes and wonders if Gavin's bike had a flat tire. It looked a little flat.

"Honey," Lindsay says, "pay attention."

The last time an ambulance was on the cul-de-sac, Nelson thinks, it was there for Roger Smith. Neither Nelson nor Lindsay hear the scream.

Esther is yelling at Shannon, "They dropped him, they dropped him, did you see that? They dropped our son," and the TV, as usual, is on full volume. They don't hear the scream.

Holly Wray stops crying for a minute about her kids, about the fact that she could be sued, about everything in her life, and looks up. She hears it through her open windows. Joe hears it. Sweetpea stops crying and looks at his mother and brother. "Fuck," he says loudly. Joe giggles. "Fuck," Sweetpea says again.

"Sure," Holly says. "You're talking now."

Mr. Walcott lets his stomach back down again and moves fast to the window. As fast as he can go. He puffs and pants. He opens the curtain slightly and looks out. His window is open in the bathroom. Just a touch. He heard something faint. A sound. A scream. He's sure he heard something. Mr. Walcott looks out at the big rundown house. The man inside must have screamed, he thinks. He shouted. Mr. Walcott heard something muted. Suddenly it doesn't matter that Jackson Kern is in the hospital. Well, it matters that Jackson is sick and Mr. Walcott is worried, but suddenly it doesn't matter that there is no one to pick up groceries for him or do all the small things around the house. That there is no one to keep him company. In Jackson's small way, he does make Mr. Walcott feel connected. But the man in the rundown house just screamed. That's all that matters. Something's breaking out. Something's different, moving, coming. There's a change in the air. A spark. Electricity. Mr. Walcott can feel it. He stretches out his hand and touches the window. It's hot.

Believe

GRACE, GAVIN, AND KATE are hanging out at the corner of Edgerow Boulevard and Blind Crescent. Grace made them stop their bikes for a cigarette and a swig out of the jam jar. Kate thinks she rides faster drunk. Occasionally a car beeps and honks. It is because of what Grace is not wearing, because she isn't wearing much. Bikini top, short shorts. Again.

"Why do you dress like that?" Kate says. Courage from alcohol.

"Like what?" Grace puffs her cigarette and looks down at her body. "I look great."

"Like a prostitute," Kate says.

Grace stares at Kate. She opens her mouth to say something and then closes it. Then opens it again. Closes it.

"Ha," Gavin says. "You do. She's right."

"I do not." Grace turns from them, looks out at the street, the dead grass. "I look great. You, Kate, are just like your mother."

"No, I'm not."

"You are. No wonder your dad is so unhappy."

"What are you talking about?" Kate says. She almost screams. "What are you talking about? They totally love each other."

Grace laughs.

"I'm going in," Gavin declares.

Grace looks at Gavin. "Huh?" She drinks from the jam jar. Stubs out her cigarette with her platform sandals, the sandals that make biking so hard.

"I've decided that I'm going into Mr. Smith's old house. See what that guy is up to. See why he has to drink out of the rain barrel."

Kate is fuming mad. She stares at Gavin. She wishes suddenly that both Gavin and Grace would go into that house and get murdered by that creepy man. She still can't believe Gavin didn't tell anyone that the guy barfed on the hill and then drank from the rain barrel. She used to play on that hill when she was a kid. Now there's barf there. It's disgusting.

"Yeah, right." Grace says. "What are you going to do? Knock on the door and ask him to let you in? There's no way you'll do it."

"You'll piss your pants," Kate says. She laughs.

"Fuck off, Kate," Grace says.

"I don't know about you anymore, Grace. You're changing," Kate drinks from the jam jar. "You're turning into a slut."

"Fuck off."

Kate feels like she's going to start crying. She drinks more and more.

"Pass that," Gavin says.

"You are chickenshit," Grace says. "Kate is right, sort of." It bothers her that everyone has to keep referring to the time Gavin pissed his pants. He saw a dead man, she keeps telling everyone. A dead man.

"Am not."

"Are too."

"I'm not going with you," Kate says. "No way."

"You're chickenshit," Gavin says to Kate. "It doesn't matter who comes with me. I just need to go in."

Grace adjusts her bikini top, gives the finger to the next beeping car, and then figures it out. Gavin needs to go in. Needs to, not wants to. It makes sense, sort of, Grace thinks. He's got to rid himself of his demons, she guesses. Go in and get out without pissing his pants. Have a story to tell. Besides, it would be kind of fun. Then she says, "Kate, come on. We only live once."

"What? No way. Are you going too?"

"Seriously, Kate. What have you got to lose?"

"I'm not going in. My mom and dad would kill me."

"Your dad's so sweet, he wouldn't kill you."

"What do you mean 'sweet'? He's not sweet." Kate stares at Grace.

"Anyway, I'll go with you, Gavin," Grace says.

"Great." Gavin looks at Grace. He smiles. She thinks he looks like their mother. The comparison makes her antsy. Her mouth is dry and pasty. She feels kind of sick. All this heat and then the booze.

"Let's go to the beach now. I'm hot."

"I'm drunk," Kate says. She giggles to herself. "And my dad is not sweet. He's gross."

"That's harsh," Grace says.

"Not gross, just—God, Grace, he's my dad. Don't you get it?"

Grace shrugs.

They cycle off up Edgerow Boulevard toward the roads that will take them to the beach. Gavin is in the lead and he feels lighter than he's felt in a long time. He's sitting on air. He has no idea why Grace decided to help him out, and he doubts that she'll follow through, but for a minute now, for this moment in time, he can believe in her and think that she is nice and kind and a good big sister. Kate, on the other hand, Gavin thinks he may be losing his crush on her. She's not impressing him that much anymore. Not really.

Gavin looks back. The girls cycle fast toward him, laughing. Wind in their hair. Grace has taken off her sandals and is riding barefoot, her sandal straps woven through her hands which are grasping the handlebars. Breeze is drying the sweat on their faces and bodies.

Well, Gavin thinks, looking at Kate in her shorts and tank top, her blonde hair sailing out behind her, her mouth open wide and her eyes shining, maybe he hasn't lost anything, actually.

"It's his brain," Esther shouts at Shannon. "The doctor says it has something to do with his brain."

Esther is holding the phone out and calling to Shannon. Shannon sits on the couch in front of the TV. His face bears a pained expression.

"*His brain?*"

"The doctor wants to know if we can come down and talk to him. Jackson is still not awake. He thinks if we talk to him, he'll wake up."

"Lazy boy," Shannon mumbles. He tries to get up, but can't. He feels dizzy.

"We can't come to the hospital," Esther says into the phone. "We don't drive."

The doctor suggests a cab.

"We don't go out alone," Esther says. "Ever. Not for anything. It doesn't matter what it is. What if we fall? Jackson has to be there to help us."

The doctor sighs.

"When is he coming home?"

"Someone has to make decisions," the doctor says.

"Who's going to feed us? Who's going to help me with my bath?"

"One of you will have to come to the hospital. We can talk to you here about home care. You'll probably have to get home care for a while."

"We can't afford home care. Not when we have a son who can do everything for free."

"That's the problem," the doctor says. "You don't have a son who can do anything right now. I don't know how long he'll be here."

"Shannon," Esther calls. "You'll have to go to the hospital. Make decisions. I need a bath."

Shannon shuffles into the kitchen and looks at his stooped wife on the phone with the doctor he assumes is inspecting his son's head, his brain. Shannon always assumed something was wrong with Jackson's brain and now it has been confirmed.

"Something called an MRI," Esther shouts. "Something called a CAT scan. What is he? A cat? I can't understand the man. He isn't speaking English." She holds the phone out to her husband. "He's got a funny accent. Like he's from some foreign country."

"Yes?" Shannon says weakly into the phone. He hasn't eaten yet. The whole episode has made him so tired. It has made him lose his appetite. The toast and marmalade and butter sit on the counter still. Without Jackson to clean everything up, nothing will get done. The whole event has made him very unhappy.

The doctor says that Shannon and Esther should come to the hospital. That the doctors will have to do lots of tests on their son, and that, as his parents, they will have to sign permission forms. The doctor is going to try to wake Jackson up. Some sort of coma, he says. Something about his head, his brain—"The boy has a brain?" Shannon says, more to his wife than the doctor. Partial paralysis?

Headaches? Drowsiness? The doctor questions Shannon, but he knows nothing about Jackson's health or about how he's been feeling lately. "Those dead flowers," Shannon suggests. "It's probably an allergic reaction to those damn dead flowers. I think he dips them in formaldehyde or something. That would make him sick, wouldn't it?"

The doctor, if Shannon could see him, is shaking his head. He is staring up at the ceiling, trying not to look at the people moving about at the nursing station. He is trying not to look at anything, trying to focus on this old man on the phone, this old man who makes him want to hit someone. "My God," he'll tell his wife later, when he gets home and loosens his tie, "the way he treated his son, it was unbelievable." The entire situation is unbelievable, he thinks now.

"Come down here any way you can," the doctor says. "Ask for me when you get here. I'm the head of neurology." The doctor hangs up the phone. He walks back into the room where Jackson lies under white sheets and he stares at the man. Jackson's face is ashen, his hair is thin and greasy. Unconscious, he looks peaceful. "I don't blame you," the doctor says. "I wouldn't want to wake up either. Not with parents like that to go home to."

"Head of neurology," Shannon says. "That's sort of funny, isn't it? Being the head of something to do with heads."

"Very funny," Esther says. "Why don't you just shut up. You're always talking."

"I'm not always talking, you're always talking." Shannon looks at his wife. "You're a nag."

"I'm going to lie down. Go to the hospital and get our son."

"I'm not going anywhere. I'm too weak."

"You've been telling Jackson you're sick for years, Shannon. You aren't sick. You're just lazy. Look at me. I'm stooped over from osteoporosis, I'm fragile, my doctor says my bones will break while I'm sleeping in bed. He says—"

"My doctor says I have cancer," Shannon says.

"You don't have cancer."

"I do. What do you think I took all those pills for? Cancer, that's what."

"You don't."

"I do. Cancer."

They stare at each other.

"I suppose we could take a cab," Esther says. "Go together. Get him out of the hospital and back home. It wouldn't take too long, would it?"

"I suppose," Shannon says. "We do go out. What you told the doctor isn't true. We do go to our doctor appointments."

"But Jackson takes us. That's what I said. Jackson takes us every-where." Esther sits down hard on a kitchen chair. "Oh," she says, "what are we going to do now?"

"Clean up this mess, for one," Shannon says, indicating the bread and marmalade on the counter. "This mess will go rotten in this heat, even with the air conditioning on, if we don't clean it up."

They sit and look at the counter. Neither of them move.

"What hospital is he at?" Shannon says.

"I don't know," Esther says. "I didn't get that information. Did you? Why didn't you?"

"That settles it then," Shannon says.

"What? What does it settle, Shannon?"

"We can't go anywhere if we don't know where we're going."

Shannon shuffles out of the kitchen. He heads back into the living room and moves over to the front window. He looks out at the houses in the cul-de-sac.

"He'll come home by himself," Shannon says. "He's a big boy."

Then he turns away and sinks back down into the couch. He turns on the TV.

Esther sits in the kitchen, slumped over, and watches the wall clock as it ticks off the seconds. She watches it for fifteen minutes and then she gets up and walks down the hall to her bedroom. She climbs stiffly onto the flowered duvet and lies down on top of it. From her position she glances around the room. She looks over at her lingerie drawer and it suddenly occurs to her how ridiculous that is—a small dresser with tiny drawers. She stares at it. Why ever would she own a lingerie drawer? The thought is baffling. Esther can't remember when she purchased it, or if it was a gift. She can't fathom what she must have been thinking. Without looking in the lingerie drawer, Esther knows what is in it. Nothing. Absolutely nothing.

It's easier, she thinks, to be mad at each other all the time. Easier than to be in love still, to remember the feeling of body next to body. They are both going to die soon, Esther knows this, and they might as well spend the rest of their time on earth mad at each other. That way neither one will miss the other.

Not too much, at least.

"Old lady, old lady," she mutters. "Old lady married to an old, old man." Esther turns her head away from the empty piece of furniture and falls slowly into a fitful sleep.

HOLLY IS WATCHING TV. She can't believe that the highway murderer took two shots this time to kill the man. They show the car with the window blasted out. The driver's window. Two shots. What'd the guy do? Holly wonders. Keep driving with a bullet in his head? Holly's heard of people who do miraculous things, like the lady who stumbled through a snowbank with fifteen stab wounds in her body and still managed to stay alive, or the woman who threw her baby to her husband just before the train ran her over, or the guy who was buried in an avalanche for twenty-two hours and dug himself out, so maybe that is what happened. A miracle. But it seems unlikely. "Each shot went straight through to the brain," the gum-chewing police spokesperson said. "One shot would have been enough." The cop said he was mangled. As if his head had exploded.

Sicko, Holly thinks.

Ivan, Holly thinks.

Ivan was a good shot. He had a pellet gun and he would shoot the squirrels on the hill behind their house. He would drink beer and shoot at the squirrels and laugh when he hit one.

Oh, God, Holly thinks.

She changes the channel. It's been too many months. Too many people dead. This endless waiting for the police to find their shooter. What happened six months ago? Holly tries to remember. What happened then that would make this guy all of a sudden turn into a sniper? Did anything happen to her? Anything Ivan would be aware of? Holly can't think of anything. Nothing symbolic.

The last postcard. The drawing of her and the kids in front of the house. Were they dead or just sleeping?

There is nothing on TV. The kids have been in bed for almost half an hour. Holly has her phone set up beside her. So far, no one has called. She watches the red light on the phone (she's turned off the ringer) but it's still black. This never-getting-a-break is wearing on her. Not a second without a screaming, snarling kid, begging, demanding, wanting—"More, more, more. Gimme." Not that, with Ivan around, she ever got a break. Not without constant pressuring. Not without begging him. Nagging him. She remembers getting a haircut once with Joe on her lap. There he was, not much older than a year, with her hair falling down on him as he sat and struggled. That had to be her worst haircut. Very uneven. The bangs chopped at an angle. The hairdresser was patient even though she got kicked in the stomach several times. Couldn't Ivan have held him for half an hour?

Holly thinks of the day that just passed and wonders how Jackson is. She worries about him for a little bit, takes a few phone calls—a woman whose teenager is driving her crazy, a man who is impotent (she wishes that were her problem)—but then her thoughts turn to the scream that came from Roger Smith's old house. That was odd. A little frightening. That man has been there for quite some time, Holly almost forgot about him. Or if not about him, then about the fact that she should have gone over and introduced herself. Said hello. A man locks himself in a house and not one single neighbour goes over to check on him, or to introduce themselves.

Holly stands and walks over to the window. She looks out at the black house. Dark. Tomorrow, she thinks, tomorrow she'll go over and say hello. Introduce herself. Ask if he needs anything.

Like furniture. Has he ever had furniture delivered?

She stands up close to the window and looks next door at Nelson Quimby's house. Nelson Quimby. A towel wrapped around his waist, his chest bare. He saw her pulling her kids around like they were sacks of potatoes. My God, Holly thinks, what have I done with my life? Even if Nelson ever thought she was worth something, now he must think she's ridiculous. Because she is. She knows it.

Holly is fiddling with the remote control. She is fiddling with an empty yogurt tube, critiquing its qualities. She is fiddling with her hair, twisting it around her finger. There is yogurt in her hair somehow. Damn tubes. It occurs to her that if she sold her ideas, her yogurt-tube-maxi-pad-drink-box ideas to someone—who? anyone—then perhaps she could get out of her rut, do something with her life. Her ideas are worth something, aren't they? Sell the idea. Forget trying to make the product. People buy ideas. People do it every day. Ideas make the world go around. She doesn't need capital to sell ideas, she only needs brains.

Brains.

But Holly has no idea how to start—who do you sell ideas to? The yogurt-tube makers? The maxi-pad corporation? Do you write your ideas down, send in a proposal, or just pitch your ideas aloud? And if so, who will listen? She has no corporate clothes.

The phone lights up. A distraught woman, worried about the sniper, worried about taking her car out anywhere. Holly reassures the woman, states statistics, the likelihood of another sniper attack so soon. It's become rote. She tries to put inflection in her voice.

"But he's not reliable anymore," the caller says.

"Men are never reliable," Holly says.

The caller laughs. Holly calms the woman and hangs up feeling good about her skills. I'm a people person, Holly thinks. I listen.

Then there is a knock at the door. A tap. A quiet knock. Someone who knows there are children sleeping in the house. Holly's legs shake as she gets up. Is it finally Ivan, coming to deliver another postcard in person? But, peeking out her curtain, she catches a glimpse of Jill McCallan on the front step.

"Oh, shit," she mumbles to herself. "I need this like a hole in the head." She opens the door.

"Hello," Jill says. Her voice is nails on a chalkboard. Holly shivers. "Yes?"

"I just—" Jill pauses. "Can I come in, Holly?"

"Why? So you can laugh at me? So you can hit my child again? I'm sorry, but he's asleep right now."

"No, Holly, listen—"

"I'm listening."

"Let me in. I can't talk to you out here."

Jill steps into Holly's house. Holly backs away, she turns toward the living room and suddenly sees the mess in front of her, really sees it. Through Jill's eyes. She sees the garbage on the floor, the toys strewn everywhere, the couch loaded with newspapers and old coffee mugs tilted at angles on chairs, the TV flashing, the blinds half-drawn, sticky with fingerprints, a marker drawing on the wall leading into the kitchen, multicoloured stains on the rugs. She sees it clearly. And she shrinks. She feels her body disappearing, like Alice when she drank from that bottle—she must stop reading that book to Joe, it's disturbing him and making her see the world in strange ways.

"I'm sorry, it's a mess in here. Normally it's not, normally—"

"No, no bother. Don't worry. I'm just here to apologize," Jill says, trying to take a seat on the couch without moving things aside. "I've been thinking a lot since...." Jill pushes over a chip bag.

"Here, let me—"

"No, I'll move it. Don't worry."

Jill perches on the edge of the couch. A newspaper falls to the floor. "I just wanted to say I'm sorry for saying those things, I'm sorry for hitting your child. I really didn't mean—you've had a lot to deal with, I—"

"It's okay," Holly sighs. "He probably deserved it. I'm not very good at giving orders, at following through."

Jill swallows. She thinks of Pearl suddenly. The way that Pearl gets drinks for Oliver, makes breakfast for Kate, but does nothing for

her. Jill is the one who writes Pearl a cheque every two weeks yet
Pearl won't even leave her any coffee in the pot. In fact, Pearl has
never cleaned Jill's bathroom. Every other room in the house, but
not Jill's bathroom. And what does Jill do? She gets down on her
hands and knees every week and cleans the toilet herself. That has to
change, Jill thinks. In fact, Jill is sure suddenly that she doesn't need
Pearl anymore. She can hire housecleaners. Kate is old enough to
take care of herself. Holly needs Pearl more than Jill does. But Holly
doesn't have the money to hire her. The world is so unfair, Jill thinks.
She shakes her head.

"But you should never do that again," Holly says. "My kids are
mine to discipline the way I see fit."

"Of course, I...." Jill reaches out and touches Holly's hand.

Holly and Jill look at each other. And then Holly begins to cry.
She slumps down to sit on the floor, in the middle of the biggest
dried stain (ketchup, she hopes), and cries. Jill leans down and
touches her hair. Then Jill pulls her hand away and holds it up
and looks at it.

"What's in your hair?"

"Yogurt," Holly cries. "In my hair. It's yogurt."

"Don't cry, Holly." Jill wipes her hand on the couch. She sighs.
"This is a sticky situation," she says and then she laughs.

"I can't help myself. I just can't seem to get anything together."

"Yes, well—" Jill looks around her. "Yes, well, keeping yourself
together is an art form. Only some people can do it. Really."

"Why can you do it?"

Jill straightens up. "Because," she says, "because I...." She wants to
say that she has support—a nanny, a husband, a child who loves her.

Holly looks at Jill. Jill looks at Holly. Jill is wearing a flowing silk
skirt, jewellery, makeup, a silk tank top, her hair swept up on her

head. Her underarms are shaved. She doesn't even look hot. Not a single line of perspiration on her body. She smells good.

"You always look so—" Holly cries louder. The phone lights up. She ignores it.

"Do you want me to get it?" Jill asks.

"No."

Jill pulls up her skirt a bit, takes a deep breath, and sits cross-legged with Holly on the floor. She takes Holly's hand.

"I was just thinking," Jill says quietly. "Do you remember when we held hands before? The only other time?"

"No," Holly says.

"When Roger Smith—"

"Oh, yes." Holly stops crying. "I suppose nothing can be that bad."

"And Jackson today," Jill says.

"Yes, poor Jackson." Holly sits straighter and stares at the wall in front of her, at the flashing lights on the TV set. The sniper shootings over and over and over. Her tears have all dried up. Jill releases her hand and Holly wipes her nose with it.

"Do you want a drink? I have some wine."

"Yes," Jill says. "A drink would be good." How quickly, Jill thinks, one can forget a hangover. Maybe Kate is right. Maybe she is drinking too much. Well, one last night.

Holly jumps up and rushes into the kitchen. She grabs two plastic kid-cups and a box of wine, the kind with a spout that drips. That's another thing Holly has ideas about—dripless wine-box spouts.

Jill stares at the box. "What is this?"

"A box of wine. Cheaper this way. Haven't you ever—"

"No, certainly not. What about the quality?"

"Who cares about the quality? It's the alcohol content and this is eleven percent." Holly squeezes two glasses out of the spout. "You can drink out of the box, too, if you put your head under the spout. That way you don't dirty glasses." She laughs a little, realizing how ridiculous she sounds.

"My God," Jill says. "That's barbaric." She takes the plastic cup from Holly's hand. It is shaped like a bear holding a lollipop and the lollipop stick is its handle.

"It's practical." Holly rejoins Jill on the floor. "But, yes, I guess it is kind of gross." Holly feels like crying again. She wipes the drip off the wine-box spout with her finger. She licks her finger clean.

The wine disappears quickly. The bear cups are large. Jill giggles.

"My life," Jill says finally, "is a facade."

"Oh," Holly laughs. "That's funny you would say that. When I first moved here I thought that the front of your house was that—a facade. Like one of those stages in Hollywood westerns—you know the kind, wooden fronts on small little buildings. They tip over during gun fights in the comedies."

"Yes, well, that's not exactly what I meant—"

"Then when I would come for your Christmas parties every year, I would see that the whole goddamn house is as nice as the front. Inside and out."

"Yes, it is. My house is beautiful, isn't it? But my life is a facade. My *life*."

"I don't understand."

"My house isn't the problem, well, the neighbourhood is—not you, of course—but really, the rest of the neighbourhood has gone downhill, hasn't it?"

"We are, literally, at the bottom of a hill." Holly giggles.

Jill stares at the floor for a minute.

"Those Christmas parties," she says quietly. "I tried so hard."

"Yes," says Holly, "they were nice."

"I was nice," Jill says. "I was nice to do those parties. For the neighbourhood."

"It's a shame," Holly begins, thinking of Roger Smith.

"Yes," Jill interrupts, "it's a shame my parties had to end."

There is silence for a minute and then Jill says, "That mystery man in the house next to mine, I just don't know what to do about him."

"I was just thinking about him. About going and—"

"I was thinking of calling the police."

"That's a little drastic. What's he done to deserve that?"

"Do you think the place even has a working bathroom?" Jill asks.

Holly laughs. "Well, where do you think he—in the basement?"

"That's precisely what I thought."

"I was kidding."

"And the fact that Celia sold her house without asking me—well!" Jill shakes her head. "She should have at least called me or something."

"Have you been in touch with her?" Holly says.

"Oh, no. That would be so awkward. But she really could have sent me a note, a brief one, telling me she was thinking of selling." Jill sips her wine. "Not very considerate, if you think about it."

"So," Holly says, "why does all of this make your life a facade? I don't get it."

Jill swallows more of the wine. "This is disgusting. I really should nip over and get us some good wine. And some snacks. I could use oysters or something."

"Jill," Holly says, "just relax for once. Everything is not about oysters and fancy wine."

"Yes, it is."

"What is?"

"Everything," Jill says. "That's the problem. Life is about appearances, Holly. You know that. I know that. And I can't seem to keep them up."

"Did you say, 'Keep him up'?" Holly is watching her phone light up and thinking that she should probably answer it. What if someone is suicidal? Or worse, what if it's the supervisor checking on her?

"What?"

"Are you talking about Oliver?"

"Oh, God, no," Jill says. "I have no problem with—well, no problem at all."

Holly sighs. She hasn't had sex in so long. "I haven't had sex in so long," she says.

"Yes, I'm sure." Jill considers Holly. Really looks at her. "You are quite pretty, though. But if you wouldn't mind some advice?"

"I don't know. I'm fragile right now. Sensitive. I don't know if I can take advice."

"Your hair," Jill says. She signals to Holly's hair on her head and she also motions toward legs and armpits.

"I really don't want to hear what's wrong with—"

Suddenly Jill thinks of Grace and Oliver and she starts to cry. "Screw him. Screw Oliver."

"What?"

"And Pearl. Bossing, always—"

"Pearl and Oliver? Isn't Pearl your nanny?"

"No, not Pearl and Oliver. Separately. Just screw them separately."

"I don't understand."

Holly's phone lights up again and Holly answers it. A woman is crying. Her dog died. She is old and alone. Jill is crying. Holly feels dizzy from all the wine. She's confused. She has no idea what anyone is talking about. She is finally able to hang up and Jill stops crying.

"I shouldn't have said anything," Jill sniffs. "It's the wine. It's so bad that I'm drunk already."

"But what about Oliver and Pearl? You haven't said anything."

Jill refills their glasses of wine. "Are you sure you don't want oysters? You know, I should drink cheap wine more often. It makes me drunk. Quicker. Faster. I'm assuming the hangover will be bad, though."

Holly nods. "You can't even imagine," she groans. She gets up and goes into her kitchen. Weaves into her kitchen. She comes back with yogurt tubes. "Here."

"Oh," Jill says. "Thanks. What are these? Little tubes?"

Holly watches as Jill struggles with her yogurt tube, blueberry, and it squirts all over her hand.

"What a mess," Jill says.

"And expensive," Holly says. "If they just sold reusable yogurt tubes that people could fill themselves, if they made them squirt-free, mess-free, easy to open, they could get rid of both problems." She sucks on her tube. "Parents would love them. They'd sell like crazy."

"But the companies don't want to make them cheaper. That goes against their policy of making money, Holly."

"But they'd sell twice as much. They'd make twice as much money. Poor people could buy yogurt tubes then."

"But then everyone would stop buying them once they had enough reusable containers. That wouldn't work, Holly."

"I thought it was a good idea."

"Mess-free. That's a good idea. Always good to improve on a product." She studies the yogurt tube in her hand, turns it over. "Yogurt and wine. Yech. It curdles in your mouth."

"I have all these ideas," Holly says. "Great ideas. And I don't know what to do with them." Holly begins to tell Jill all about her ideas for comfortable maxi-pads, for juice boxes that don't spill, for refillable yogurt tubes and dripless wine-box spouts. The list is endless. All the things that Holly uses daily, monthly, yearly, that don't work, aren't practical, don't make sense, aren't convenient. Jill listens.

"Well, you've got something, Holly. The mother angle. There probably aren't that many real mothers on the design teams for these companies. I remember hearing a program on the radio once about designing cars and some woman called in and said, 'Why is there never a place to put my purse?' and the designer was dumbfounded. He said that they just never thought of that." Jill thinks for a minute. "I wonder if you could talk to this guy I know. I'll call him."

"It's true," Holly says. "There's never anywhere to put your purse."

"More wine," Jill says, filling them both up. "I'll call him on Monday, okay? You'll like him. He's quite nice. Handsome too. But he's married."

"That doesn't stop some people."

And Jill begins to cry again. "Oliver," she says.

"What? Is he having an affair, Jill? Is that it?"

"Not yet," Jill says. "Just not yet. But he might, and until now, for some reason, I didn't care if he did."

"Well," Holly says. She studies Jill's face. "He might not, too, if you look at it that way."

"Yes, I guess so." Jill stops crying. "I guess you are right about that. It's funny, isn't it?"

"What?"

"Well, marriage. One minute you hate your spouse so intensely you feel like killing him, the next minute you can't bear to see him gone."

"I guess," Holly says. "I can't really say anymore."

Jill and Holly look at the TV where, suddenly, there is a flurry of activity on the news. Something has happened. Holly and Jill watch intently and Holly turns the volume back on.

"A composite sketch," the news reporter says. "The sniper. Witnesses."

"Oh, my," Holly says. "That looks like every man I've ever met."

Jill laughs. "You're right, you know. It does. It looks a bit like Jackson Kern, actually. Even Oliver. Even a bit like Nelson."

"Not as cute as Nelson," Holly says. "It looks like Ivan."

"God, it does. And a bit like Roger Smith. The whole damn neighbourhood. I told you it's going downhill."

"Maybe," Holly says breathlessly. "Maybe the sniper is all these men. Maybe they take turns, one at a time."

"Men aren't that organized," Jill says.

"You're right."

"They'd have to plan. Make phone calls. Set up schedules." Jill laughs.

Holly laughs.

Holly and Jill drink the rest of the wine. They watch the news. They eat more yogurt. They toast each other. And men. And kids. And yogurt tubes.

"Ideas," Holly keeps saying, "ideas make the world go around."

"You know," Jill slurs, as she's leaving, "in the big picture, it doesn't really matter about your own life. I mean, my life. It doesn't really matter."

"What do you mean?"

"I mean, there are bigger things, Holly. Like the sniper. Bigger things out there that'll get you. It's the small things. Families, affairs, facades, kids. Those small things don't really matter, if you think about it."

Holly nods wisely and sees Jill out. She watches her weave across the street and up the steps to her own house, tripping several times.

"No," Holly says suddenly. "Wait." She smacks the window, but Jill is already inside her house. "That's wrong." Jill has it wrong. She has it backwards. It's the small things that do matter. The big things will happen no matter what. It's the small things that can make a difference.

Or something like that. Holly can't think straight. Maybe that's what Jill said in the first place. Who knows? She looks at her phone and the red button is flashing wildly. Holly ignores it, turns off the living-room lights, and stumbles up the stairs to her empty bed.

Duck

MR. WALCOTT HAS STAYED quiet in his house. He has been hoping to hear another scream from the Roger Smith house. But there's been nothing. No sound. Now it's night again and he's hungrier than a horse. He wonders if horses are often hungry— it's a strange saying. Why not hungrier than an Ethiopian kid with a distended belly? He guesses that wouldn't work as a saying, it's a mouthful. Ha, Mr. Walcott thinks, a starvation joke is a mouthful. That's funny. Mr. Walcott is happy that he still has the capacity to make himself laugh. If he lost that, he doesn't know what he would do.

He wonders how Jackson is doing in the hospital. He tried phoning the Kerns over and over, but there was no answer. He assumes that Esther and Shannon are with their son. Mr. Walcott wonders what they will do with themselves. How they will take care of themselves. He supposes they will be forced to do what he will be forced to do eventually. If Jackson doesn't come home soon, all three of them, the old people on the street, will have to be taken care of by someone else. Or put somewhere. The thought terrifies him, but there is nothing he can do about it. He knew that this day would

220

come. He just didn't think it would come so quickly and unexpectedly. He assumed Jackson would eventually move out, find a wife maybe. Instead, it's Jackson's health that has jeopardized the finetuning of Murray Walcott's life. Poor Jackson Kern.

"Ah, well," he says as he bumbles around the kitchen, searching out a second dinner. There are always delivery services. Groceries On Wheels, that kind of thing. He'd just have to get used to seeing another body in his house every week. Mr. Walcott wonders if he could request the same delivery person each time.

But his thoughts keep returning to the Smith house and to that scream. It sounded like the man shouted, "Duck," but Mr. Walcott isn't sure. Why would he say "duck" to himself? Unless he was shouting for someone to watch out. As in, "Duck, that beam is falling on your head." But he's all alone in there, isn't he? At first Mr. Walcott thought it meant there's a duck in the house. But that made no sense. Now he thinks it definitely was: "Duck, something is falling." Just warning himself, that's what he was doing. Construction. Fixing things up. It's all a matter of being there, seeing the person say it. Mr. Walcott once got Judy a Far Side card that had several tall animals in a car going under a very low bridge. One of the animals shouts, "Duck!" and all the animals look up in the sky, and one animal says, "Where?" There was some caption on the bottom, something like, "Animal miscommunication." It was a funny card, but Judy just smiled politely and propped it up on the mantelpiece with the rest of her get-well cards. Even now, years later, thinking about it, Mr. Walcott still knows it's a funny card. The giraffe was about to lose his head under that bridge. Although he does have to admit that, next to the floral, glossy, high-end cards that her friends had sent, Hallmark cards, the ones that said, "May God be with you," sweet sentiments like that, his card did look out of place. Looking back on it, Mr. Walcott now sees that when someone you love is diagnosed with cancer, it's not an appropriate time to make jokes. Which is a funny thing, really, because what you want to do more than anything else is cheer someone up when they are feeling down. Make someone laugh.

Mr. Walcott wonders if he should send a card to Jackson. But who would take it to the mailbox for him?

Mr. Walcott reaches into the fridge and pulls out an avocado and some defrosted chicken breasts and a jar of mango chutney. He can make something with this. Use the chutney as a glaze, slice the avocados around the chicken for beautiful colour and presentation.

Mr. Walcott's mouth waters. It's a bit cooler now at night. He has enough food for several more days. Jackson probably has the flu or is just rundown. He's been working so hard. The man up the street is doing renovations and instinctively yelled "duck" when something fell. Everything will be fine. It's a quiet night. Nothing much happening.

A peaceful summer night—some television, another good meal, and early to bed. And Jackson won't wake him up tonight.

It was silly of Mr. Walcott to think that something was up, that something exciting was about to happen on Blind Crescent. He merely has plots in his head—book plots, movie plots—he seems to always be expecting a climax when, really, there isn't going to be one. Life isn't like that. Mr. Walcott whistles as he pops the chicken out of the wrapper and into the frying pan.

KATE IS WATCHING TV down in the basement with Pearl. They rented a scary movie and Oliver can sometimes hear them scream. He is sitting in the kitchen, drinking a beer, and wondering what happened to Jill. She left for Holly's house about an hour ago and she's still not home. Oliver wonders if Holly might have killed her or something. Lately, he's been feeling like killing Jill. She's become so annoying. Well, more annoying than usual. Always questioning him: "What's wrong, Oliver?" "What are you thinking about?" "Is anything bothering you?" "Have I done something?" And making him feel guilty.

He hasn't done anything.

He shouldn't feel guilty.

Every day he brings flowers home. They are all over the house in vases half full with stagnant water. Pearl is complaining about the smell. "Like a funeral home," she keeps saying. She says it isn't in her contract to change water in vases every day. "Ms. McCallan can do it herself," Pearl says. And Jill grumbles under her breath, "That's another thing I have to do. Why do I have to do everything?"

Women, Oliver thinks. He knows he's stereotyping, but women really can be annoying. He can't understand them. His daughter has taken to wearing second-hand clothing (doesn't he give her enough money?) and slouching around the house looking tired all the time, his wife is afraid, defiant, angry, sweet, and bitchy all at the same time, his nanny complains continuously about everything even though she's pocketing about one-third of his salary, and the teenage girl across the street is driving him mad with lust.

Grace.

He can't stop thinking about Grace. The way she touched his arm, his waist.

That's why he feels guilty.

But thinking isn't doing, Oliver reminds himself. He gets another beer from the fridge. That's three now. He lines the bottles up in front of him. "Thinking isn't doing," Oliver says aloud.

Kate comes into the kitchen to get three cans of pop and a bag of chips.

"Are you talking to yourself?" she says.

"Why do you have three cans of pop?"

"Grace is coming over. Can you let her in when she knocks?"

Kate goes down the stairs again.

Oliver swallows hard. He gulps at the beer. "Shit," he whispers.

Of course, when Grace knocks quietly and Oliver lets her in and she follows him into the kitchen and stands up close to him and pretends to grab his beer—and then does grab it and takes a gulp—when her lipstick mark is on his beer bottle, and his next swallow tastes like cherries and wax, and she says, "Look at the burn I got at the beach today, Mr. Rafferty," and pulls her tank top up off her pierced belly and, at the same time, down off her shoulder, and Oliver sees the white lines of a string bikini (brilliant white against savage pink), and Grace says, "Touch this, it burns," and when he touches her flat stomach—he can't stop himself—and she shudders and her nipples are suddenly visible and she moans, "Oh, God, your hand is cold from the beer," and when he backs away, terrified, his eyes open wide, and she walks back with him, closely, smiling coyly, when all of this is happening he can't stop whispering, "Shit," over and over and over.

"Shit, shit, shit, shit."

"Shhh. Stop swearing," Grace giggles and presses herself up close to him.

"No," Oliver says, as soon as he gathers himself, realizes "shit" isn't what he really wants to say. He pushes Grace away. "I can't. I'm married. You're too young."

"Just a kiss," Grace says. "There's no harm in that."

"It's not just a kiss," Oliver says as Grace moves up close to him again and takes his beer again, takes another sip.

"A small peck on the cheek then?"

"No, I—"

"I won't hurt you." Grace laughs quietly.

"This isn't right, Grace. I can't."

Grace moves closer to him. Oliver can smell her. She smells like candy and coconut tanning oil. She smells like cigarettes and beer.

Oliver's heart feels weak. He's breathless. Confused. I'm being seduced, he thinks. Help me. Someone.

"What good will this do?" Oliver says. "Think of the future."

"*Future?*" Grace laughs. "What future?"

She has a point, Oliver thinks.

"Oliver," Grace says, in her deep big-girl voice, and she touches his face with her hand and suddenly he doesn't see her anymore, he sees instead a woman in a glossy magazine, a cover girl. He sees everything he wants to see and finally he pulls her up to him and she smiles as he kisses her hard on her soft mouth, her full lips. She pushes him aside to take the gum out of her mouth (Oh, God, he thinks, gum?) and place it on the top of his beer bottle, and when all of this is happening, Oliver thinks to himself nothing.

Absolutely nothing.

His mind is one big fat zero. One blank. Whiteness. He focuses on the kiss. That's it. Nothing else there. Nada.

Grace's lips are wet and full and Oliver loses himself in them, in the feel of her young body pressed hard against his. He can feel every curve of her. Her thighs, her pubic bone, her hips jutting into him, her stomach tight and flat, her belly-button ring—God, he can feel her belly-button ring—her breasts. Everything.

Kate calls up, "Grace? Dad? Is Grace here?"

And then Oliver's mind fills up. Expands. All sorts of horrible things come crashing in, moving around, squeezing tight inside his head.

"Oh, God, oh, God, oh, God," he murmurs.

But Grace just casually turns away from him. She calls out, "Yep, coming down. I'm here," and starts to walk down the stairs. She turns then, to Oliver, and, his heart stopping, she moves again toward him. She smiles and reaches around him, to the counter, to the gum stuck to the top of his beer bottle. She pops it back into her mouth.

"My gum," she says, and cracking her gum against her teeth, she disappears below.

Oliver sits down.

Now he's done it, he thinks. He's sold his soul, hasn't he?

Oliver runs his fingers through his thinning hair, wipes the lipstick off his mouth.

Six bottles of beer later it occurs to Oliver that all of this is Jill's fault. Where the hell is she? If she had been here, none of this would have happened.

Every time he hears one of them scream from deep in the basement, Oliver jumps half off his stool. His nerves are shot. His body tense. And no matter how many bottles of beer he drinks, he doesn't loosen up.

WHEN JILL FINALLY CRASHES into the house, Oliver is already passed out in their bed, snoring loudly. Pearl and Kate are asleep in theirs. Grace has gone home.

SHANNON AND ESTHER are sitting in front of the TV. The phone has been ringing off and on, but neither of them have the energy to answer it.

"He's probably dead," Shannon says suddenly.

The sound from her husband startles Esther. She looks away from the TV.

"What are you talking about?"

"The phone ringing. Jackson probably died."

Shannon looks down at his hands in his lap. His old-man, shaking hands. Age spots. And then he begins to cry. Soft, warm tears fall into these hands. He watches them curiously.

Esther stares at her husband.

"No," she shouts. "No. It's not true. Don't say that."

In the middle of the night Gavin wakes up with another nightmare. The dead man hanging from his beam in the basement. As usual, when Gavin gets up close to his swinging feet, the man opens his eyes, smiles, and says something. Tonight it was something about mowing the lawn. Then Gavin's mother was there, her face became the face of the dead man.

And Gavin wakes sweating and crying.

He does what he always does when he cries. He gets up and goes over to his mirror and watches himself cry. Watching himself he realizes quickly how silly he looks and the cry begins to look fake and soon peters out. It always happens. He did this when he was really small too. He did this when his mother left and didn't come back. He would stand in front of the mirror just when his sobs were the heaviest and the funny expression he was making would, inevitably, stop his tears. He became merely curious then, not sad or hurt.

It's like watching TV, Gavin thinks. That's not really me. That's someone else crying.

And then Gavin hears something from downstairs. He creeps down the stairs and looks into the living room. His father is sitting on the couch, crying. Not loudly, but softly and quietly. His shoulders shake. Gavin wants to get a mirror, hold it up to his father, he wants to show his father how ridiculous he looks. He wants to shout, "We're men. We're men, Dad," but instead he tiptoes down the hallway and through the kitchen and, quietly, quietly, opens the kitchen door and heads outside into the night. Gavin feels helpless and scared and he hates these feelings.

IN THE LIVING ROOM, Nelson wonders if his ex-wife will ever want to see the children again. He wonders if he's having a nervous breakdown, if this is what it's like to have a mid-life crisis. Nelson is so afraid for his children, of his children, he suddenly doesn't want them to grow up, move on, or move away. He wants to keep them tight to the house. He wipes the tears off the sides of his face. He wants his kids to come back to him. Nelson thinks, Yes, this must be a mid-life crisis. Why, all of a sudden, does he want his children by his side? Why, all of a sudden, does he want them to be small again? Why, all of a sudden, does he feel like crying at every little thing? It makes no sense.

Nelson stands and walks over to the front window. He looks out at the dark street. He sees Jill leaving Holly's house and he thinks for a minute that it's odd those two are doing something together. Jill is walking crazy, as if she's drunk. She is drunk. Nelson watches her stumble down the street. He smiles. She looks funny. Usually so poised and in control, Jill crashes up the stairs, holding on to the sides of her skirt, lifting it up slightly as if it's an evening gown.

Beside her the empty house sits. Nelson thinks that he's never gone over there, never gone up to see who is living there, what is going on. It occurs to him that this is mean. This is the kind of mean behaviour that leads people to shoot small children, or the kind of behaviour that leads wives to pack up and leave their husbands, or the kind of behaviour that leads kids to become teens who are bitter and angry and want to get away.

And then the street is silent. Still. Quiet. Nelson thinks his children are upstairs in bed. Lindsay is asleep in his bed. The houses are all dark on the cul-de-sac—all but Mr. Walcott's, which is lit up like a Christmas tree. It is still. It is hot. A storm seems to be hovering nearby, ready to crash. Nelson can feel it. He shivers and feels the perspiration on his back begin to dry.

Something, Nelson thinks to himself, has to change.

Here

FROM BEHIND HIS HOUSE Gavin watches Kate's mom come out of Holly Wray's house and stumble up the street to her own. He watches her trip on the stairs and then slam the front door. He creeps out and starts to walk behind the other houses over to his tree. His feet are bare but rough from the summer. He walks carefully. In the backyard of the empty house, Gavin stops and stands still and looks around. He can feel the air pressure changing. A storm is coming. He scratches his stomach and then remembers he is wearing only boxer shorts and a T-shirt, his pyjamas. He hopes no one will see him. But then he thinks that he wants to see someone, he wants to see this man in Roger Smith's house—or not someone, really, but something, he wants to see the basement—and so Gavin walks close up to the empty house, up to the kitchen door, and tries to peer in. He wipes the dirt off the window. He presses his head against the glass.

Heat lightning flashes. Gavin jumps. Steadies himself. Decides that he wants to go into the basement more than the kitchen. So he tiptoes to the basement window on the side closest to the Rafferty house. What he wants is not to disturb the man, really, but to sneak in and sneak out quickly. Test himself. Replace his memory with something new.

Gavin pushes at the window. It is locked or stuck or painted shut. He rubs at the glass and looks in. He can see nothing in the dark. He pushes again. This time he feels some movement. Surely, Gavin thinks, kids at his high school have been inside, surely there is a way. Another push.

The window swings open. It swings into the basement making a creaking sound. Gavin's heart thumps wildly in his chest. He looks around outside. The night is still. More heat lightning. A rumbling of thunder in the background.

Gavin steadies himself on the windowsill and then, with one leap, he jumps into the basement and lands on the floor with a thump. Looking up in the darkness, Gavin identifies the beam that Roger Smith hanged himself on. He walks over to it. Something moves in the shadows under the stairs. An animal. Gavin wants to cry. He wants to run. But he pulls himself together and stands stiffly under the beam. Letting his eyes adjust to the darkness, he looks around. The basement is empty. Where the bikes stood, the wine rack stood, the tools and workbench, there is nothing.

And where Roger Smith was hanging, there is nothing. Not even a frayed rope. Nothing.

Gavin hears a noise upstairs. Someone shouts out. He hears something heavy hit the floor. Gavin runs over to the window and pulls himself out into the night. Thunder booms. Gavin runs like the wind through his backyard, up through the kitchen door, and into his house. He scurries up the stairs, looking once at the empty living room, and up to his bedroom where he quietly shuts the door and flops down on his bed.

He did it. He really did it.

Things will be different, Gavin thinks, from this point on.

Rain crashes down outside. Gavin's curtains blow wildly into his room. A cool breeze billows in. Gavin stares at his ceiling. He did it.

Hell-oh

INDIGESTION FROM THE MANGO CHUTNEY. It must have been rotten. He has no idea how old it was.

Mr. Walcott can't sleep. Instead, he turns off a few of the lights in his well-lit house, and in the dark of night, he props his chair up to the front window and peers outside. What drew him into his living room, he can't say. But there is something happening around him on this night, something strange, he can feel it. He was right before. Something feels like it's coming. Mr. Walcott likes to look at the house at the end of the street whenever he feels nervous. Its shape tastes like peppermint or ginger, one of the soothing spices. It relaxes his gut. Coats the acid.

So here he is in his chair in the middle of the night, occasionally thumping his chest to get down the acid reflux that's creeping up, occasionally shrugging his large back up and down the chair to scratch the itch, when he sees Jill shuffle drunkenly out from Holly's house and stumble down the street toward her own. He watches as she climbs the rickety stairs and then pushes herself in through her front door.

Something about the way Jill moves down the street reminds him of Judy, of the way his wife moved.

Judy wasn't ever comfortable in her body. She clothed herself in material shaped like bags, long tunics, long shirts, loose pants, anything to hide what she was ashamed of. What could she have been ashamed of? It still baffles him. A thin, small, lovely woman. Okay, Mr. Walcott thinks, this line of thought is making him much too sad and so he turns his thoughts instead to the man in the deserted house.

He is interrupted by the Quimby boy who slips out from behind his house and moves around to the house next door. The boy isn't wearing shoes. Mr. Walcott shakes his head. At least he isn't carrying his basketball. The boy disappears behind the Smith house.

Mr. Walcott hopes the boy isn't bothering the man inside, and again his thoughts turn to him, his twin, his reclusive friend. Mr. Walcott knows he is identical to the unknown man in that house. Both of them hiding from the world. Needing to hide from the world. One reason or another. It really doesn't matter.

Eventually, for both of them, all will be quiet.

Heat lightning strikes. Mr. Walcott watches.

It takes him by surprise when, suddenly, he sees a shape looming in the front window of the house. A distinct figure. And then he sees the shape come close to the window, put his forehead against the glass, and look out. Mr. Walcott stands up and knocks over his chair. He holds onto the curtains for balance and he can hear, feel, and see the curtain rod bending with his weight.

What's going on?

The man looks horrible. Sick. Tired. Drawn. Thin.

Interesting, Mr. Walcott thinks. Sad. He wonders why the man looks so sad.

And then—look at that—the man looks right at him, right at Mr. Walcott. He stares. Mr. Walcott stares back.

It's a party, Mr. Walcott thinks. The beginning of a party.

And then Mr. Walcott sees a miraculous sight. It is superb. It buoys him. Lifts him up. He knows it's only his imagination, some triggering, firing or misfiring, of his synapses, his synesthesia acting up—but Mr. Walcott sees something glowing behind the man. A fine white powder, a dust, floating up behind him and reflecting from the moonlight outside. It's a ghostly trail. Mr. Walcott holds his breath. An earth-shattering, eerie, beautiful sight. As if spirits are floating behind the sad man.

Mr. Walcott waits, standing there in his window, waits for the man to do something, to acknowledge the particles behind him. He doesn't know what he expects the man to do. Come out of his house? Turn toward the light? Something. Anything. But there is no movement from the man. Mr. Walcott wills the man inside to do something. Move.

The Quimby boy is nowhere to be seen.

More heat lightning. A rumble.

A minute passes.

Then Mr. Walcott has an idea. He raises his hand and waves. A small wave. He acknowledges the sad man in the house, the man with the spirits behind him. And the man waves back. Just slightly. The energy it takes to move his arm is obviously fierce. It shows on the man's face.

Mr. Walcott smiles.

The man nods once and then slowly, slowly, walks backwards, out of sight. He disappears. The glowing dust remains in the empty air.

Mr. Walcott opens wide his front door. He steps one fat foot out, then the other. Takes the releasing heat of the night full on. Blink. The wind picks up. Wearing slippers, polyester pants, a shirt the size of a tent, Mr. Walcott stands, for the first time in years, right out on his front step.

Dizzy, he feels dizzy.

His back. That itch. He's on fire.

But he continues on.

A connection was made.

One, two, three … down the stairs. Panting, wheezing. Shaking. Breathing so heavily it feels to Mr. Walcott as if there is a vacuum cleaner working in his lungs, sucking air in violently. He begins his journey to Roger Smith's old house. Toward the end of the street. Ever so slowly. Shapes coming at him, flavours surrounding him. His mouth waters. He drools. So hungry for another dinner, for a snack, for anything that will stop the flow of chocolate, mint, peppers, chicken, zucchini, bread, cheese, cinnamon, cherry liqueur, milk, fried egg-and-mustard sandwich, chutney (coming up his gorge—he can actually taste that one), pumpkin pie, roast-beef submarine sandwich, pizza, Chinese takeout, thumbprint cookies, green lollipops.…

What if, he thinks, what if he has a heart attack? Right here. In the middle of the cul-de-sac. Before he can do any good. Before he can meet the man.

Itchy, itchy.

In San Francisco, Mr. Walcott thinks, forcing his mind to focus, the public utilities commission hired a herd of four hundred goats to eat the weeds and brush from the slopes of its rights-of-way. They were rented from a company called Goats-R-Us, if he remembers correctly, and they ate about an acre a day.

Lightning.

The moon disappears behind a cloud.

Fear of criticism is called enissophobia.

Remember? A cab driver in L.A. eats twelve lettuces a day smothered in chocolate sauce. Just because he can. Remember this, Mr. Walcott thinks.

Fear of long waits is called macrophobia.

Being in a gloomy place: lygophobia.

"When the chips are down, the buffalo are empty."

Thunder.

Judy. Judy with her cancer. Lungs. Lungs. Breathe. Her body beautiful to him, even sick. His body disgusting to her.

He can't breathe. His whole body itches.

He makes it up the front porch before almost collapsing. The door opening amazingly easily, Mr. Walcott moves into the front hall. The stench hits him. Stale and rotting. A smell that is nauseous and sorrowful.

"Hello," he shouts. "Are you okay?" The hall is dark, a rat scurries and hides. Mr. Walcott falls heavily to his knees. "Hello?" And then his knees buckle and he falls forward onto his face. It takes all the effort he has left to roll onto his back.

"Hell—" Mr. Walcott says. "Oh."

So Much More

"I'll get help. Just wait." He stumbles around the hallway, not knowing what to do.

The fat man lies on the hallway floor in the heat. He is barely breathing, he is almost unconscious.

"Don't die," he says. His voice is hoarse from little water, from no food, from not talking to anyone but the rats.

One sad eye looks straight at him. The fat man smiles. "Who are you?" he whispers.

"My name is Aaron. Aaron Cotton," the man says. He is so weak. "Just hold on. I'll get someone."

Outside it begins to rain. The wind blows wildly around the house, coming in through the open front door.

"Why?" the fat man whispers.

"Why what?" Aaron says.

"Why bother?"

"Too many people die," Aaron says. But he doesn't know what to do. He doesn't know where to go. Where to turn. Who to turn to. He's exhausted.

"There's blood on your hands," the fat man says.

Aaron holds up his hands. Dried blood, black, the creases on his palms stained. "Rats," he says. "Just rats. Don't worry."

He sits beside the fat man on the floor. The walls spin around.

"Rats," the fat man says. He sighs. Then, "Of course, everyone dies." The fat man closes his eyes. Lashes flutter.

"No," Aaron says. Almost shouts. "No. It doesn't have to be this way."

The fat man breathes deeply. Once. Twice. "I enjoyed it," he whispers.

"What?" Aaron says, frantic now. "Tell me what you enjoyed. What?"

"Going outside."

And then, suddenly, the fat man is dead. One moment he is breathing, talking, the next moment he is dead. Aaron thinks there should have been so much more. When people die, there should always be something more. Like fireworks. Or like the heat lightning outside. Lighting up the sky. The boom isn't only what you wait for, it's also the light, the glow, the colours. Night to day to night.

"Where are all the colours?" Aaron says. He stares at his stained hands. Blood dried in his fingernails.

"A bang," he whispers. "A crack." The universe should open.

This way seems so unfair, Aaron thinks. Like The Others. One minute they were there with him, the next minute they were gone. He begins to cry but is dehydrated and so his tears are dry.

The fat man smells of food. And something else. Sweat.

Aaron Cotton stands up. The fat man there below him, on the floor. He steadies himself on the hall closet door. The fat man's eyes are closed. He looks comfortable. Aaron thinks that's good. The Others looked comfortable in death too.

More comfortable than Aaron is in life.

Maybe that's something.

With bent knees that are stiff from sitting he hobbles back upstairs to retrieve his belongings. It's time to go. It is time to move on. To another house, perhaps, or maybe back to where he came from. He isn't sure. Aaron feels lighter somehow. Just slightly. He grieves for the fat man, but there is nothing he can do for him now. There was never anything he could do for him. Or for anyone. He has no power to make any changes in the past or in the future. He has to just ride it out. Aaron thinks that he can't carry the fat man along with him, he has The Others riding heavy on his shoulders already.

The Others.

Aaron doesn't know if the sorrow will ever leave him. He has to carry on, move somehow, continue. Small steps, Aaron thinks. Very small steps.

On the stairs a rat comes rushing out at him, rushes at his feet. He raises his hand, makes a gun with his thumb and forefinger, and shoots him dead.

"Bang."

The rat disappears around a corner.

There is no satisfaction, Aaron thinks, in killing anything.

Part Five

Tomorrow

IT IS HOT AND STILL. The brief storm in the night brought in a humidity that is stifling. There is the smell of sulphur in the air from the factories by the water.

Oliver opens the front door of his house to get the paper. It is Sunday morning. There is no paper. Oliver stands at the door, overwhelmed by the heat. His hangover is so intense that he's glad there is no paper. He's afraid if he had to bend down to pick it up he might fall down. Breathing in deeply, he feels full of wet air. Oliver is pleased that even though he drank a lot last night, this morning when he woke up his pee was normal, a normal colour. This buoys him up, makes him grateful to be alive. Even with the heavy hand of guilt on his heart. Even with a head almost bursting, a stomach ripe with bile.

Across the street, Nelson opens his front door. He reaches out for the paper before he, too, realizes it's Sunday and there is no paper. He straightens and looks across at Oliver. Oliver waves.

"Hot, isn't it?" Oliver shouts. He feels he has to say something to Nelson, say something that will fill the chasm that opened in his soul when he kissed Grace. His voice cracks.

A bird startles in the hill behind the houses and caws and cries and flies up into the air. Nelson shrugs.

Shannon Kern opens up the front curtains in his living room and looks out on the street. He sees the two men on their porches, both wearing shorts and T-shirts. In his time, men didn't wear shorts. It was considered unmanly. But maybe it wasn't as hot back then. Shannon can't remember. Behind him, Esther is moving around, attempting to get breakfast herself. They are going to the hospital to pick Jackson up at ten o'clock. The doctor called again and offered to send a taxi. Shannon feels excited and scared. He feels sad. He feels hungry. The air-conditioning unit in the hallway hums and whirrs.

Grace is suddenly awake. She doesn't know why. Perhaps it was the sound of the bird screeching outside, or the door opening downstairs. She looks at the clock. Nine in the morning. Too early, she thinks. She stands and stretches and looks out her window at the street. She sees Oliver at the front door of his house and she stares at him. He looks skinny and tall and old, the remains of his hair sticking up haphazardly. Grace remembers the kiss last night and wonders suddenly how she could have kissed him, how she could have thought he was attractive or desirable. Look at him, she thinks. What was I thinking? He's an old man. Grace crosses her arms in front of her chest and hugs herself. She squinches up her eyes. She feels suddenly so sad. School will start again soon, she thinks. This is no fun. Absolutely no fun at all.

Initially she wanted Kate's things—a mother, a nice house, wealth, even a nanny (someone who at least cared where she went)—but now she isn't so sure. It's weird that she kissed Kate's father like that. Too weird. And scary. And depressing. Grace feels uncomfortable. She throws on a tank top and shorts and heads downstairs for something to eat. Gavin walks downstairs just behind her.

"Beach today?" he says.

"Sure. Why not?"

Nelson meets them in the hallway. He shuts the front door and steps back into the air-conditioned home.

"God, it's hot," Grace says.

"You're going to the beach today?" Nelson says.

Grace and Gavin shrug.

Gavin remembers seeing his father cry last night. It dampens his mood for a minute, but then he thinks about how he went into that house and came out alive. A new man. He feels proud and big. A big man. He puffs up his chest a bit. Stands tall. His father looks at him and smiles. Gavin can't wait to find the right time to tell Grace and Kate what he did.

"Can I—can I come to the beach with you?" Nelson says. "I could drive you."

Grace imagines her father lying there beside her on his own beach towel. She imagines the looks she'll get.

"Well," she says.

"Where's my coffee, honey?" Lindsay calls down from upstairs.

Nelson shrugs.

"Yeah, Dad, sure," Gavin says. He smiles. "Of course. That'd be great."

Grace says, "Gavin."

"He can come, Grace. Why not?"

"Because it'd be so embarrassing." Grace looks at her father's fallen face, thinking, What have you ever done for me? You are finally tired of your girlfriend, you're bored and lonely, now you want to go to the beach with me? But she says nothing. She wants to cry because, oh, God, she kissed Mr. Rafferty. Her mind is crazy these days. Maybe Kate is right. Maybe she does dress like a prostitute.

"Shit," she says. "I guess you can come." It's Sunday, she thinks. Not many people will be there in the morning. As long as they leave right after lunch to come home.

"Don't swear, Grace," Nelson says, smiling. "Who wants pancakes? I could make pancakes."

"Coffee?" Lindsay calls. "Nelson?" She peeks her head over the bannister, her hair sticking up, her eyes half shut from sleep.

"I'm making pancakes for the kids," Nelson says. "Why don't you make your own coffee?"

"What? What did you say?" Lindsay asks. "Pancakes?"

Nelson ignores her. "You know, Grace, you're looking more and more like your mother every day."

Grace shrugs. "Who cares?" Grace thinks, What are you going to do? Get rid of me too?

But Gavin is looking out the front window. He is looking across the street at Mr. Walcott's house.

"Dad?"

"Yes?" Nelson calls from the kitchen as he shuffles around looking for pancake mix. Surely his ex-wife would have bought pancake mix at some time in the past, wouldn't she?

"Mr. Walcott's front door is open."

Grace moves to the front window. Nelson joins them.

"You're right." They look at Mr. Walcott's door. "That's odd."

Across the street Jill looks out to the side of her house and sees that Mr. Walcott's front door is open at the same time Nelson and Gavin and Grace see it. She calls Oliver to the window. She is nursing her headache with an ice pack—Boxed wine, she thinks, what was I thinking?—and her upset stomach with Pepto-Bismol.

"Oliver—look."

Kate, Oliver, and Pearl all come to the window. Everyone is up early because of the heat. Pearl's air conditioning turned off in the basement for some reason—"You bought the cheapest one," Pearl said. "I told you not to buy the cheapest one. All your money and still you're cheap"—and Pearl marched up the stairs onto the second floor to complain loudly to anyone who could hear it. Jill was jolted out of bed by her voice. Oliver said he'd get the air conditioner fixed and that, for now, she could sleep in the guest room.

Kate spent half an hour helping Pearl carry some of her things up the stairs from the basement and now she's standing, rubbing her eyes, by her father and mother and Pearl, looking out the front window at Mr. Walcott's open door. Across the street she can see Gavin and Grace staring out too. She waves. They wave back.

And, in the bungalow, Esther Kern points out the side window, a piece of dry, plain bread in her hand, and through a mouthful of sticky bread, she says, "Murray's door is wide open." Shannon gets up from his chair and looks out. He turns and contemplates the door. And then he walks over to his own front door and opens it. He steps out into the heat.

"It's hot outside, Esther," he says. "Very, very hot."

"What are you doing? You're letting the cold air out."

Esther follows him onto the front mat. She gasps when the heat hits her. She puts her bread down on the porch railing and steadies herself.

Shannon looks at his wife, at her age spots, her crooked back, her shrunken frame. He remembers how beautiful she used to be. Small and thin, erect, her back straight. She was a proud woman. Now he sees her face is lined so deep it looks like it has been carved. Her skin is sallow from lack of sunlight.

He wonders when it was that she changed so dramatically. Was it when he was turned down for the first promotion at work, or the second one, or when he lost his job at the one construction company and took a lower-paying job at another?

Or was it when Jackson left each day for school and Esther would stay home alone and count their money, balance the budget? One day Shannon remembers Esther putting down the cheque book and saying, "That settles it. We can't have another baby. We have absolutely no extra money."

But Shannon doesn't remember ever wanting another baby—maybe a different child, one who liked sports, perhaps, or tools instead of dried flowers—but not a second child.

Today they have to take a taxi to the hospital and pick up their only son. Jackson regained consciousness. He is coming home. Roles have been reversed. Now he and Esther will have to look after Jackson. And there'll be no one to look after them.

"Let's go," Shannon says.

"Where? Shut the door."

"To see what's happened to Murray, I guess." And Shannon starts to move carefully down the porch. He holds tight to the railing.

"We have to get Jackson soon," Esther wails. "All this adventure is killing me, Shannon. I'm too old for all of this."

"Come on, old woman," Shannon grumbles. "Get a move on."

Just then, Holly Wray comes down her stairs and rushes across the street—"Hurry up, Joe. Come on"—over to Mr. Walcott's open front door. The children pad along after her. She climbs the steps and goes inside.

"No hesitations," Jill says to Oliver from their front window. "She's incredible." Jill smiles. She thinks she likes Holly's impulsiveness now.

All of Blind Crescent comes out into the street. They stand first on their front porches and then begin to walk down the steps and walk out into the street.

Oliver sees Grace and his face heats up. He turns pink.

"What's wrong, Oliver?" Jill says, and then she sees the way he's looking at the girl and she feels a lump rise in her throat. "Come on, Oliver."

Kate is watching. Oliver and Grace look at each other. And then Grace turns abruptly away and Oliver knows he's been rejected. She won't look at him. He feels crushed, flattened. What have I done? he thinks. She looks like a little girl wearing those clothes, looking sleepy. Rubbing her eyes. No makeup. A girl. She is a little girl.

Jill looks at Kate. Kate shrugs her shoulders high, up to her ears, and tries to smile at her mother. It's a girlish look, her shoulders up like that, the grin silly and big. Jill smiles back. And then Jill clears her throat and whispers to her husband, "Get over it, Oliver, she's only sixteen," and Oliver feels humiliated and angry at himself. How, Oliver thinks, how can they change so quickly? How can women do that? Be both young and old at the same time? He looks closely at Jill and thinks that even she doesn't stay constant most of the time. Some days she is girlish and giggly, other days she is a business woman, and then still some days she is her mother. Oliver looks at his hands. They are shaking. Stupid, he thinks, I'm so damn stupid.

"This is a cool summer," Kate says to Gavin. "Everything has happened on this street. Do you think we'll see another dead body?"

Gavin says nothing. He doesn't have to defend himself anymore.

Holly comes out of Mr. Walcott's house. She has Sweetpea on her hip and Joe is standing beside her. She looks down at everyone standing on Mr. Walcott's front lawn.

"He's not here," she says. "I looked in every room. He's gone."

"He can't just disappear," Nelson says. "Let's walk around a bit and see if he went out for some air. Maybe he collapsed somewhere."

"The heat," Jill says. "The storm last night. Does he have air conditioning?"

"No," Holly says. "It's like an oven in there."

"Disappear?" Grace says. "But he's so fat."

They fan out and start looking around. The kids go toward the hill behind the houses, the adults mull around the front. Sweetpea finds a shovel in the dirt in front of his house and sits down and begins to dig up the lawn. Shannon and Esther sit on the steps at the bottom of Mr. Walcott's front porch. It's a small cul-de-sac and soon everyone is back again, sweaty and out of breath.

"Oh, my God," Holly says. "I hope he's okay."

"Where is he?" Oliver asks.

Joe notices it first.

"Look—" he says. He points toward Roger Smith's old house. The door is open there too.

"How did we not see that?" Jill says.

Gavin thinks back to last night and the shouts he heard. The noise of something falling.

Everyone begins to walk to the old house. Up the stairs, the two old and the two young holding the rickety railing, trailing behind.

"Something about this house," Oliver says. He shrugs. "I don't know. It's just…."

A taxi pulls up in front of the Kern residence. Everyone turns to look. Jackson Kern gets out of the taxi and looks at all of them, the whole of Blind Crescent, standing on the steps of Roger Smith's old house. He walks over.

"Hello," he says. "What's going on?"

"You're back," Shannon says. "We don't have to go and get you."

"What's happening?"

"Come help me stand up, Jackson," Esther says. "My knees are weak."

"Give him some air, woman," Shannon says. "Give him some room."

"The fat man is gone," Pearl says. "How are you feeling?"

Jackson shrugs. "I'm okay, thanks. Mr. Walcott? Gone?"

"Mr. Walcott is missing," Jill says. "His front door was open this morning. So was this front door. We thought maybe—"

"*Missing?*" Jackson says. "How can such a huge man disappear?"

"That's what I said," says Grace. "I said the same thing."

Jackson was determined to come home, pack his suitcases, crate up his flower-drying things, and disappear into the sunset. He was determined to tell his parents to go to hell—the doctor said they were causing the headaches, that it was stress-related, even that ache in his hand that never seemed to go away, that to live with them any longer would most probably cause Jackson to have some kind of stroke—and walk out the front door.

Maybe visit occasionally. See how they were doing.

They are adults, the doctor had said. They can get help on their own.

But now, Jackson comes home and sees the entire neighbourhood, including his parents—who haven't been outside in months—standing on the front steps of Roger Smith's old house, looking for Mr. Walcott. He walks up the steps and takes hold of his mother's arm. He feels her bones through the soft, weak skin. No muscle.

"Jackson's here," Esther says. "He'll find Murray. He always knows where Murray is. 'Everything for Murray,' we say. Jackson takes good care of that man, don't you, Jackson?" Esther tries to laugh.

"Mother."

Nelson is the first one in the house. He finds Mr. Walcott lying in the front hall. He cautions the others to stay back. Gavin, however, comes up close to his father and looks down at the huge, fat man. Behind him Gavin can hear the women beginning to cry. He can hear Oliver take his cellphone out of his pocket and call the police. This time, however, no one is screaming. Gavin looks around at the dust everywhere, at the decay of the house. He smells an awful smell—the smell of human waste, of Mr. Walcott. If only he'd come upstairs last night when he heard the shouts. But Gavin knows there is nothing he could have done anyway.

"It's all right, Gavin," Nelson says. "Don't worry. It's okay. I'm here for you."

"I'm okay, Dad," Gavin says. He moves over toward Joe and Sweetpea. He shuffles them out onto the front porch, away from Mr. Walcott's body.

"Lord," Pearl says loudly. "Heart must've given out. It was bound to happen. Look at the size of him."

WHILE THEY WAIT for the police to come, and then wait for the coroner, everyone mulls about on Roger Smith's front porch, on his front lawn, and on the Raffertys' front porch. Jackson sits with his parents on the bottom step of the old house. His head is fairly clear right now. It must be the drugs they gave him in the hospital.

Joe and Gavin work together to entertain Sweetpea, to keep Sweetpea from the back of the ambulance. Joe was told he would get a dollar if he kept Sweetpea from crying. But Sweetpea just sits cross-legged on the Rafferty porch and cries softly. His mother is on the front lawn talking to Gavin's father. No one has fed him breakfast.

Gavin finally gives up and moves over to Kate and Grace. Grace puts her arm around his shoulders.

"Shut up," Joe says. "Sweetpea, just shut up. I want a dollar."

Sweetpea cries loudly now.

"I'm at the end of my rope," Joe says, mimicking his mother. "Why do bad things always happen to me?" Joe pauses and looks out at the street.

"Okay," he says, focusing back onto Sweatpea. "How about this? I've got an idea of what we can do. Let's give you a real name. Sweetpea isn't a real name."

Sweetpea stops crying. He looks at his brother.

"Okay, I'm Joe. Mom is Holly. Dad is Ivan. What about … what about—can you think of anything?"

Sweetpea shakes his head.

Joe thinks about Sweetpea's stuffed animals. A bear. "What about Bobo? Like your bear."

"No," Sweetpea says.

"No? Good. You can talk." Joe smiles. "Dicky?" Joe mimics Sweetpea's walking robot toy. "Wilbur? Walrus Head? Mr. Hanky? Ordinary Frank?"

Sweetpea giggles.

"Alice? Lucy? Zulu?"

"No."

"We'll think of something," Joe says. He tries TV show characters, names in books. "What do you want to be called? Something different or something everyone is called?"

Sweetpea nods his head.

"Something the same as everyone? Okay. Bill? Bob? Nick? Thomas? Peter? Simon?"

"No."

"What about Walcott? Or Jackson? Or Gavin? Or Nelson?" Joe points to each man in turn.

"No."

Joe lies back and looks at the ceiling of the porch. "I give up," he says. "You'll have to think of it on your own."

"Joe," Sweetpea says.

"What? What about Rudolph?"

"Joe," Sweetpea says again.

"No, you can't be Joe. I'm Joe."

"Joe."

"Hey, that's my name, Sweetpea. You can't have it. That's my name."

"Joe," Sweetpea says and giggles.

Joe looks at his little brother. "Two Joes."

"Joe."

"Yeah, okay. Let's call you Joe."

They laugh. Little Joe lies down next to Big Joe. "Joe," he says. They both laugh some more.

The ambulance attendants take Mr. Walcott's body out of the house. It's awkward work as he is so large, but the men do it carefully and professionally. They hoist Mr. Walcott into the ambulance and Grace is sure she can see the tires deflate a bit.

It isn't until the police look around a bit that they start to ask questions about the squatter.

"Oh, my God," Jill cries. "I forgot about the man who lives there."

Holly and Nelson and Oliver all look up toward the house.

"Is he in there?" Holly whispers.

"No one else is in the house," a police officer says. "But the place is a mess."

Holly shakes her head. The rest of the neighbours shake their heads.

"From the looks of it, he was here quite a long time," the police officer says.

"Yeah," Gavin says.

"And none of you reported him? None of you went over to see if he was okay? Who he was? What he was doing in this house? It's an empty house, right? Did he have any right to live here?" The police officer jots notes down in his little book.

"We assumed—" Jill begins.

"I thought about it," Nelson says.

"I saw him get water from the rain barrel out back," Gavin says. "But it was too dark to see his face."

"I've got two kids," Holly says. "I thought he bought the house."

"I was working," Oliver says. "Privacy and all that...."

"Haunted," Pearl whispers.

Jackson looks down at his feet and says nothing.

Gavin says quietly, "He wanted to be left alone." But no one hears him.

"Who lived here before?" another officer asks. He has just come down from the upstairs of the house. "This house should be condemned. Torn down. It's a mess. The squatter was using the upstairs bathtub as a toilet."

"Gross," Kate says.

Jill looks at Holly. "Oh, my God," Holly mouths. "The bathtub."

"Can any of you describe him to me?"

Everyone shrugs, shakes their heads.

"Not very neighbourly," the cop mumbles, "are you?"

The ambulance pulls off, lights flashing, and heads down the cul-de-sac.

Joe and Sweetpea begin running after it. Gavin rushes to stop them. When he catches them and carries the two boys under each arm like footballs, Holly says, "Thanks, Gavin," with such emotion that Gavin feels good. Really good.

The police officer looks disdainfully at everyone in front of him.

He stretches police tape across the front door. "Nobody go inside," he says. "The city will condemn this place, I'm sure of it. Then they'll probably tear it down. We'll have to get in touch with the owners. You do know who owns this, don't you? That is something you are aware of?"

"Maybe he was the highway sniper," Holly says. "Could he have been the sniper?"

The cop looks up at the house. He shrugs. "I doubt it."

"Why not?" Holly says.

"Did he have a car? A truck?"

"No," Jackson says. "And he never left the house."

"Maybe at night," Nelson says. "When we were sleeping."

"He could have been the sniper," Oliver says. "You never know."

"Probably just some bum," the cop says. "The sniper is more tricky than that. The sniper is fitting in, not sticking out like a sore thumb."

"That's true," Holly says. "That's why he's getting away with so much."

"We'll get the sniper eventually. We've got a lot of manpower on it. This guy, however"—he points at the house—"he was probably just sick of the world."

"'The world'?" Nelson asks.

"Yes," says Esther.

"Or just sick," Holly says.

"Or sad," Jackson whispers.

"Yeah," the cop says and shrugs. "You can't account for some people's behaviour, you can't ever know what makes some people tick."

Holly looks at her children standing quietly next to Gavin Quimby. He is talking to them, telling them something she can't hear. She thinks of Ivan. She thinks of how Gavin has already spent more time with Sweetpea than Ivan ever did.

"Some people just snap, I guess," she says softly.

When the police officers leave, everyone stands around looking lost. And then they split up, go back to their homes.

Jackson Kern takes his parents back home. He feeds them an early lunch and then tucks his mother into her bed for a nap and turns the volume up on the TV for his father.

"I can't believe Murray's dead," Shannon says.

Then Jackson retires to his shed to work.

For once, Jackson's head does not hurt. The doctor gave him some painkillers that seem to be working. In fact, he feels alert and clear. His head has stopped buzzing. Maybe tonight he won't have to go out for his drive. Although he is missing the open highway. The freedom it gives him. Release from his boring life. Maybe he will go tonight anyway. Maybe the experience will be different now that he has no headache. Maybe he'll see everything clearly now. With no pain. Jackson can understand the man from Roger Smith's house. He can understand wanting to get away from the world. That's what he does on his highway. His own highway. Just his. Open road. That empty feeling of nothingness.

It saddens him too that Murray is gone. Slowly Jackson's world is getting less cluttered. Soon he'll be all alone.

Oliver stands beside his car, feeling strange. Feeling dejected. He feels like an idiot. He wants to smack his hands hard on his forehead, knock some sense into himself. Instead, he walks up the front steps of his house.

"Jill," he calls into the front door. "Do you want to do something today? Go out for lunch? Go for a drive? Check out some houses?"

Jill comes to the door. "Houses?" She looks at Oliver.

He looks at her carefully, tries to see her for who she is, tries to remember.

"God, yes," Jill says. "Let's check out some houses. But first let's get something greasy to eat. French fries," she says. "I need greasy french fries for this hangover."

Oliver gets into the car and puts down the roof.

"Can we get a house with only two bedrooms?"

"But what about Pearl?" Oliver says as he starts the engine. "Where will she sleep?"

"It's time, Oliver," Jill says, "we make some changes."

Nelson ushers Grace and Gavin into the car.

"I haven't been to the beach in so long," he says.

Grace feels ill. She sits in the back seat. She can't believe she agreed to this. At least Lindsay's not coming. That's something.

"Listen," Nelson says to Gavin when they are out on the open highway. "If you need to talk about this morning, or about your mom, or about that suicide ... Well, I know we haven't talked about anything. If you need to—"

"I know," Gavin says. "I'm okay now. Thanks."

Gavin keeps his eyes open wide on the highway, watching out for the sniper.

Holly and the two Joes sit outside on the front lawn. Holly turns on the sprinklers and watches her sons as they run in and out of the spray and then as they slide in the mud that soon forms. She can't help but laugh. They are having a great time. And the spray from their bodies as they race past her keeps her cool enough.

Poor Mr. Walcott, Holly thinks. I'm alive, she thinks. That's what matters. That's what's good. Holly stands and walks over to her mailbox. She didn't check the mail this morning, but something tells her there's another postcard in the box. This time there is a picture of just the beach on the card. Just the white sand and the blue water. No women in bathing suits. And on the back, in Ivan's scrawl, it says, "I miss you and the boys. Love, Ivan."

There is no postmark or stamp, but Ivan has put his phone number down on the back of the card and Holly notices it's a local number. She puts the card in her pocket.

Only a couple weeks left of summer and then Joe will be going to kindergarten. Holly settles back into the grass and laughs when a muddy, wet, and slippery Sweetpea comes rolling down toward her.

Much later, when Oliver and Jill drive back into the cul-de-sac, Holly invites them into her house for coffee. She cleaned, she tells them, laughing, and she wants to show that off.

"Look at that," Pearl says.

She is lying on the guest-room bed with Kate beside her, the air conditioning turned up full blast, the TV on loud. They are both shivering. Pearl is pointing to the TV. Kate looks.

On the TV is a list of the names and ages of the highway sniper's victims.

"That sure makes it real, doesn't it?" Pearl says, watching the names roll down the screen. "Remember those poor kids and that mom?" she asks. "There must be a daddy somewhere out there grieving like mad."

REBECCA COTTON, AGE 39
TODD AARON COTTON, AGE 3
SUSAN MARIE COTTON, AGE 6 MONTHS

The Christmas Party

AS IF A SWITCH *has been turned on, the entire cul-de-sac is illuminated. Christmas lights on every house. From the wildly ornate cascading icicles at the Raffertys' house, to the twinkling colours at Holly Wray's, to the musical lights—mechanical and tinny—at the Quimbys', to the simple strand of twenty-four lights along the tops of both Mr. Walcott's and the Kerns' front doors, to the lit-up wreath and blinking red-and-green lights of the Smiths' house. Six houses glow.*

It is two days before Christmas. The last day of work and school before the holidays. Almost everyone is happy. Festive. In good spirits.

The McCallan/Raffertys' Sixth Annual Neighbourhood Christmas Party—embossed invitations, champagne and caviar, elaborately decorated trees in every room, pine-scented potpourri on every table—is about to begin. At seven o'clock sharp.

Jill is rushing through her house, through the living room, the hallway, the dining room, into the kitchen. She is happily checking everything one last time. Humming a Christmas carol. She turns on the gas fireplace in the living room. Click. She turns on

260

the mechanical device that makes the fireplace sound like it's crackling. She refills the crystal nut bowl on the coffee table. She sips her wine and fixes her hair in the dining-room mirror.

"Kate, sweetheart, you look lovely. I'm so glad we bought that dress. Oliver? Where's Oliver? Has anyone seen Oliver? Pearl?"

Outside, down the street, Jackson bundles his old parents into their coats and steers them slowly and tenderly toward the party. Esther wobbles. Shannon limps. Jackson is careful with them, guiding them patiently, encouraging them on.

The doorbell rings. Jill checks her lipstick in a compact she has hidden in a drawer in the kitchen. She moves toward the front door, Pearl just behind her, grumbling about her duties. ("Taking coats," she says. "It's just the neighbours. I never." "Shush up, Pearl. Really, now," Jill hisses. "Be polite for once.")

"Oliver? Honey? The guests are here."

Jill throws back her head, flicks her hair, and opens the door just as Oliver descends the stairs. She grins broadly. "There you are. You look wonderful."

"Hello, welcome. Merry Christmas. Happy holidays."

"Hello, Jackson," *Oliver says.* "Mr. and Mrs. Kern. Welcome. Good to see you again."

"Oh, I'm so glad the Kerns came," *Jill whispers to Oliver as he hangs their coats in the hall closet, Pearl having disappeared.* "They are getting so old." *She kisses Oliver on the cheek.* "Not much time left."

Jackson and his parents stand for a minute by the powder-room door until Pearl shuffles them into the living room and seats them on a white sofa. Jackson admires the orchids in a vase next to the nut bowl. He would prefer them if they were dried, but still, they look pretty anyway. He helps his mother hold her drink.

Water. Jackson has a 7 Up. The bubbles distract him from his headache. Pearl leaves the Kerns to themselves. Shannon clears his throat and Esther plays nervously with her watch and samples everything the Raffertys bring her. Cheese balls, shrimp with tails, fruit plate, liver pâté. The Raffertys bustle around them.

Outside, Nelson walks out the door of his house. He stands back and looks up at the decorative lights above his windows. Many of the bulbs are out and those that are working are so old he can hear them crackle. Grace comes out of the house in a flowered dress and black tights. Her hair is in ponytails. She isn't wearing a coat.

"It's too bright out here. Turn off the lights."

"Aren't you cold? You need a coat."

Grace shrugs. "I'm fine. It's just across the street." She looks out and across the circle toward the Rafferty house. She sighs. She can see people in the window. Old people. She can see Jackson Kern and his parents moving slowly.

"Some lights are out," Nelson says. "I'll have to get more. We can't have a tacky Christmas this year."

Nelson has had several beers already and is glowing almost as bright as the lights. This is his first Christmas without his wife since the children were born and it's coming up fast. He still has gifts to buy and it just occurred to him yesterday that Santa, perhaps, uses different wrapping paper. Doesn't he? Nelson doesn't know. There were so many things Anna did that Nelson didn't realize—even though she spent most of their marriage saying, "You have no idea what I do around here," it never sunk in before. Busy, he's so busy these days.

Another Christmas, Grace thinks. In the back of her head it occurs to her that she may be too young to be so cynical. Is fourteen too young to stop caring? She stopped caring about six weeks ago and doesn't know why. The counsellor at school says it's her hormones, but Grace doesn't think so. Besides, what does she really care about her hormones anyway?

Gavin makes his way out the front door. He slouches past Grace.

"Stick with me, okay?" Grace whispers. "I hate these things." Grace particularly hates Kate Rafferty's house, all prettied up and perfect.

"We'll just find a TV somewhere," Gavin says. "We'll eat and watch TV. Are you wearing lipstick?"

Grace plays with her earrings. She sighs. The Quimbys make their way toward the Rafferty house.

Gavin stops at the front door when he sees Kate. He somehow forgot she would be here. Of course she would be here. She lives here. Kate Rafferty always seems so alien to him, with her glowing blonde hair, her long-leggy beauty, the fancy clothes she wears. Seeing her in the halls at school is like walking headfirst into the sun.

"Hey, Grace," Kate says. "Come on in. Are you wearing makeup? God, I wish my mom would let me wear makeup."

"Since my mom took off, I can do what I want now," Grace says smugly.

Gavin closes his mouth and sucks his tongue into a roll. He works it like it's candy.

"Come on." Grace pushes Gavin ahead. She wants to be anywhere right now but here. Mr. Rafferty says hello to them as he passes in the hall. Nelson strolls toward Jill Rafferty and she holds out her hands and pecks him on both cheeks.

"So good of you to come," Jill says. "Let me get you a drink. Pearl, where are you? A beer, Nelson? Listen, I'm so sorry about

you and Anna. I always thought you were such a good couple. How are you doing?"

Outside and down the street, Holly Wray is helping Joe out the front door. She zips up his coat. She picks him up and props him on her hip in order to turn and shut the door. He is three and a half years old and big for his age. Ivan follows behind. He turns off the Christmas lights.

"Leave the outside ones on, Ivan," Holly says. "They're pretty."

"That's a waste of electricity."

"It's Christmas, Ivan. Leave them on."

"Two more days," Ivan says, slamming the door. "In my family, we only turned on the outside lights on Christmas Day. We didn't waste."

Joe says, "I want to stay home." He sticks his hands in his pockets and scowls. He sticks his tongue out at his father.

Ivan raises his hand, threatening a slap. Joe puts his tongue back in his mouth.

"Joe," Holly says as she cups his face in her hand, "that's not nice. And, Ivan, you stop. Listen, we'll just go for a bit and then we'll come home. There'll be cookies, I'm sure, and other sweet things." She looks at Ivan, at his unruly hair and his unshaven face. He looks tired, worn, drawn. He is wearing a sweater that has holes under the arms. Holly sighs.

"I want to watch TV," Joe says. His little body quivers with anger. He tries to stamp his feet and ends up kicking his mother in her stomach. The baby inside her kicks too. She groans.

"This is ridiculous," Ivan says. "We don't even like these people."

"I don't know," Holly says. "I've never really given a relationship with them a chance. Have you?" Holly holds the squirming Joe and can feel the new baby moving.

"Relationship—ha."

Joe screams. Holly adjusts him on her hip. "We'll watch TV when we get home. Screaming won't change anything."

"I don't want to go," Joe hisses.

Holly looks up at the Rafferty house and then at her child, and down at the other child in her belly. At Ivan. He's scowling.

"You don't have to come," she whispers.

"Can you get him to stop screaming?"

"He's a baby, he screams—"

"He's not a baby, he's three years old. If you wouldn't baby him. If you'd treat him like the kid he is. Treat him his age. It's all your fault he screams."

Holly sighs. She'll get them up there, give Joe a cookie, and talk to an adult who isn't always negative, who doesn't always yell at her. She is organized tonight. She is in control. Joe has had his dinner, she's as dressed up as possible. She even has makeup on ("You look like a clown," Ivan says). Holly tries to do up her winter coat, but her belly is much too large, and it's tight and awkward. Her breasts feel squished in the bra she put on for the party. But she's going to a party. Her new baby will be born in two weeks. Nothing can spoil her mood.

Up the street they go, Ivan lagging behind, Joe heavy and mad on her hip, Holly's back breaking. They cross the street, walk through the centre of the circle, and climb the stairs to the Rafferty house. Nelson Quimby is on the front porch, a beer in his hand. Holly smiles at him. Anna Quimby left four months ago, Holly thinks, poor Nelson. Ivan walks into the house and goes straight for the drinks table. Holly stays to talk to Nelson.

"Hey," Nelson says. He holds up his beer and toasts the sky.

"Merry Christmas, Holly. You look great. Pregnant women always look so great. Full of life."

"Thank you," Holly says. She pats her stomach. "I am full of life." She laughs. "And you too. You look great, Nelson."

"Another Rafferty party."

"Yes, another year. How are you doing? Everything okay? Have you heard from Anna yet?"

"It's hot in there." Nelson signals to the front door. "No, she hasn't been in touch. But, yeah, I'm fine, I guess." Nelson admires Holly's breasts. He loves large-breasted women. He feels the urge to reach out and touch her shirt.

"Good." Holly's face is flushed. Joe is wriggling around, trying to get down. Holly's never really noticed how nice looking Nelson is. She feels hot.

Joe clambers down and then looks up at his mother and pulls at her arm. Momentary quiet. "I want a cookie," Joe says. "A big cookie."

"I mean," Nelson says, "there's something about a pregnant woman. Something so beautiful."

"We glow," Holly says. "Although that's just because we're hot all the time." She laughs.

"No, really," Nelson moves close to Holly. She can smell beer on his breath. "So sexy, really."

Holly swallows hard. The last thing she can imagine doing right now is having sex. Everything is sore, swollen. Nelson is so attractive. Lovely, she thinks. She smiles.

"He's got great lungs," Nelson says, pointing down to Joe, who is hollering up at his mother. "Healthy."

"I guess that's a good way to look at it," Holly shouts over the noise. "If you were in trouble, in an accident, he'd be helpful." She

sees Ivan in the window. He is talking to Jill and holding a beer in his hand. Drinking out of the bottle even though Jill has an empty glass right there, a glass she's waving awkwardly in front of Ivan. Ivan looks out toward Holly, sees Holly with Nelson standing so close, and he glares at her.

"Have you thought of a name for the baby yet?" Nelson says. "It's a boy, right?"

"Yes. But no," Holly says quietly. "Not yet. I'm working on it. Ivan, well, we just don't agree on any choices." She laughs. "Any ideas?"

"What about Nelson?" Nelson puts an arm around Holly. She smells his beer breath, his cologne, and something else. A heat he's giving off. She feels woozy.

Nelson smiles, backs away, and then tips his beer to Holly. He goes back inside to the party. Holly and Joe follow behind. That, she thinks, was some come-on. Here she is, nine months pregnant, and a gorgeous man was coming on to her. Holly's face is pink. Her bra straps are tight. She feels wonderful. Joe pulls her straight to the dessert table.

Nelson watches Gavin and Grace as they stand in the corner by the piano. Good-looking kids. A bit awkward, maybe. Grace is growing up so fast. Nelson looks at Holly, trying to get Joe to take only one cookie. She looks great pregnant. He loves her swollen stomach, its tightness. It's been weeks since his last date. Four months since Anna left him for her boss. Nelson isn't used to being alone, he isn't used to having to work at companionship. For God's sake, Nelson thinks, look at me. I'm great looking. I'm nice. I'm fun. He takes a sip of his beer. He stands in the living room, looking at his kids. Then he turns and looks out the window at the street. Across at his house. He'll find someone. He knows he will.

He's never been out of the game for long. It'll be a good year. He's sure of it. Nelson raises his glass of beer and drinks. He knows it's not New Year's Eve yet, but this year, he thinks, is starting out just fine.

Mr. Walcott peeks out from behind his curtains at the lit-up street. He clears his throat. He shifts his bulk a bit and then turns from the window toward his TV. It's a Wonderful Life is playing and Mr. Walcott loves this movie. It always brings a tear to his eye. But tonight he is going out. To the Raffertys' party. Just to be nice. He does this every year. He'll stay for ten minutes and then he'll disappear, head home, eat the roast turkey that is waiting for him on his counter. He will sit in front of the TV and watch It's a Wonderful Life *and cry and laugh. He'll toast Judy and toast himself, his synesthesia, his aches and pains.*

There are a few things he wants to discuss with Roger tonight anyway, always an interesting person to talk to. Mr. Walcott wants to talk to Roger about what appears to be a squirrel infestation in his attic—squirrel or raccoon, he isn't quite sure—and see if Roger knows anything about how to get rid of them. Roger's always been a fountain of information. Always reading, studying up on things. He's almost as well read as Mr. Walcott himself.

At his front door, Mr. Walcott pauses and reflects on the coming winter. He thinks he's not getting any younger. He'll have to be better prepared this year. He'll have to stock up on supplies. Make sure everything is working properly in the house. The furnace, the water heater, the laundry machine, the dryer. He is sure Roger could come look at everything for him. Roger likes to bring his kids over—nice boys—to study appliances. Roger knows everything about everything, it seems. It's good to have a useful neighbour. And Roger's wife, Celia, well, she's a wonder with pies.

Something about her crust. Mr. Walcott's mouth waters. That family. The Smiths. They are people who are really in touch with reality. The good things in life. Solid as rocks, they are. Mr. Walcott was pleased as punch when they moved into the big house several years ago. He's been so lonely without Judy, but Roger and Celia have been so kind. He just wishes Judy could have met them. She would have spoiled the boys rotten. No one else on the cul-de-sac has bothered to befriend Mr. Walcott. The Kerns are so sickly now, they barely go outside. And Jackson doesn't talk at all when he delivers Mr. Walcott's groceries.

As Mr. Walcott leaves the house, his mood considerably lighter, a cold rain begins to fall. He lumbers up the street, his bulk shifting back and forth, and up the Raffertys' staircase, careful not to slip. He blinks rapidly because of the lights and the laughter coming from within the house. Everything is full volume, everything is bright.

At the top of the steps Mr. Walcott hears a piercing scream. He turns toward the Smiths' house, to where the sound came from. It was an animal scream. Something in pain. Mr. Walcott wonders if there is a fox on the hill out back. Maybe a fox caught a cat or a rabbit. Sometimes that happens.

Mr. Walcott hears the scream again—no, it's human, not animal—and sits down on the top step. His knees snap. He sits so hard with all his weight that later he'll discover he has bruised his tailbone.

Behind Mr. Walcott the party is in full swing. He turns and looks at the lit window. Someone is playing "Santa Claus Is Coming to Town" on the piano. People are singing. He can see Jackson Kern and his parents sitting on the sofa, looking awkward. A platter crashes in the kitchen.

Celia Smith comes running out of her house, runs out to the front porch, half-dressed, her arms waving in the air, her face contorted. Mr. Walcott stares at her. And then Jill Rafferty, surrounded by friends and family in her beautiful party house, her hand clasped in Oliver's, waiting for the song to end, calls out, "Merry Christmas," and the sound is sweet and full of life. The front door is open wide to let in the damp air. Her voice echoes out on the street, into the new falling rain.

"Merry Christmas," she shouts happily, just before everything else happens. She holds up her glass for a toast. "Merry Christmas, everyone."

Acknowledgments

THERE ARE many people to thank.

The editor: Barbara Berson, first and foremost, for her editing advice, her keen eye, and her ability to communicate changes in such a direct and straightforward way. Also for her leap of faith and quirky sense of humour.

The experts: Janet Miller for her flower-drying expertise and rapid email response. Whatever mistakes I've made I hope can be considered creative licence. Michael Kesterton for the back page of *The Globe and Mail*, "Social Studies: A Daily Miscellany of Information," without which Mr. Walcott would not be who he is.

The agents: Hilary McMahon, for such strong support and conviction over the years. Nicole Winstanley, for her positiveness and strength. And Natasha Fairweather (at A.P. Watt) for all her help.

The copy editor: Bernice Eisenstein. I wouldn't use anyone else.

The managing editor: Tracy Bordian. For putting it all together.

The readers: Ann Ireland, who took time out of her busy schedule to offer brilliant comments on this book. I'm indebted to you. Michele Hutchison, who whipped off such intelligent edits only days before giving birth. And Natalee Caple, for her fine insights.

The friends and family: Beverly and David Baird for their support, and the new Peterborough gang, for being so welcoming.

And finally, thanks goes out to my family: Mom, Dad, Dave, Stu, Abby, and Zoe. Without whom I couldn't have written a word.